Niels Lyhne

JENS PETER JACOBSEN

Niels Lyhne

Translated from the Danish
by Tiina Nunnally

With an Afterword
by Eric O. Johannesson

Fjord Modern Classics No. 2

Seattle
Fjord Press
1990

Title of Danish edition: *Niels Lyhne*
Originally published in 1880 by Gyldendalske Boghandel, Nordisk Forlag,
Copenhagen.

This edition was translated from the definitive edition in the Danish Classics
series of the Danish Language and Literature Association, edited by Jørn
Vosmar, published by Borgens Forlag, Copenhagen, in 1986.

Grateful acknowledgment is given to the National Endowment for the Arts
and the Danish Ministry of Cultural Affairs for their generous support.

Published and distributed by:
Fjord Press
P.O. Box 16501
Seattle, Washington 98116
(206) 625-9363

Editor: Steven T. Murray
Cover design: Bonnie Smetts Graphic Design, Berkeley
Cover painting of the author by Ernst Josephson, 1879. Reproduced by
    permission of the Museum of National History at Frederiksborg Castle.
Design & typography: Fjord Press Typography, Seattle
Proofreading: Julie Carter
Printed by Malloy Lithographing, Ann Arbor

Library of Congress Cataloging in Publication Data:

Jacobsen, J. P. (Jens Peter), 1847–1885.
    [Niels Lyhne. English]
    Niels Lyhne / Jens Peter Jacobsen ; translated from the Danish by Tiina
Nunnally ; with an afterword by Eric O. Johannesson.
        p.   cm. — (Fjord modern classics ; no. 2)
    "This edition was translated from the definitive edition in the Danish
Classics series of the Danish Language and Literature Association . . .
published by Borgens Forlag, Copenhagen, in 1986" — T.p. verso.
    Includes bibliographical references.
    ISBN 0-940242-30-3 : $19.95. — ISBN 0-940242-29-X (pbk.) : $9.95
    I. Nunnally, Tiina.   II. Title.   III. Series.
PT8140.N5E5   1990   839.8'136 — dc20   89-82139
⊗   CIP

Printed in the United States of America
First edition

GUIDE TO
PRONUNCIATION

For those readers who are unfamiliar with Danish pronunciation, here are a few guidelines to assist you in correctly pronouncing the Danish names in this book.

The final *e* in Danish is always pronounced, like *a* in *Linda*. The Danish *y* sounds like German *ü* or French *u*. Danish has three special vowels too. The first, *aa*, sounds like the long *o* in *go*; *æ* sounds like *e* in *get*; and *ø* is similar to German *ö* or French *eu*. The Danish *j* and *hj* are both pronounced like the *y* in *yes*.

For instance, *Niels Lyhne* is pronounced *Nils Lü-ne*; *Lønborggaard* is *Lön-bor-gor*; *Frithiof* is *Frit-yof*; *Edele* is *E-de-le*; *Te-ma Bo-ye* is four syllables; *Hjerrild* is *Yer-ril*; *Fjordby* is *Fyor-bü*; and *Mariager* is *Ma-ri-a-er*.

Niels Lyhne

I

S he had the black shining eyes of the Blid family, with fine, straight eyebrows; she had their strongly contoured nose, their powerful jaw and full lips. She had also inherited the odd, painfully sensual creases at the corners of her mouth and the restless movements of her head, but her cheeks were pale and her hair was soft as silk, curving gently and smoothly to the shape of her head.

The Blids were not like that; their colors were rose and bronze. Their hair was rough and curly, heavy as a mane; and they had full, deep, supple voices, strangely suited to the family traditions of their fathers' raucous hunting expeditions, solemn morning prayers, and thousands of love affairs.

But *her* voice was flat and toneless.

I am describing her as she was at seventeen; a couple of years later, after she was married, her voice had more fullness, the color of her cheeks was fresher, and her eyes had become duller and yet somehow bigger and blacker.

At seventeen she was quite different from her siblings, and her relationship with her parents was not a close one either. The Blids were a practical family who took life as it came; they did their work, took their rest, and never dreamed of demanding any more or any other pleasures than the harvest feast and three or four Christmas parties. They were not religiously inclined, but it would have been as difficult for them to think of neglecting to pay their taxes as not to give God his due, so they said their evening prayers, went to church on holy days, sang their hymns on Christmas Eve, and received communion twice a year. They were not inquisitive either, and as for their sense of aesthetics, they were by no means insensitive to little sentimental songs. When summer arrived and the grass was thick and lush in the meadows and the grain was maturing in the wide fields, they would often remark to each other that it was a beautiful time to be traveling through the countryside. But they did not have particularly poetic temperaments; beauty did not intoxicate them, and they had no vague longings or daydreams.

But it was different with Bartholine; she had no interest in the events of the stables or the fields, no interest in dairy work or housekeeping — none at all.

She loved poetry.

She lived in poetry, she dreamed in poetry, and she believed in it more than almost anything else.

Her parents and siblings, neighbors and acquaintances never said a word that was worth listening to, for their thoughts never soared higher than the earth or the task they had at hand, just as their glance never sought higher than the situations and events right before their eyes.

But poems, on the other hand! For her they were full of new ideas and profound wisdom about life out in the world, where sorrow is black and joy is red, and they glittered with images, foaming and beaded with rhythms and rhyme. They were all about young girls, and the young girls were noble and beautiful — they themselves did not realize how beautiful. Their love and their hearts were greater than all the riches in the world, and men worshipped them, held them up high, up in the sunlight of happiness, honored and adored them, happy to share their thoughts and plans, their victories and fame with them, and even said that it was these joyous girls who had inspired all their plans and won all their victories.

And why shouldn't one be that kind of girl? They're so . . . and they're so . . . and they don't even know it. What do I know about how I am? And the poets expressly said that *this* was life and that life was not sewing and hemming, helping around the house, and paying stupid visits.

But after all, there was really nothing hidden in this but a somewhat morbid urge to realize oneself, the longing to find oneself which is so often awakened in a young girl of above-average intelligence. But the worst part was that in her circle of acquaintances there was not a single superior individual to be found who could have given her a kind of direction for her intelligence. There was not even a single kindred spirit, and thus she came to regard herself as something extraordinary, unique, like a kind of tropical plant which had shot up beneath inclement skies and which now could only manage to unfurl its leaves patethically; while in warmer air, beneath a more powerful sun, it would have been able to shoot out proud stalks with a wonderfully rich and shining abundance of flowers. That, she felt, was her true nature—that was what the proper surroundings would make her into, and she dreamed thousands of dreams about those sun-bright places and was consumed with yearning for her true, rich self, and forgot what it is so easy to forget: that even the fairest dreams, even the deepest longings do not add a single inch to the stature of the human spirit.

Then one fine day a suitor came to her.

It was young Lyhne from Lønborggaard, the last male in a family lineage that for three entire generations had been among the most intelligent in the province. In their old age, as mayors, district revenue officers, or royal commissioners (frequently granted the title of Councilor), they served king and country actively and with honor. In their younger days, during sensibly planned and thoroughly executed study trips to France and Germany, they had enriched their easily susceptible minds with the knowledge, aesthetic pleasures, and impressions of life that those foreign lands offered in such rich measure. And when they returned home, these years of exile were not pushed aside among old memories, as the memory of a party is pushed aside: the last candle blown out and the last note faded away. No, life at home was built up around these years, and the interests that had been awakened were not allowed to deteriorate in any way, but were nourished and developed with all the means at their disposal; and exquisite copperplate engravings, valuable bronzes, volumes of German poetry, French legal negotiations, and French philosophy were everyday items and common topics in the Lyhne household.

As far as their temperament was concerned, they moved with an old-fashioned ease and graceful charm which often formed an odd contrast to the crude pomposity and clumsy stateliness of their peers. Their speech was broadly rounded, with meticulous diction, but somewhat affectedly rhetorical — that was undeniable — yet it was well-suited to these large, broad figures with the high, domed foreheads, the receding hairline, the curly black hair, the light blue, calmly smiling eyes, and the finely formed, slightly crooked noses; but their jaws were too heavy and their mouths too wide, and their lips were also much too full.

Just as these outward traits were less pronounced in the young Lyhne, the mind seemed to have grown weary in him too, and the intellectual tasks or serious artistic pleasures he had encountered had far from awakened any kind of zeal or desire in him; rather, he had tackled them with a dutiful tenacity, which had been neither lightened by any joy in feeling his powers come alive, nor rewarded with any proud self-confidence when it turned out they were effective. Satisfaction that the work was done — this was all the reward he had.

He had inherited his farm, Lønborggaard, from a recently deceased uncle, so he had returned from the traditional trip abroad and was going to manage the operation of the farm himself. Since the Blids owned the nearest neighboring estate and his uncle had had a close relationship with the family, he paid them a visit, saw Bartholine, and fell in love with her.

That she fell in love with him almost goes without saying.

Finally here was someone from out in the world, someone who had lived in the great, distant cities where the forests of spires and towers were silhouetted against the clear, sunny sky, where the air vibrated with the clanging of bells, the roar of organs, and the fleet tones of mandolins, while radiant processions in gold and many colors wound festively through the wide streets; where marble buildings gleamed and the variegated coats of arms of proud families perched in pairs over the wide portals while banners waved and veils fluttered up on the balconies with their ornamental stone foliage. Someone who had wandered in those realms from which victorious armies had marched forth along the roads, where mighty battles had crowned the names of the villages and fields with an immortal glow, where the smoke from the gypsies' campfire rose languidly over the treetops in the forests while red ruins up on the vineyard-wreathed heights looked down on the smiling valley where the mill-wheel roared, and clattering herds returned home over wide, arched bridges.

He told her about all these things, but not the way the poets did — far more realistically and with such familiarity, just as her family talked about the towns in their diocese and the neighboring parishes. He also talked about painters and poets, and there were names he praised to the heavens that she had never heard mentioned before. He showed her their pictures and read their poems with her in the garden up on the hill where they could look out over the smooth waters of the fjord and the brown undulations of the heath. Love made him poetic, and there was beauty all around; the clouds turned into the clouds that sailed through the poems, and the trees of the garden assumed the foliage that sighed with such melancholy in the ballads.

Bartholine was happy, for her love caused the entire day to dissolve into a series of poetic situations. Thus, it was poetry when she walked along the road to meet him, their meeting was poetry, and their parting was too; it was poetry when she stood up on the hill in the glow of the setting sun and waved to him a last farewell and then, feeling wistfully happy, went up to her lonely room to think about him undisturbed; and when she prayed for him in her evening prayers, that was poetry too.

She no longer had those vague desires and yearnings; her

new life with its shifting moods was enough for her, and her thoughts and perceptions had become clearer now that she had someone to whom she could turn without reserve, without fear of being misunderstood.

She had changed in another way too: happiness had made her kinder toward her parents and siblings, and she discovered that they actually were more sensible and had more feeling than she had presumed.

And then they were married.

The first year was very much like their engagement, but after they had lived together for a while, Lyhne could no longer hide from himself that he had grown weary of constantly giving his love new expression, of constantly having his wings spread for flight, clothed in the plumage of poetry, through all the heavens of emotion and all the depths of thought. He longed to sit still on his branch in peace and quiet, dozing, and hide his head beneath the warm feathers of his wing. He did not think of love as an eternally vigilant, blazing flame, which with its powerful, flickering glow shone into all the peaceful folds of life and in some fantastic way made everything seem bigger and stranger than it was. For him love was more like the calm, smoldering ember that gives off an even heat from its soft bed of ashes and in the muted twilight tenderly forgets what is distant and makes what is near seem twice as close and twice as intimate.

He was tired, exhausted; he couldn't stand all that poetry, he longed to plant his feet on the solid ground of daily life — just as a fish suffocating in the hot air must long for the clear, fresh cold of the wave. It had to end, it had to end of its own accord. Bartholine was no longer innocent about life and books; she was just as familiar with them as he was. He had given her everything he had, and now he was supposed to keep on giving. It was impossible, he had no more — his only consolation was that Bartholine was with child.

For a long time Bartholine had noticed with sorrow that her view of Lyhne had been gradually changing and that he no longer stood on the dizzying heights where she had placed him during their engagement. She did not yet doubt that he was what she called a "poetic temperament," but she had grown frightened, because prose had begun to stick out its horse's hoof now and then. With even greater zeal she strove for poetry and tried to recapture the old feeling by overwhelming him with even greater emotional riches, even more enthusiasms; but she found so little response that she almost thought that she herself was sentimental and affected. For a time she still tried to sweep the resistant Lyhne along with her; she refused to believe what she suspected. But when the fruitlessness of her exertions finally began to awaken doubt in her about whether her own spirit and heart really encompassed as great a wealth as she had believed, she suddenly released him, became cool, silent, and reserved, and sought solitude in order to grieve in peace for her lost illusions. For she now saw that she had been bitterly disappointed and that deep within, Lyhne was actually no different from her old acquaintances, and that what had betrayed her was the quite ordinary fact that for a brief moment his love had surrounded him with an ephemeral aura of spirituality and loftiness — something that often happens with inferior temperaments.

Lyhne was both distressed and anxious about this change in their relationship, and he tried to remedy it with unsuccessful attempts at the old, romantic flight; but this only served to show Bartholine even more clearly how great her delusion had been.

That is the way things stood between the couple when Bartholine brought her first child into the world. It was a boy, and they named him Niels.

I I

I n a certain way the child brought the parents together again,
for they always met beside his little cradle in mutual hope,
mutual joy, and mutual fear. They both liked to think about
the boy and talked about him often, and each was so grateful to
the other for the child and for their joy and love for him.

But there was a great gap between them.

Lyhne was absorbed in his farming and parish affairs,
though without appearing to be a leader or even a reformer in
any way. But he participated conscientiously in the established
order, looking on as an interested spectator, and agreeing to
the sober-minded improvements that his old foreman or the
elders of the parish suggested after careful consideration, very
careful consideration.

It never occurred to him to make use of the knowledge that
he had acquired in earlier days; he had too little faith in what he
called theory and too much respect for the empirical maxims
made venerable through time-honored custom, which the
others called the truly practical. In general, there was nothing
about him to indicate that he had not lived his whole life here
and in this fashion. But there was one small thing: the fact that
he would often sit still on a gate or a boundary stone for half an
hour or more and, in a strange vegetative trance, stare out over
the lush green rye or the golden, top-heavy oats. He had that
from somewhere else — it was a remnant of the old Lyhne, the
young Lyhne.

In *her* world, Bartholine did not adjust in that way —
immediately, all at once, without fumbling or making a fuss.
No, through the verse of a hundred poets she first complained,
with all the broad generality of the day, about the thousands of

barriers, bonds, and chains of human life. At times her lament was clothed in the mighty rage that slings its froth of words at the thrones of emperors and the prisons of tyrants; at other times it was the calm, sympathetic sorrow that sees the rich light of beauty turn away from a blind and servile generation, subdued and broken by the vapid preoccupations of the day; and sometimes the form of her complaint was the quiet sighing for the free flight of the bird or for the cloud that sails so easily into the distance.

But she had grown tired of complaining, and the annoying powerlessness of her complaint goaded her into doubt and bitterness. Just as certain believers strike down their saint and tread him underfoot when he refuses to demonstrate his power, she now derided her adored poetry and asked herself with a sneer whether she really thought that the Roc was going to show up at any moment down in the cucumber patch, or whether Aladdin's cave was going to open up under the floor of the dairy cellar, and with childish cynicism she amused herself by making the world overly prosaic, calling the moon a green cheese and the roses potpourri, all with the feeling that she was avenging herself, but also with a half anxious, half titillating feeling that it was blasphemy.

The attempt at liberation implied by all this was not successful. She sank back into her dreams, the dreams from her girlhood, but the difference now was that no hope shone through them. And there was the fact that she had learned they were only dreams — distant, illusory visions in the air — which no longing on earth would have the power to pull down to *her* world; so whenever she surrendered to them now, it was with restlessness and in spite of a reproachful voice within, which told her she was like a drinker who knows that his passion is destructive and that each new intoxication is energy taken away from his weakness and added to the power of his passion. But the voice spoke in vain, for a life lived soberly, without the light burden of dreams, was not a life worth living — life, after all, had only the value that dreams gave to it.

So different were the father and mother of little Niels — the two friendly powers who, without knowing it, were fighting a battle for his young soul from the moment that a glimmer of intelligence appeared for them to seize hold of. And the older the child became, the fiercer was the battle, because of the richer choice of weapons.

Imagination was the gift through which the mother sought to influence her son, and he had an abundance of imagination, but even as a little boy he demonstrated that for him there was a significant difference between the fantasy world created by his mother's words and the world that really existed. More than a dozen times, when his mother told him fairy tales and described how agonizing was the hero's plight, Niels could find no escape from all that agony, had no idea how to end it — all that misery, walling him in tighter and tighter inside an impenetrable ring, and the hero too. Many a time Niels would press his cheek against his mother's, and with tears in his eyes and quivering lips whisper, "It's not *really* true, is it?" And when he had received the consoling response he was hoping for, he would breathe a deep sigh of relief and listen to the rest of the story comfortably reassured.

But his mother did not really appreciate this desertion.

When he grew too old for fairy tales and she was also tired of thinking them up, she told him, with slight embellishments, about all the wartime and peacetime heroes whose lives were suited to demonstrating the power that resides in the human soul, if only he seeks the One, the Great One, and does not let himself be frightened into faintheartedness by the shortsighted doubt of the day, or let himself be lured down into the soft inertia of peace. The stories were told in that tone, and since there were not enough suitable heroes in history, she chose a fantasy hero whose deeds and fate she could control com-pletely — a hero after her own heart, spirit of her spirit, yes, flesh of her flesh and blood of her blood too: a couple of years after Niels was born she had brought a stillborn male child into the world, and he was the one she chose. Everything he could have become and could have accomplished was now paraded before his brother with intentional vacillation — Promethean longings, Messianic courage, and Herculean strength — in naive travesty and uncontrollable distortion, a world of cheap fantasies that had no more flesh of reality to them than that poor little baby skeleton moldering and rotting up in Lønborg cemetery.

Niels did not miss the moral of these stories; he understood completely that it was contemptible to be like ordinary people. He was also prepared to accept the harsh destiny of the heroes, and in his imagination he suffered willingly the scathing battles, the stiff adversity, the martyrdoms of ingratitude, and the victories without peace, but it was still an incomparable relief to him that it was all so far in the future — that all of it would not happen to him until he was grown up.

Like dream-visions of the night, dream-sounds can haunt the broad daylight and, in hazy forms, mists of sound can call on the mind, which seems to listen for a fleeting moment, wondering whether it was really called — this is how notions about the dream-borne future whispered softly over the childhood days of Niels Lyhne and reminded him gently but without respite that there was a limit set for this happy time and that one day it would be no more.

His awareness of this gave birth to an urge to enjoy his childhood to the fullest, draw it in through all his senses, not waste a drop, not a single drop, and so there was an intensity to his play that bordered on passion, under the pressure of the restless feeling that time was running away from him without his having salvaged from its rich waves everything that it brought, wave upon wave. So he would throw himself to the ground and sob with despair when he was bored because something or other was lacking: playmates, ingenuity, or warm weather; and that was also why he was so reluctant to go to bed, because sleep was the lack of activity, the complete lack of feeling. But it was not always like that.

Sometimes he would wear himself out and his imagination

would lose all its colors. Then he would feel thoroughly unhappy, too little and too wretched for those ambitious dreams — yes, he felt that he was a worthless liar who had arrogantly pretended to love Greatness and to understand it, while in reality he could only empathize with the Small, while he loved the ordinary and had all the basest longings and desires alive inside him. Yes, it even seemed to him that he had the vermin's class hatred of the sublime, and that he would willingly take part in stoning those heroes who were of better blood than he was, and knew that they were.

On such days he avoided his mother, and with a feeling that he was obeying an ignoble instinct he would seek out his father and lend a willing ear and a receptive mind to all his earthbound thoughts and dreamless explanations. And he felt so at ease with his father, was so glad that they were equals, that he almost forgot that this was the same father whom he usually looked down on with pity from the pinnacles of his dream castle. Of course this was not as clear and definite in his childish consciousness as words can express it, but it was all there, unfinished, unborn, in a vague and intangible fetal form. It was like the strange vegetation of the lake bottom, seen through milky ice. Break up the ice or pull what is dimly alive out into the light of words, and the same thing happens — what can now be seen and grasped is, in its clarity, no longer the obscurity that it was.

I I I

And the years passed. Christmas after Christmas filled the
air with its shining, festive glow until long after Twelfth
Night, one Whitsuntide after another passed over the spring
meadows teeming with flowers, and summer vacation after
summer vacation drew near, celebrated its orgy of the open air,
its layers of sunshine, and poured its summer wine from full
cups; and then one day, with a setting sun, it vanished and the
memory remained: the sunburned cheek, the dazzled eyes, and
the blood still dancing.

And the years passed, and the world was no longer the
world of wonder it had been before. Those murky corners
behind the rotting elder trees, those secretive attic rooms, and
that gloomy culvert beneath Klastrupvej — the terror of the
fairy tale no longer dwelled there. And that long embankment
which, at the first song of the lark, hid its grass under the
crimson-edged stars of the asters and the yellow bells of the
primrose, the stream with its fantastical treasures of animals
and plants, and the wild hillsides of the sand pit with their
black flint and silver-glinting blocks of granite — they were
nothing but poor flowers, animals, and stones: the fairy's
radiant gold had withered to leaves again.

Game after game had become old and absurd, stupid and
boring like the pictures in an ABC, and yet they had once been
so new, so persistently new. There they had rolled barrel
hoops, Niels and Frithiof, the pastor's son, and the hoop was a
vessel that shipwrecked whenever it fell over, but if they caught
it before it fell, then it meant they were dropping anchor. The
narrow alley between the outbuildings, through which it was
so difficult to pass, was called Bab el Mandeb or the Gate of

Death; on the stable door it was scribbled in chalk that this was England, and on the barn door it said France. The garden gate was Rio de Janeiro, but the smith's house was Brazil. There was also the game of playing Holger Danske, which *could* be played among the big sorrel bushes around behind the barn, but up in the miller's field there were a couple of sinkholes that were called "the Snappers," and that's where Prince Burmand himself and his wild Saracens lived, with reddish-gray turbans and yellow crests on their helmets, burdock and mullein in great profusion. That was their first real Mauritania; for this boundless exuberance, these teeming masses of the most luxuriant life stimulated the destructive urge, intoxicated the mind with the voluptuousness of annihilation, and the wooden swords flashed with the luster of steel, the green plant juice colored the blade blood-red, and the severed stalks were squashed underfoot like the bodies of Turks beneath horses' hooves with a sound of bones being crushed inside flesh.

They had played down by the fjord; mussel shells were sent out as ships, and when they were stopped by a clump of seaweed or landed on a sandbar, then it was Columbus in the Sargasso Sea or the discovery of America. Harbors were constructed and mighty dams, the Nile was dug out of the firm beach sand, and once they built Gurre Castle out of pieces of flint — a little dead fish in an oyster shell was the dead Tove, and they were King Valdemar, who sat grieving alongside her.

But all that was over.

Niels was a big boy now, twelve years old, going on thirteen, and he no longer needed to chop away at thistles and sorrel in order to indulge his chivalric fantasies, nor did he have the need to set his explorer dreams sailing out to sea in mussel shells. A book and a corner of the sofa were enough now, and if they weren't sufficient, if the book would not lead him to a coast he loved, then he would find Frithiof and tell him the story that the book would not provide. Arm in arm they would walk along the road, one of them narrating, both listening; but whenever they really wanted to enjoy themselves, really give their imagination free rein, they would hide in the aromatic darkness of the hayloft. But soon these stories, which would end just as they felt most comfortable with them, turned into one long story that never ended, but lived on for generation after generation: whenever the hero grew too old or they carelessly allowed him to die, then he was given a son who inherited everything from his father and was even equipped with whatever new skills they especially valued at the moment.

Everything that had made an impression on Niels, what he saw, what he understood and what he misunderstood, what he admired and what he knew ought to be admired — it was all included in his story. Just as gliding water is colored by every image that comes near its mirror and sometimes may reflect the image in undisturbed clarity or pull the picture crooked and distort it, or cast it back with a wavy, erratically dancing outline, or else drown it entirely in its own colors and play of lines — that is how the boy's story seized hold of feelings and thoughts, both his own and others', seized hold of people and events, life and books, as tightly as it could. It was like a life played out alongside real life, it was like a cozy, secret hiding place where the wildest journeys could be sweetly dreamed, it was like a fairy garden that opened at the slightest gesture and embraced him in all its magnificence, shutting everyone else out. From above it was enclosed by whispering palms, and below — among flowers of sun, beneath starry leaves, on rows of coral — thousands of paths diverged to all regions and all ages. If he went down one of them he would arrive at one place, and down another he would arrive somewhere else, with Aladdin and Robinson Crusoe, with Vaulunder and Henrik Maynard, with Niels Klim and Mungo Park, with Peter Simple and with Odysseus — and all he had to do was wish and he was home again.

A month after Niels' twelfth birthday a pair of new faces appeared at Lønborggaard.

One of them was the new tutor; the other was Edele Lyhne.

The tutor, Mr. Bigum, was a theology graduate, on the threshold of his forties. He was rather short, but hefty, built almost like a draft horse: broad-chested, with hunched shoulders and a stooped neck. His arms were long, his legs short and powerful, his feet wide. His walk was lumbering, heavy, and emphatic, his arm movements vague, expressionless, and requiring a lot of room. He was red-bearded like a wild man, his complexion fair and freckled. His large, high forehead was flat as a wall with a couple of vertical wrinkles between his brows; his nose was short and ugly, his mouth large with thick, moist lips. His most attractive feature was his eyes, which were bright, gentle, and clear. From the movement of his pupils you could tell that he was somewhat hard of hearing. But this did not prevent him from being a great lover of music and a passionate violinist; because, he said, the notes were not merely heard with the ears — the whole body listened: the eyes, the fingers, the feet, and if the ear failed once in a while, the hand, with a strange, instinctual genius, would know how to find the right note without the help of the ear. In the long run, all audible notes were false anyway, but whoever had the gift of perfect pitch had an invisible instrument within (compared with which the loveliest Cremona was like the calabash violin of the savage), and on that instrument played the soul, from its strings rang the ideal tones, and on that instrument the great composers had created their immortal works. The external music, that which quavered through the air of reality and which the ear heard, was merely a poor imitation, a stammering attempt to say the unsayable; it resembled the music of the soul the way the statue — formed by hands, shaped with a chisel, measured with a gauge — resembled the sculptor's glorious marble dream, which eyes would never be allowed to see and lips never praise.

Music, however, was by no means Mr. Bigum's chief

interest; he was above all a philosopher, but not one of those productive philosophers who discover new laws and construct systems. He laughed at their systems, those snail shells they dragged around with them through the endless field of thought, in the simple-minded belief that the field exists inside the snail shell. And those laws: the laws of thought, the laws of nature! As if discovering a law was anything more than finding a definite expression for how narrow-minded one is: I can see so far and no farther, there is my horizon. That is what the discovery signified and nothing more, for wasn't there a new horizon beyond the first one, one after the other, horizon beyond horizon, law beyond law, on into infinity? He was not that kind of philosopher. He didn't think that he was conceited or that he overestimated himself, but he could not close his eyes to the fact that his intelligence encompassed wider fields than that of other mortals. When he immersed himself in the works of the great thinkers, it seemed to him as if he were passing among a group of slumbering giants of thought, who, bathed in the light of his spirit, awoke and realized their strength. And everything was like that: all the foreign thoughts, moods, or feelings that were allowed to awaken in him would awaken with his mark on their brow — ennobled, purified, their wings braced, and with a greatness inside them, a power about them of which their creator had never dreamed!

How often he had marveled, almost humbly, at the wondrous richness of his soul and at the divinity of his spirit, secure in its power; for the days might find him judging the world and the things in it from completely opposite perspectives and find him observing them (the world and its things) from preconceived ideas that were as different as night and day. However, these chosen points of view and chosen preconceptions that he had taken for his own never, even for a second, took *him* over — just as the god who has taken the form of the bull or the swan never for a moment becomes the bull or the swan, or ceases to be a god.

And no one had any idea what dwelled within him; everyone

passed blindly by him. But he rejoiced in this blindness, contemptuous of humanity. The day would come when his eyes
would be closed and the glorious temple of his soul would
burst its pillars and collapse and vanish as if it had never existed, but no work from his hand, not a scrap of writing would
he leave behind that might reveal what had been lost with him.
His genius would not be crowned with thorns by the world's
failure to appreciate it, nor would it surrender to the defiling
purple cape of the world's admiration. And he rejoiced at the
thought that generation after generation would be born and
would die, and the greatest of each generation throughout the
ages would devote their lives to attain what he could have given
them if he had deigned to open his hand.

The fact that he lived in such humble circumstances afforded
him a certain pleasure because it was so magnificently prodigal
that his soul should be employed in the teaching of children, so
insanely disproportionate that his time was rewarded with the
paltry daily bread, and so enormously wrong that he was per-
mitted to earn this bread on the recommendation of pitiful,
ordinary human beings who could vouch for his being clever
enough to take on the miserable occupation of tutor.

And they had given him a third-rate grade when he took his
university exams!

Oh, there was a strange pleasure in feeling the brutal fool-
ishness of life cast him aside like lowly chaff, treasuring the
empty and the hollow as golden grain, and knowing himself
that his slightest thought was worth an entire world.

But there were also times when the loneliness of his greatness lay heavy and oppressive upon him.

Alas, how often he listened to himself for hour after hour in
sacred silence, and then began to hear and see the life around
him again and found it foreign to him in its wretchedness and
vanity — how often he felt like that monk in the cloister forest
who had listened as the bird of paradise sang a single trill, and
who, when he returned, found a hundred years had passed!

For if the monk was lonely in this unfamiliar generation that was living among the graves of those he had known, wasn't Bigum all the more alone, whose rightful time had not yet been born?

In such desolate moments he would sometimes catch himself in a cowardly longing to sink down to the multitudes of ordinary mortals and to share their base happiness, become a citizen on their large earth, a citizen in their little heaven.

But he was soon himself again.

The farm's other guest, Miss Edele Lyhne, the elder Lyhne's twenty-six-year-old sister, had lived in Copenhagen for many years, first with her mother, who had moved to the capital when she was widowed, and after her mother's death with her rich uncle, Councilor Neergaard. The Councilor and his wife kept a large household and were quite active in society, so that Edele found herself living in a whirl of balls and parties.

She was admired everywhere, and envy — admiration's faithful shadow — followed her too. She was as talked about as it is possible to be without having done anything scandalous, and when gentlemen discoursed about the three beauties of the city, there were always many who voted to erase one of the names and put in Edele Lyhne's instead, but they could never agree on which of the two lesser beauties should give up her place — considering the first was out of the question.

Very young people did not admire her, however; they were a little afraid of her, and in her company they felt twice as stupid as they were, for she listened to them with a gently crushing expression of patience in her eyes, a patience marked with meanness that clearly stated that she had heard it all before, everything they were saying, and all their exertions to elevate themselves in her eyes and in their own by feigning nonchalance, by dreaming up wild paradoxes, or, when their despair reached its peak, by making bold declarations — these attempts, which pushed and tugged at each other in youthful, poorly executed transitions, were all greeted with the shadow of a smile, a fatal smile of recognition that made the unfortunate one blush and feel like the hundred-and-eleventh fly in the same merciless spider's web.

And her beauty had none of the gentle or the passionate about it, which is so enchanting to young hearts.

But for older hearts and colder minds her beauty exercised a particular attraction.

She was tall.

Her heavy, thick hair was blonde with the dull reddish sheen of maturing wheat, and it grew on the nape of her neck in two narrowing tendrils, a little lighter than the rest and tightly curled. On her high, sharply contoured forehead the rather fair eyebrows were sketched faintly and indistinctly. Her eyes, light gray, large, and clear, were not emphasized by her eyebrows, nor was there any shifting interplay of shadows from the delicate, thin eyelids. Her eyes had something indefinite and indeterminate in their expression, always looking at you directly and openly, with none of those sidelong glances fraught with nuance, or coy, fleeting looks; they seemed unnaturally alert, indomitable, unfathomable. The whole play of expression lay in the lower part of her face, borne by her nostrils, mouth, and chin. Her eyes were merely spectators. Her mouth was especially expressive with its deep corners, its sharply etched outline, and the lovely sinuous line of the lips where they met. Only in the attitude of her lower lip was there something harsh, which in her smile would at times practically melt and at times harden into an almost brutal expression.

The rather violently curved line of her back and the great opulence of her bosom in relation to the severe form of her shoulders and arms lent her an air of boldness, charmingly tropical, which was emphasized even more by her dazzling pallor and the sickly, powerful blood-red color of her lips, so that the impression was provocative, but also alarming.

There was in general a kind of refined stylishness about her tall, slim-hipped figure which she knew how to accentuate, particularly in her ball toilettes, with a resolute and clearly intended art; and because it spoke so *highly* of her knowledge of art, which here signified self-knowledge, it hinted at bad taste, totally controlled in style though it was. And there was an even greater loveliness to it.

Nothing could be more irreproachably proper than her behavior. In everything she said and everything she allowed to be said to her, she kept herself within the bounds of the strictest propriety, and her coquettishness consisted of not being the least bit coquettish, incurably blind to the impression she made, and not making the slightest distinction between her suitors. But that was precisely why they all dreamed intoxicating dreams of the face that must be behind the mask, believed in a fire beneath the snow, detected a scent of depravity in the innocence. None of them would have been surprised to discover that she had a secret lover, but neither would any of them have dared to guess at his name.

That is how they saw Edele Lyhne.

The reason for her leaving the capital for Lønborggaard was that her health had suffered from this continual social activity, the thousand-and-one nights of balls and masquerades, and toward the end of the winter it had become apparent that her lungs were quite strongly affected; so the doctor had ordered country air, quiet, and milk, which were all to be found in great abundance at her present residence. But she also found a constant boredom there, and hardly a week had passed before she started to feel a consuming homesickness and longing for Copenhagen. She filled letter after letter with pleas to put an end to her exile, and she let it be understood that her longing was doing her more harm than the air was doing her good. But the doctor had so frightened the Councilor and his wife that they felt it their duty to turn a deaf ear, no matter how bitterly she complained.

It was not only the amusements themselves that she missed so much; it was feeling her life resound audibly in the sound-filled air of the great city, and here in the country there was a silence in thoughts, in words, in eyes, in everything, so that you perpetually heard yourself with the same inescapable certitude with which you hear the ticking of the clock on a sleepless night. And knowing that back there people were living as they had lived before — it was like being dead and hearing the notes from a ballroom dying out over your grave in the still night air.

There was no one here with whom she could talk, for they didn't grasp the nuances of her words, the very life of the words; they presumably understood them, since they were Danish words, but with that dull approximation with which you understand a foreign language that you're not used to hearing spoken. They had no idea to what or to whom the precise stress of a sentence referred, didn't dream that one little word was a quote or that another word, used in just that way, was a new variation on a popular witticism. They themselves spoke with an honest spareness so that the rib of the grammar could be felt through their phrases, and with a literal use of the words, as if they had taken them fresh from the columns of a dictionary. Just the way they said: "Copenhagen"! Sometimes with a mysterious intonation, as if it were a place where people ate small children, sometimes with a faraway sound in their voices, as if it were a city in the heart of Africa, and sometimes in a solemn voice that trembled with history, almost the way they might have said Nineveh or Carthage. The pastor always said "Axelstad" with nostalgic delight, as if it were the name of one of his former sweethearts. None of them could say "Copenhagen" so that it became the city which extended from Vesterport to Toldboden, on both sides of Østergade and Kongens Nytorv.

And that's the way it was with everything they said; and it was the same with everything they did, too.

There was not a single thing at Lønborggaard that pleased her — those mealtimes that were regulated by the sun, that smell of lavender in the drawers and cupboards, those spartan chairs, all that provincial furniture crowded up against the walls as though it were afraid of people. Even the air displeased her; she couldn't take a walk without bringing a robust perfume of

meadow hay and flowers back with her in her hair and clothing, as though she had been shut up in a weighing-house.

And it was so exquisitely pleasant to be called "aunt" —
Aunt Edele.

How awful that sounded!

She got used to it, however; though in the beginning the relationship between her and Niels was rather cool because of this.

Niels didn't care.

But then one Sunday, in the beginning of August, Lyhne
and his wife had driven off on a visit, and Niels and Miss Edele
were home alone. In the morning Edele had asked Niels to pick
a bouquet of cornflowers for her, but he had forgotten; it
wasn't until afternoon that he remembered, as he was saunter-
ing about with Frithiof. So he picked the flowers and ran up to
the house with them.

The silence in the house made him think that his aunt was
asleep, and he tiptoed carefully through the rooms. On the
threshold of the parlor, he stopped in order to prepare himself
to walk especially quietly over to Edele's doorway. The parlor
was full of sunshine and a large flowering oleander made the air
inside heavy with its sweet almond fragrance. The only sound
to be heard was a muted splash now and then as the goldfish
moved about in their glass bowl on the table with the plant.

Niels walked quietly across the floor, balancing with his
arms, his tongue between his teeth.

He cautiously took hold of the door handle (warmed by the
sun, it burned in his hand) and turned it, slowly and gingerly,
his brow furrowed and his eyes squinting.

He pushed the door ajar, leaned in through the opening,
and placed the bouquet on a chair just inside the door. It was
dark in there, as if the shades were pulled down, and the air
seemed moist with scent, the scent of rose oil.

In his bent-over position, he could see nothing but the
light-colored straw carpet on the floor, the panel under the
window, and the enameled foot of a gueridon, but when he
straightened up to step back, he saw his aunt.

She was stretched out on the sea-green satin of the chaise longue, dressed in a fantastic gypsy costume. She lay there on her back, her chin in the air, her throat extended, her forehead tilted back, and her long, loose hair flowing over the end of the chaise longue and onto the carpet. An artificial pomegranate flower had washed ashore on the island formed by a bronze-colored leather shoe in the middle of the dull-gold stream.

The colors of her costume were many, though all muted. A waistband of a matte, striped material, designed with multi-colored flames of dark blue, pale rose, gray, and orange, was fitted around a white silk shift with very wide sleeves that reached down past the elbow. The silk had a slightly reddish sheen to it, and it was sparsely shot through with threads of red gold. Her skirt of primrose-colored velvet, without any trimming, was not pulled tightly around her but lay loosely spread out with the folds falling obliquely over the chaise longue. From the knee down, her legs were bare, and she had bound her crossed ankles together with a heavy necklace of pale coral. Out on the floor lay an open fan with pictures of a series of playing cards arranged in an arc, and farther away lay a pair of leaf-brown stockings, one of them rolled up, the other spread out flat, revealing its shape and the reddish seam along the leg.

At the same moment that Niels had caught sight of her, she had also seen him. She made a little involuntary movement, as if to stand up, but stopped herself and remained lying there as before, simply turning her head slightly and looking at the boy with an inquisitive smile.

"Here they are," he said, going over to her with the flowers.

She stretched out her hand for them, hastily compared their color to the colors of her costume, and then, with a wearily murmured "Impossible," she let them fall.

With a dismissive motion of her hand she stopped Niels from picking them up.

"Give me that over there," she said, pointing to a red bottle lying on a crumpled handkerchief by her feet.

Niels went over to it; he was beet-red, and as he bent over

those matte-white, gently curving legs and those long, narrow feet that had something of a hand's intelligence in their finely cradled contours, he felt quite faint; when, at the same moment, the tip of one foot curled downward with a sudden movement, he was just about to collapse.

"Where did you pick those cornflowers?" asked Edele.

Niels pulled himself together and turned toward her. "I picked them in the pastor's rye field," he said with a voice that surprised him, there was such a resonance to it. Without looking up he handed her the bottle.

Edele noticed his emotion and looked at him with astonishment. Suddenly she blushed, raised herself up on one arm, and pulled her legs up under her skirt. "Go, go, go, go," she said, partly annoyed, partly embarrassed, and with every word she sprinkled some of the essence of rose at Niels.

Niels left.

When he was out the door she slowly let her legs glide down from the chaise longue and gazed down at them with curiosity.

With hurried, uncertain steps Niels raced through the house and up to his room. He was completely bewildered, he felt such a strange weakness in his knees and nausea rising in his throat. Then he threw himself on the sofa and closed his eyes, but could find no peace. There was an incomprehensible restlessness in him, his breathing was so heavy, as if in fear, and the light tortured him even though his eyes were closed.

Gradually things changed; it was as if a hot, oppressive breath were blowing over him, making him so helplessly weak. He had a feeling like the one you have in dreams: something is calling and you want to go to it so badly but you can't move your feet and you panic at your impotence, wilt from your longing to escape, compelled to madness by this calling that does not understand that you are trapped. And he sighed impatiently like an invalid and looked around the room in despair; never had he felt so unhappy, so alone, rejected, and forsaken.

Then he sat down at the window, in the midst of sunshine, and wept.

From that day on Niels felt anxiously happy in Edele's presence. She was no longer a human being like everyone else, but a wonderfully exalted creature, made divine through a strange mystery of beauty, and he felt a heart-pounding joy in observing her, kneeling before her in his heart, crawling at her feet with self-effacing humility. But at times the need to worship would grow so great that it demanded expression in an outward sign of submission, and then he would look for an advantageous moment to tiptoe into Edele's room and — a premeditated, infinite number of times — kiss the little rug in front of her bed, her shoes, or whatever other keepsake offered itself to his obsession.

He regarded it as great fortune that his Sunday shirt was just at that time demoted to an everyday shirt, for in the scent left behind by the sprinkling of rose oil he had a powerful talisman which, as if in a magic mirror, showed him Edele as he had seen her, reclining on the green chaise longue, dressed in the masquerade costume. In the story that he shared with Frithiof, this image reappeared again and again, and from then on poor Frithiof was never safe from bare-legged princesses: if he was dragging himself through the depths of the primeval jungle, they would call to him from their hammocks of lianas; if he sought refuge from a hurricane in a mountain cave, they would rise from their beds of velvety soft moss and bid him welcome; and if, with a mighty slash of his saber, he sprang into the pirate's cabin, powder-stained and blood-spattered, he would find them there too, lounging on the captain's green sofa. They bored him to tears, and he could not fathom why they had suddenly become so necessary to the beloved heroes.

However high a human being may have placed his throne, however tightly he may have pressed the crown of the exceptional — signifying genius — onto his brow, he can still never be absolutely certain that one day he might not be suddenly seized, like King Nebuchadnezzar, by an unnatural desire to walk on all fours and eat grass alongside the quite ordinary animals of the field.

This is what happened to Mr. Bigum, in that he quite simply fell in love with Miss Edele. And it was no help at all that he altered world history in order to excuse his love, nor did it help that he called Edele Beatrice or Laura or Vittoria Colonna, for all the artificial halos with which he crowned his love were extinguished just as quickly as he could light them by the intractable truth that it was Edele's beauty he was in love with, and that it was not the qualities of her soul or her heart that had enchanted him, but rather her elegance, her easy worldly tone, her self-confidence—yes, even her gracious shamelessness. It was in all respects a love that was sent down to fill him with a shameful astonishment at the fickleness of the children of humanity.

Yet what did that matter? What did they have to say, all those eternal truths and provisional lies that clasped each other ring by ring and were linked together into that weighty coat of mail he called his convictions; what did they have to say against his love? They were the strength, marrow, and core of life, so let them show off their power: if they were weaker, then they would break; if they were stronger . . . But they were shattered, pulled apart like the weave of tender threads they were. What did she care about the eternal truths? And the mighty visions — what good were they to him? Ideas that plumbed the boundless depths—could he win her with them? All that he owned was worthless. If his soul shone with a glory a hundred times greater than the sun's, what good would it do, since it was hidden beneath the felt of a Diogenes cloak hideous with poverty? Form, form, give me form's thirty pieces of silver for my content, give me the body of Alcibiades, the cloak of Don Juan, and the rank of a *Kammerjunker*!

But he did not have that, and Edele did not feel at all moved to sympathy by this awkward, philosophical person who had only regarded life's emotions in the barbaric nakedness of the abstract; so there was something brashly absolute about his utterances, something that asserted itself with an unpleasant confidence, rather like a misplaced drum in a *dolce* concert. The tenseness in him, the fact that his thoughts about every little question immediately assumed a position of muscular strength, like a strong man playing with barbells, made him ridiculous in her eyes. And he irritated her when, driven by a carping morality, he would indiscreetly reveal every feeling — faintly intimated yet incognito — by boorishly calling it by its true name, as it would race past him in the course of a conversation.

Bigum knew full well what an unfavorable impression he presented and how completely hopeless his love was, but he knew it the way you do when, with all the power of your soul, you hope that your knowledge is false. There was still a chance for a miracle, and miracles don't happen, but they might. Who knows? Perhaps you make a mistake, perhaps your reason, your instincts, your senses with all their daylight clarity still lead you astray, perhaps the thing to do is to possess the reckless courage to follow the will-o'-the-wisp of hope that burns above the lust-laden ferment of your passion. It is not until you hear the door of decision slam that the iron-cold claws of wisdom dig into your breast, slowly, slowly closing around the nerve-fine thread of hope in your heart from which your world of happiness hangs; then the thread is cut, and what it was holding falls, then it is crushed, then comes the sharp scream of despair through the emptiness.

In a state of doubt, no one despairs.

One sunny September afternoon Edele was sitting on the terrace of the wide, old-fashioned wooden stairway, which had five or six steps leading down from the conservatory into the garden. Behind her the glass doors stood wide open, thrown back against the wall's motley, shiny red, shiny green covering of wild grapevines. She was leaning her head up against the seat of a chair burdened by large black portfolios, and she was holding a copperplate etching in front of her with both hands. Colored etchings, depicting Byzantine mosaics in which blue and gold were dominant, lay spread out on the withered-green rush mat of the terrace, on the threshold, and on the oak-brown parquet floor of the conservatory. At the foot of the stairs lay a white sun hat, for Edele was bareheaded, with no other ornament in her hair than a flower of gold filigree, matching the design of the bracelet she wore high up on her arm. Her white dress of a translucent material, with thin, silky-smooth stripes, had a double border of gray and orange chenille and was covered with little rosettes in the same two colors. Light-colored gloves without fingers covered her hands and arms past her elbows. They were of pearl-gray silk, just like her shoes.

Through the forward-drooping branches of an ancient ash, the yellow sunshine seeped in rays down over the stairs, forming in the cool translucent shade a radiant lattice of lines that filled the air with a golden dust and sketched out clear spots on the steps, on the door and wall, one spot of sun next to another, as if everything were shining toward the light through a template full of holes in its own color: white from Edele's white dress, blood-crimson from her crimson lips, and gold like amber from her amber-blonde hair. And round about in hundreds of other colors — in blue and gold, in oak-brown, in glass-smooth mirror flashes, and in red and green.

Edele let the copperplate etching fall and raised her eyes hopelessly, the sigh she was too weary to utter mutely pleading in her glance. Then she straightened up with a movement as if she were shutting out her surroundings and hiding inside herself.

At that moment Mr. Bigum came walking up.

Edele looked at him with a drowsy blinking, exactly like a child who is lying too comfortably and is much too sleepy to want to move the slightest bit, but at the same time is too curious to close her eyes.

Mr. Bigum was wearing his new felt hat; he was completely engrossed in himself and gesticulating so energetically with his tombac watch in his hand that the thin silver chain it was attached to threatened to snap at any moment. With a sudden movement he literally shoved the watch into his pocket, shook his head impatiently, grabbed hold of the lapels of his coat with a gesture of annoyance, and walked on with an angry twist of his body, and with his face clouded by all the hopeless fury that boils in a man who is fleeing from his own tormented thoughts and knows that he flees in vain.

Edele's hat, lying there at the foot of the stairs, white against the black earth of the pathway, stopped him in his flight. He lifted it carefully with both hands, at the same moment catching sight of Edele, and as he searched for something to say, he remained standing there with the hat, without handing it to her. Not a thought could he find in his mind, not a word would come to his tongue, and he looked straight ahead with a hollow expression of paralyzed profundity.

"It's a hat, Mr. Bigum," Edele remarked in order not to feel embarrassed herself in all that embarrassing silence.

"Yes," said the tutor eagerly, as if delighted to hear her confirm a similarity that had just struck him too; but at the same instant he blushed at the clumsiness of his reply.

"It was lying here," he hurried to add, "here on the ground, like . . . like this," and he bent down and showed her how it had been lying there, with all the thoughtless verbosity of embarrassment and almost happy at what a relief it was to show some sign of life, no matter how meager that sign might be. And he was still standing there with the hat.

"Are you going to keep it?" asked Edele.

Bigum didn't know what to say.

"I mean, would you give it to me?" she explained.

Bigum took a few steps up and handed her the hat. "Miss Lyhne," he said, "do you think . . . You must not think, Miss Lyhne . . . I beg you to let me speak; I mean . . . I'm not saying anything, but have patience with me! I love you, Miss Lyhne, inexpressibly, inexpressibly, I can't tell you how much I love you. Oh, if there were a word that contained the admiring fear of a slave, the ecstatic smile of a martyr, the nameless homesickness of the banished, the exiled — that is the word I would use to say I love you. Oh, let me speak, hear me, hear me, don't push me away yet. Don't imagine that I insult you with an insane hope, I know how lowly I am in your eyes, how coarse I am and repulsive, so repulsive. I'm not forgetting that I am poor — yes, you must hear this — so poor that I have to let my mother live in a poorhouse, and I must, yes I must, I am that impoverished. Yes, Miss, I'm just a humble servant in the service of your brother, and yet there is a world where I am ruler, with power — proud, rich, I tell you, with the glow of victory about me, and noble, ennobled by the drive that allowed Prometheus to steal fire from the heavens of the gods, and there I am their brother, all of the great in spirit whom the earth has borne, and who bear the earth — oh, I understand them as only equals can understand each other; no flight they have flown has been too great for the might of my wings. Do you understand me, Miss? Do you believe me? Oh, don't believe me, it's not true, I am only the base goblin form you see. It's all over; for the terrible delirium of this love has paralyzed my wings, the eyes of my spirit are losing their power to see, my heart is withering, my soul is bleeding itself dry to the bloodlessness of cowardice. Oh, save me from myself, Miss, don't turn away in scorn, weep for me, weep, it's Rome that is burning!"

He had sunk down on both knees in the middle of the stairs, his hands twisting together. His face was pale and drawn, his teeth clenched in pain, his eyes drowning in tears, and his whole form rippled with suppressed sobbing, which could be heard only as wheezing gasps.

Edele had not risen from the terrace. "Pull yourself together, sir!" she said in a somewhat sympathetic tone. "Pull yourself together, don't let yourself be so overwhelmed. Be a man. Do you hear me? Get up, go down into the garden for a while and try to get hold of yourself."

"So you can't love me at all?" Bigum gasped almost inaudibly. "Oh, that's terrible, there is nothing in my soul that I wouldn't murder or degrade, if only I might win you by doing so. No, no, if I were offered madness and in the visions of that madness I possessed *you, possessed* you, then I would say: look, here is my mind, dig down into its wondrous construction with a careless hand and tear asunder all the fine fibers with which my soul is bound to the shining triumphal chariot of the human spirit, let me sink down into the temporal mire, beneath the chariot's wheel, and let the others pass by on their paths of glory up toward the light. Do you understand me? Do you comprehend that even if your love came to me stripped of all its brightness, all the majesty of its purity, yes, even if it came to me debased, sullied, like a travesty of love, like a sickly phantom, I would receive it, on my knees, as if it were a holy host. But the best in me is in vain, the worst in me is in vain. I shout to the sun, but it does not shine, to the cloudy pillar, but it does not reply. Reply! What is there to reply to? That I am suffering? No, this inexpressible torment that is splitting my innermost being down to its deepest roots, this agony just repels you, offends you like a cold little insult, and you laugh scornfully in your heart at the poor tutor's impossible passion."

"You do me an injustice, Mr. Bigum," said Edele and stood up. Bigum stood up too. "I'm not laughing at you. You ask me whether there is any hope, and I reply: no, there is no hope. That is certainly nothing to laugh about. But let me tell you one thing. From the first moment you began to think about me, you have known what my answer would be; you *have* known it, haven't you? You have known it the whole time, but still you have driven all your thoughts and desires toward the goal you knew you could never attain. I'm not offended by your love, Mr. Bigum, but I condemn it. You have done what so many others do. People close their eyes to real life, they don't want to hear the 'no' it shouts at their wishes, they want to forget the deep chasm it shows them between their longing and what they long for. They want to realize their dreams. But life doesn't take dreams into account, there is not a single obstacle that can be dreamed away from reality, and so in the end they lie there wailing at the chasm, which has not changed but is the same as it has always been. But they themselves have changed, for with their dreams they have goaded all their thoughts and inflamed their longings to the very highest pitch. Yet the chasm has not grown narrower, and everything in them longs so painfully to cross over it. But no, always no, never anything else. And if only they had watched out for themselves in time, but now it is too late, they *are* unhappy."

She fell silent, as if awakening from a spell. Her voice had been calm, searching, as if she were talking to herself, but now it turned hostile, cold, and hard.

"I can't help you, Mr. Bigum; for me you are nothing of what you wish to be. If it makes you unhappy, then you will have to be unhappy. If you are suffering, then suffer; there has to be someone to suffer. If you turn a person into your god and master of your fate, then you must bow to the will of that divinity, but it is never wise to create gods who will not come down from their pedestal. Be sensible, Mr. Bigum. Your god is so small and so unworthy of worship; turn away from her and be happy with one of the country daughters."

With a faint little smile she went in through the conservatory; Bigum dejectedly watched her go. He continued pacing back and forth in front of the stairs for a quarter of an hour — all the words that had been spoken still rang in the air where she had been so recently; it was as though a shadow of her still lingered, as though she were still within reach of his prayers and everything did not yet look so hopelessly, totally over. But then the maid came out and gathered up the copperplate engravings, took in the chair, the portfolios, the rush mat — everything.

Then he was free to go.

Up in the open dormer window Niels sat and stared after him. He had heard the whole conversation from beginning to end, and there was a frightened expression on his face and a nervous trembling all over his body. For the first time he had felt fear about life, for the first time he had truly understood that when life had sentenced you to suffer, this sentence was neither a pretense nor a threat — you were dragged to the rack and then you were tortured, and no fairytale liberation came at the last moment, no sudden awakening as if from a bad dream.

This was what he understood with terror and foreboding.

It was not a good autumn for Edele, and the winter completely broke her strength, so that when spring arrived it did not find a poor, weak germ of life that it could be kind and gentle and warm toward; it found only a withering that no gentleness, no warmth, could stop or even deter. But it could shine its flood of light down over the languishing woman and lovingly follow with its fragrant warmth the waning life-force, just as the lingering crimson of evening pursues the dying day.

It was in May that it ended, a day full of sunshine, the kind of day when the lark is never silent and when the rye is growing so you can see it with your own eyes. Outside her window the big cherry trees stood white with flowers. Bouquets of snow, wreaths of snow, domes, arches, garlands, a fairyland architecture of white flowers with a background of the bluest sky.

She felt so weak that day, and yet so light in her weakness, so strangely light, and she knew what would come, for in the morning she had summoned Bigum and said farewell to him.

The Councilor had come over from Copenhagen, and the whole morning the handsome, white-haired man sat by her bed with his hand clasped in hers. He did not speak; once in a while he would move his hand, then she would press it and look up and then he would smile at her. Her brother was with her the whole time too, giving her medicine and otherwise making himself useful.

She lay so still, with eyes closed, and images from home passed before her from her life in Copenhagen. The drooping willows of Sorgenfri, Lyngby's red church on its pedestal of

graves, and the white farm by the little sunken road down to
the lake where the dock was always green, as if it were painted
with dampness; all this appeared before her, grew in clarity,
diminished in clarity, and disappeared. And other images followed. There was Bredgade as the sun set and darkness slowly
rose over the buildings, and there was the strange Copenhagen
she discovered when she came in from the country one morning. It seemed so fantastic in its bustle and sunshine, with its
whitewashed window frames and the smell of fruit in the
streets; the buildings looked so unreal in the bright light, and it
was as if a silence lay over them which the noise and rumbling
of wagons could not disturb. Then there was the warm, dark
parlor in the autumn evenings, when she had gotten dressed for
the theater and the others were not yet ready: the smell of
incense, the fire in the tiled stove that shone onto the carpet,
the patter of rain against the window, the horses stamping at
the gate, the melancholy cry of the shellfish vendor down in
the street... and waiting beyond it all: the theater's lights,
music, and grandeur.

With images such as these, the afternoon passed.

In the parlor were Niels and his mother. Niels was kneeling
in front of the sofa with his face pressed into the brown velvet
and his hands folded over his head; he was crying loudly and
moaning, without any attempt to control himself, completely
gripped by his sorrow. Mrs. Lyhne sat with him. On the table
in front of her lay a hymnbook open to the funeral hymns.
Now and then she would read a couple of verses, now and then
she would bend over her son and say consoling words to him
and admonish him; but Niels would not be comforted, and she
could stop neither his tears nor the wild prayers of his despair.

Then Lyhne appeared in the doorway to the sickroom. He
made no sign, he simply looked at them somberly, and they
both stood up and followed him in to his sister. He took each
by the hand and stepped up to the bed with them, and Edele
looked up, looked at each of them and moved her lips as if to
speak; then Lyhne led his wife to the window and sat down

with her, while Niels threw himself to his knees at the foot of the bed.

He wept quietly and prayed with folded hands, fervently and unceasingly in a muted, passionate whisper; he told God that he would not give up hope. "I won't let you go, Lord, I won't let you go until you say yes, you mustn't take her from us, because you know how much we love her, you mustn't, you mustn't. Oh, I can't say: 'Thy will be done,' because you'll let her die; oh, but let her live, and I will thank you and obey you, I'll do everything I know you want me to do, I'll be so good and never do anything against you, if only you will let her live. Do you hear me, God? Oh, stop it, stop it and make her well, before it's too late. I will... I will... oh, what can I promise you? Oh, I will thank you and never, never forget you; oh, but just listen to me! You can see that she's dying, you can see that she's dying, listen to me, take your hand away, take it away, I can't lose her, God, I can't, let her live, won't you, won't you? Oh, it's so unfair of you..."

Outside, beyond the window, the white flowers blushed like roses in the glow of the setting sun. Arc after arc, the profusion of blossoms formed itself petal-light into a rose palace, into a choir of roses, and through the airy vault the evening-blue sky evoked the dawn, as golden light, and lights of gold with crimson fire, shot out in glorious rays from all the swaying garlands of the flower temple.

Pale and still, Edele lay with the old man's hand in both of hers. Slowly she breathed her life away, breath after breath; fainter and fainter lifted her breast, heavier and heavier grew her eyelids.

"Send my greetings to... Copenhagen!" was her last faint whisper.

But no one heard her very last greeting. It didn't even come as a breath across her lips, her greeting to him, that great artist whom she had secretly loved with all her soul, but for whom she had been nothing, just a name his ears recognized, just one more unfamiliar face among a large, admiring public.

And the light vanished in the bluish twilight, and her hands slipped exhausted from each other. The shadows grew — the shadows of evening and death.

The Councilor bent over the deathbed and placed his hand on her pulse and waited quietly, and when the last breath was gone, the last faint ripple of blood silenced, he raised the pale hand to his lips.

"Little Edele!"

I V

There are those who can take up their sorrow and bear it, strong temperaments who feel their strength in the very weight of the burden, while those who are weaker give in to the sorrow, as powerlessly as one surrenders to an illness; like an illness, grief penetrates them, seeping its way into their innermost being and becoming one with them; it is transformed within them in a slow battle and then lost inside them in a full recovery.

But there are also those for whom grief is a violence directed against them, a cruelty that they never learn to regard as a test or a prayer or merely as simple fate. For them it is a manifestation of tyranny, something personally hateful, and there will always be a thorn left in their hearts.

It is not often that children grieve like this, but Niels Lyhne did. For in the fervor of his prayer it was as if he had been face to face with his God, he had crawled on his knees at the foot of the throne, the hope within him trembling in fear, and yet firmly believing in the omnipotence of his prayer, bold enough to implore that his prayer be heard. And he had been forced to rise up from the dust and go away with his hope crushed. With his faith he had not been able to call down the miracle from its heaven; no god had answered his cry. Death had stridden toward its prey, without stopping, as if there were no rampart of prayers built as protection from fear.

A silence came over him.

His faith had flung itself in blind flight against the gates of heaven, and now it lay on Edele's grave with broken wings. For he had believed, he had had that straightforward, dazzling, fairytale faith that a child so often has. It is not the coherent, subtly nuanced God of the catechism that children believe in; it is the mighty Old Testament God, the one who was so fond of Adam and Eve, and for whom the entire human family — kings, prophets, pharaohs — are merely well-behaved or naughty children; that violent, patriarchal God who has the anger of a giant when angered and is generous with the generosity of a giant, who barely has created life before He goads death toward it, who drowns His world in waters from His heaven, who thunders down laws that are too weighty for the people He has created, and who then in the days of Caesar Augustus develops sympathy for them and sends His son to death so that the law may be broken, even as it is obeyed. That God, who always has a miracle as an answer — He is the one the children talk to when they pray. Then the day will probably come when they understand that, in the earthquake that shakes Golgotha and throws opens the graves, they have heard His voice for the last time, and now that the curtain of the Holy of Holies has been rent asunder, it is the God Jesus who reigns, and from that day on they pray in a different way.

But Niels had not come that far.

With a believing mind he had followed Jesus on his wandering of the earth. But the fact that Jesus still was subordinate to his Father, walked so powerlessly, and suffered so humanly, had concealed his godliness from Niels; in him Niels had seen only the one who did his Father's will, only the son of God, not God Himself, and thus it was to God the Father that he had prayed, and it was God the Father who had betrayed him in his bitter need. But if God had turned away from him, then *he* could also turn away from God. If God had no ears, then Niels would have no voice; if God had no mercy, then Niels would have no adoration, and he defied God and turned Him out of his heart.

On the day Edele was buried, he stomped his foot in the earth of the grave with contempt every time the pastor mentioned the Lord's name; and later, when he encountered it in books and in conversation, he would wrinkle his child's brow with rebellious spirit. When he lay down to sleep at night a strange feeling of forsaken greatness would be awakened in him as he realized that now all people — both children and adults — were praying to Our Lord and closing their eyes in His name, while he alone kept his hands from folding, he alone refused God His homage. He was shut out from the safekeeping of heaven, no angel kept watch at his side; solitary and unprotected he drifted on the mysteriously murmuring waters of darkness, and loneliness spread around him, outward from his bed in ever more distantly receding circles. Nevertheless, he did not pray — though he yearned to do so to the point of tears, he did not call out.

And thus it was for all his days, because in defiance he freed himself from the way of seeing to which his upbringing had bound him, and with his sympathies he fled to the side of those who had used their powers in vain to fight against adversity.

In the books he had been given to read and in what he had been taught, God and all that was His — peoples and ideas — passed by in an unceasing victory procession; and Niels had rejoiced along with the rejoicing, swept up by the happy feeling of being counted among the proud legions of the victorious. For is victory not always just, and is the victor not the liberator, the innovator, the light-bringer?

But now the rejoicing inside him had been silenced, now he did not speak. He thought with the mind of the conquered, felt with the heart of the defeated, and he understood that if what wins is good, what surrenders is not necessarily bad; and so he took sides, said that his side was better, felt that it was greater, and called the victorious force tyrannical and violent. He took sides, as completely as he could, against God, but like a vassal who takes up arms against his rightful master, for he still believed and could not banish his faith.

His tutor, Mr. Bigum, was not a man who could help a soul back to the fold. On the contrary. His temperamental philosophy, which allowed him to be enthralled by and enthusiastic about *all* sides of an issue — today one side, tomorrow the opposite — set all dogmas adrift for his students. He was no doubt actually a Christian man, and, if you could have made him say definitely what was firm ground for him amid all this flux, he certainly would have said that it was the faith and teachings of the Lutheran evangelical church, or something along that line, at any rate. But he had so little interest in propelling his students forward along the clearly marked path of the church faith or in shouting to them at every step that the slightest movement outside the signposts was a step into lies and darkness, toward hell and the damnation of the soul. For he completely lacked the passionate concern of righteousness for trivial details. He was religious in that rather artistic, superior manner which such minds permit themselves, not afraid of a little compromising, and easily lured into semi-involuntary rewritings and adaptations because above all else they must promote their own personality, and in whatever spheres they fly, they must hear the rush of their own soul's wings.

These kinds of people do not lead their students, but there is a fullness in their teaching, a complexity and a somewhat reeling versatility which, if the student is not confused by it, develops his independence to the highest degree and almost forces him to form his own opinion, since children are never satisfied with anything vague or ambiguous, but out of an instinct for self-preservation they always demand a pure "yes" or a pure "no," a for or against so they will know which way to direct their hatred and which way their love.

So there is no steady and intractable authority, eternally establishing facts and showing the way, who is able to maneuver Niels back. He has taken the bit in his teeth and is running down every new path that appears, as long as it leads away from what was previously the home of his emotions and his thoughts.

There is a new feeling of power in seeing with one's own eyes and choosing with one's own heart like this, in participating in creating one's own self; and so many things spring up in Niels' mind, so many unfathomed, scattered sides of his being gather so wondrously into a sensible whole. It is a thrilling time of discovery during which, little by little, with apprehension and uncertain jubilation, with disbelieving joy, he discovers himself. For the first time he sees that he is not like the others; a spiritual modesty stirs in him, making him shy and reticent and embarrassed. He is suspicious about all questions and finds references to his most secret thoughts in everything that is said. Because he has learned to read inside himself, he thinks that everyone else can also read what is written within him, and he withdraws from the adults and wanders around alone. All at once people have become so strangely intrusive. He feels slightly hostile toward them, as if they were creatures of a different race, and in his loneliness he begins to take them to task and examine them, searching and judging. Before, the names "Father," "Mother," "the pastor," "the miller" contained a completely satisfactory explanation. The name had totally hidden the person from him. The pastor was the pastor, there was no more to be said about it. But now he saw that the pastor was a short, jovial man who was as quiet and subdued as possible at home in order not to draw his wife's attention, and away from his house he always spoke with a rush of excitement and freedom-thirsty exuberance, in order to forget the yoke at home.

That was what the pastor had become.

And what about Mr. Bigum?

Niels had seen him prepared to throw everything aside for Edele's love, heard him deny his self and his soul during that hour of passion down in the garden, and now Mr. Bigum still talked about the philosophical person's Olympian calm amidst life's vague whirlwinds and vapor-borne rainbows. What painful contempt this aroused in the boy. And how alert and easily awakened it made the doubt in him! He did not know that what Mr. Bigum called inferior in other people was called something else when it concerned himself, and that Mr. Bigum's Olympian calm toward what roused human emotions was the contemptuous smile of a Titan, full of memories of the Titans' longings and the Titans' passions.

V

Six months after Edele's death one of Lyhne's cousins lost her husband, pottery manufacturer Refstrup. Business had never been good; her husband's lengthy illness had brought it even closer to collapse, and there was not much left between the widow and destitution. Seven children were more than she could support. The two youngest and the eldest, who helped out in the factory, stayed with her; relatives took in the rest. The Lyhnes took the next-oldest boy; his name was Erik, he was fourteen years old, and he had had a scholarship to the town's private Latin school. Now he studied with Mr. Bigum along with Niels and Frithiof Petersen, the pastor's son.

It was not of his own free will that Erik continued his studies, for he wanted to be a sculptor. His father had said that that was a lot of nonsense, but Lyhne didn't have anything against it. He thought the boy had talent. But he wanted him to graduate first; then he would always have something to fall back on. And besides, for a sculptor a classical education was essential, or at least to be highly recommended. That was the situation for the time being, and Erik had to console himself with the not insignificant collection of fine copperplate engravings and pretty bronzes to be found at Lønborggaard. At any rate, they seemed great to someone who had only seen the junk that a more eccentric than knowledgeable cabinetmaker had bequeathed to the parish library, and Erik was soon busy with pencil and sculpting tools. No one appealed to him as much as Guido Reni, who in those days was more famous than Raphael and the greatest masters. And there is perhaps nothing better to open young eyes to the beauties of a work of art than the certain knowledge that their admiration is validated on the highest levels. Andrea del Sarto, Parmigianino, and Luini, who later, when he and his talent had found each other, would mean so much to him, now left him cold; while the vigor of Tintoretto, the bitterness of Salvator Rosa and Caravaggio delighted him. For sweetness in art has no appeal for the very young: the painter of the loveliest miniatures has started out in the footsteps of Buonarotti, the warmest poet has sailed his first voyage with black sails in the blood of tragedy.

But this trifling with art was still only a game for him, little better than other games, and he was no prouder of a successfully modeled bust or a cleverly carved horse than he was of hitting the church weathervane with a rock or of swimming out to Sønderhagen and back again without stopping; these were his kind of games, requiring physical ability, strength, endurance, a sure hand, and a practiced eye — not like Niels' or Frithiof's games, where fantasy played the main role and where the plot and the success of the plot were all imagined. But soon they abandoned their old pastimes to follow Erik. The novels were put aside, and at their last secret meeting in the hayloft, their endless story came to a rather violent end; and deep silence brooded over its hastily erected grave, for they did not want to say anything about it to Erik. After knowing him for only a few days they had already realized that he would make fun of both them and their story, degrade them in their own eyes, and make them feel ashamed of themselves. He had that power, because he was free of anything that could be called dreaming or exaltation or fantasizing. And since the clear, practical common sense of a boy, with its irreproachable health, was just as quick to scorn and ruthless toward spiritual flaws as children generally are toward physical defects, Niels and Frithiof were afraid of him, and they patterned themselves after him, denying much and concealing more. Niels was especially quick to suppress everything in himself that was not part of Erik's world, and with the passionate zeal of a renegade he mocked and ridiculed Frithiof, whose slower and more loyal nature could not all at once abandon the old for the new. But what actually drove Niels to this unkind behavior was jealousy, because from the very first day he had fallen in love with Erik, who, shy and reserved, only reluctantly and somewhat contemptuously tolerated allowing himself to be loved.

Of all the emotional relationships in life, is there any more delicate, more noble, and more intense than a boy's deep and yet so totally bashful love for another boy? The kind of love that never speaks, never dares give way to a caress, a glance, or a word, the kind of vigilant love that bitterly grieves over every shortcoming or imperfection in the one who is loved, a love which is longing and admiration and negation of self, and which is pride and humility and calmly breathing happiness.

Erik stayed at Lønborggaard only a year or a year and a half, for during a visit to Copenhagen Lyhne had spoken with one of the most prominent sculptors and shown him the boy's sketches, and Mikkelsen, the sculptor, had said that he had talent and that studying was a waste of time; you didn't need much of a classical education to think up a Greek name for a naked figure. So it was decided that Erik should be sent there at once to enter the Academy and work in Mikkelsen's atelier.

On the last afternoon, Niels and Erik were sitting upstairs in their room. Niels was looking at pictures in a penny magazine. Erik was engrossed in Spengler's descriptive catalog of the art collection at Christiansborg Palace. So many times he had leafed through that book, trying from the naive descriptions to form an impression of the paintings, almost sick with yearning actually to see all that art and beauty, with his own eyes actually to enjoy and to grasp all the loveliness of the color and line, so that in admiration they would become his; and so many times he had closed that book, weary of staring into the swirling, fantastical fog of the words that would not catch hold, would not take shape, would not give birth to anything but merely billow and glide, billow, glide, in vague, delirious alternation.

Today was not like that, today he had the knowledge that soon they would no longer be shadows from dreamland, and he felt himself so rich because of all the book's promises, and the images took shape today as never before and broke forth — a fleeting glimpse like brilliant suns through a fog, gilded and dancing gold.

"What are you looking at?" he said to Niels.

Niels showed him Lassen, the war hero from the 2nd of April, in his book.

"He's sure ugly!" said Erik.

"Ugly! He was a hero. Would you call *him* ugly too?"

Niels had turned the pages back to the picture of a great poet.

"Incredibly ugly!" Erik assured him with a grimace. "Look at that nose! And that mouth, and those eyes! And look at those wisps of hair all around his head!"

Niels *saw* that he was ugly and fell silent; it had never occurred to him that what was great was not always cast in a form that was beautiful.

"Oh, that's right," said Erik, closing his Spengler, "I've got to remember to give you the key to the wheelhouse."

Niels made a melancholy, deprecating gesture, but Erik put a little padlock key on a wide cotton ribbon around Niels' neck. "Shall we go down there?" he asked.

They went outside. They found Frithiof by the garden fence; he was lying there eating sour gooseberries, and he had tears in his eyes because of Erik's departure. He was also hurt that they hadn't sought him out before. Of course, he usually came of his own accord, but on a day like today he thought things ought to be more formal. Silently he held out a handful of the green fruit to each of them, but they had had their favorite dishes for lunch and were finicky.

"Too sour," said Erik, shuddering.

"What unhealthy stuff!" added Niels haughtily, looking down at the proffered berries. "Why do you bother? Throw that stuff away. We're going to the wheelhouse." And he pointed with his chin at the key ribbon, because his hands were in his pockets.

Then the three of them went off together.

The wheelhouse was an old, green-painted ship's cabin that had once been bought at a beach auction. It stood down by the fjord and had served as a storage house while the dam was being built, but it wasn't used anymore, and the boys had taken possession of it, keeping their toy boats, bows and arrows, fishing poles, and other treasures there, especially such forbidden but essential items as gunpowder, tobacco, and matches.

Niels opened the wheelhouse door with a kind of gloomy ceremoniousness, and they went in and brought out their things from the dim corners of the empty bunkrooms.

"Do you know what?" said Erik with his head completely inside a distant corner. "I'm going to blow mine up."

"Mine and Frithiof's too," Niels replied, underlining his words with a sweeping movement of his hand as if taking an oath.

"No, not mine, by God!" yelled Frithiof. "Then what would we have to sail after Erik is gone?"

"That's true," said Niels, turning away from him in scorn.

Frithiof felt a little uncomfortable, but when the others had gone outside, he moved his boat to a more secure hiding place.

Outside they quickly placed the gunpowder in the small vessels, in a nest of tarred oakum; then they set the sails, arranged the fuses, lit them, and jumped back. And they ran along the shore, waving to the crew on board and loudly explaining to each other the ships' haphazard turns and movements, which were the result of the nautical intelligence of the worthy captains.

But the ships ran aground near the point without the desired explosion having taken place, so Frithiof had the opportunity to sacrifice magnanimously the stuffing from his cap for the preparation of new and better fuses.

At full sail the vessels turned toward Sjælland's Reef; the

Englishman's heavy frigates approached, slowly making for land in impenetrable circles, while the waves foamed brightly beneath the black bows and the flying jib cannons filled the air with their sharp roar. Closer and closer... blue and red it gleamed, golden it glistened from the fathom-high bows of *Albion* and *Conqueror*. The grayish sails hid the horizon, the smoke of gunpowder billowed forth in white clouds and was carried low like a veil of fog over the sunlit flashing of the waves. Then the deck of Erik's boat exploded with a weak little poof; the oakum caught fire, the red blaze advanced, and the nimble flames ran up the shrouds and along the yards, eating their way smoldering along the ropes of the sails, and then, with long lightning flashes, they reached the canvases which, on fire, rolled and shrank from one another and flew in great black flakes far out over the sea. Dannebrog, the Danish flag, still flew from the sky-high, slender spire of the schooner's mast; the flag line was burned through so it flapped wildly, as if it were striking out with red wings, ready for battle, but the flame erased it in a blaze. Without direction and without a navigator the smoke-blackened ship now drifted, dead and powerless, a toy for the wind and the waves of the beach. Niels' boat refused to burn like that; the gunpowder was lit and smoke had poured out, but that was all — and it wasn't enough.

"Avast, mateys!" Niels shouted out on the point. "Scuttle the ship! Point the starboard cannons down through the aft hatchway and give it to her good!" At the same moment he bent down for a rock. "Ready, aim, fire!" and the rock flew out of his hand.

Erik and Frithiof were quick to help, so the hull was soon in splinters, and Erik's was too.

The wreckage was brought ashore, because now it was going to be burned in a bonfire.

The wreckage, dried seaweed, and withered grass soon formed a burning heap thick with smoke, and the small pieces of flint entangled in the seaweed kept cracking and exploding from the intense heat.

The boys sat silently around the bonfire for a long time, but suddenly Niels, still gloomy, jumped up and took all of his things from the wheelhouse, smashed them to pieces, and threw them on the fire. Then Erik got his things, and Frithiof got some of his. Now the flames reached high in the air from the sacrificial bonfire, so Erik began to worry that it might be visible from up in the field, and he started to put it out with wet seaweed, but Niels stood calmly and stared sadly at the smoke drifting along the beach. Frithiof stayed back a little ways, humming to himself a heroic ballad, which he secretly accompanied now and then with wild, bard-like strumming on the strings of an invisible harp.

After a while the bonfire was put out and Erik and Frithiof headed for home, but Niels stayed behind to close up the wheelhouse. When that was done he cautiously looked around for the others and then threw the key and ribbon far out into the fjord. Erik turned around at just that moment and saw it fall, but he quickly turned his head away and set off in a race with Frithiof.

The next day he left.

At first he was badly missed, bitterly missed, for everything seemed to stand still for the two who were left behind. Life had gradually taken shape with the assumption that there were three of them to live it. Three was company, multiplicity, change; two was loneliness and nothing at all.

What in the world could two find to do?

Could two go skeet shooting? Could two play ball? They could be Friday and Robinson Crusoe, the two of them, but who would be the savages?

What Sundays! Niels was so sick of life that at first he set about studying and then, with the help of Mr. Bigum's huge atlas, expanding his knowledge of geography well beyond the prescribed boundaries. Finally he began to read through the whole Bible, and he kept a diary; but Frithiof, in his utter desolation, sought a disgraceful solace in playing with his sisters.

Later on, the past became less distinct and the longing grew milder; it might appear on a still evening when the red of the sun would light up the wall in the lonely room, and the distant, monotonous song of the cuckoo would stop completely and make the silence broader and greater. Then the longing would appear and turn everything sickly, and its dullness would steal into Niels' mind; but it did not hurt anymore, it came so unnoticed and weighed so gently that it was almost sweet, like a soothing pain.

Their letters tended to follow the same course. In the beginning they were full of complaints, questions, and wishes, loosely intertwined, but later they grew longer, more circuitous and descriptive, and now they were completely stylish, well written, and hidden between the lines there was a certain joy in being able to write so well.

The way things were going now, many things showed up again that hadn't dared raise their heads while Erik was present. Imagination sprinkled its glittery flowers down through the languid silence of Niels' uneventful life, the air of dreams lay upon his mind, urging and corrosive with its scent of life, and with the fine poisons of intimations thirsty for life hidden in the scent.

And that is the way Niels grew up. All childhood influences shape the soft clay; everything shapes it, everything has significance, whatever exists and whatever is dreamed, whatever is known and whatever is sensed — it all imposes its light but surely drawn network of lines, which must be reshaped and deepened, and then must be smoothed away and erased.

V I

"**M**r. Lyhne — Mrs. Boye. Mr. Frithiof Petersen —
Mrs. Boye."

Erik was the one who made the introductions, and they
took place in Mikkelsen's atelier — a large, bright room with a
hard-packed earthen floor and six yards to the ceiling, with
two huge doors leading to the outside on one wall and, on the
other, doors leading to small studios behind. Everything was
gray with dust from the clay and plaster and marble: it had
formed cobwebs high up as thick as rope and painted river
charts on the great windowpanes; it lay in the eyes, mouths,
and noses, and in the bands of muscle, the curly hair and
draperies of the jumble of castings that stretched, like a frieze
of the destruction of Jerusalem, around the entire room on
long shelves. And the laurel trees in the corner near the doorway, the tall laurel trees in their large tubs, had been powdered
grayer than the gray olive.

Erik was standing in the middle of the studio working with
clay, wearing a smock and with a paper cap on his dark, rather
curly hair. He had grown sideburns since they had last seen
him and he looked quite manly next to his pale, exam-weary
friends, who seemed so provincially well-mannered in their
much-too-new clothing and with their cropped hair in the
quite roomy graduation caps.

A short distance from Erik's modeling stand, Mrs. Boye
was sitting on a low, high-backed wooden chair with an elegant
book in one hand and a little lump of clay in the other. She was
petite, quite petite, a brunette with clear brown eyes and a fair
complexion, which in the shadow of her features turned a dull

gold and went so well with her shining hair, whose darkness, in the light, took on a sheen of sun-burnished blonde.

She was laughing when they arrived, as only a child can laugh, so unrestrained and gleefully loud, so happily free, and there was also a child's undaunted look in her eyes, a child's candid smile on her lips, which seemed even more childlike since her upper lip was so thin that her milk-white teeth were almost never hidden and her mouth was almost always slightly open.

But she was no child.

Was she a little over thirty?

The full form of her chin did not deny it, nor the mature blush of her lower lip; and she had a full figure with lush but firm lines that were strongly emphasized by a dark blue dress, tight-fitting like the bodice of a riding habit, tight at the waist, breast, and arms. Around her neck and over her shoulders was draped a dark, blood-red silk cloth, the corners of which disappeared in the V-shaped neckline of her dress, and in her hair she wore carnations the same color as the cloth.

"I'm afraid we're interrupting your pleasant reading," said Frithiof with a glance at the elegant book.

"Not in the least, not at all! No, we've been fighting for the last hour about what we've been reading," replied Mrs. Boye, gazing with big, inescapable eyes at Frithiof. "Mr. Refstrup is such an idealist about all art, and I find that so boring — all that about raw reality which has to be purified and clarified and reborn or whatever it's called, so that it becomes mere nothingness in the end. Do me a favor and look at that *bacchante* by Mikkelsen that deaf Traffelini is standing there copying; if I were to describe it in a catalog . . . Good God! 'Number 77. A young woman in a negligée stands thoughtfully, uncertain what she should do with a bunch of grapes.' She should crush the bunch of grapes, if I might suggest, crush them so the red juice runs down her breast. Well? Shouldn't she? Am I right or not?" And with childish eagerness she caught hold of Frithiof's sleeve and practically tugged at it.

"Well, yes," Frithiof agreed, "yes, you're probably right, it's lacking that... freshness... spontaneity..."

"Oh, it's lacking naturalness, and good God, why *can't* we be natural? Oh, I know full well that courage is what's missing. Neither artists nor poets have the courage to acknowledge human beings for what they are — but Shakespeare did."

"You know very well," said Erik from behind his sculpture, "that I can't abide Shakespeare. I think he overdoes it, I think he runs you around in circles so you don't know what's what in the end."

"I wouldn't say that," Frithiof objected reprovingly. "But," he added with an apologetic smile, "I wouldn't rightfully call the berserk fury of the great English writer the truly conscious, intelligent courage of an artist."

"You wouldn't? Oh God, you're so amusing!" And Mrs. Boye laughed as hard as she could, and stood up and moved across the atelier. Suddenly she turned, stretched her arms out toward Frithiof, and exclaimed, "God bless you!" and then doubled over almost to the floor with laughter.

Frithiof was on the verge of feeling insulted, but it was so troublesome to go away angry, and besides, he was completely right in what he had said — and the lady was so beautiful too. So he stayed and started talking with Erik, and with his thoughts on Mrs. Boye he tried to inject a tone of mature tolerance into his voice.

In the meantime Mrs. Boye was walking about in the far end of the studio, humming thoughtfully; she would occasionally break out in a few hearty, laughing trills, or would sweep past slowly in a solemn recitative.

A youthful bust of Augustus stood on a large wooden crate. She began to dust it off, and then she found some clay and made sideburns and a beard for the head, and rings too, which she hung on its ears.

While she was busy with this, Niels, on the pretense of looking at the shelves with the castings, had come over to Mrs. Boye. She had not even turned her glance in his direction, but she must have known he was there all the same, for without looking up she stretched out her hand toward him and asked him to get Erik's hat.

Niels put the hat in her still extended hand, and she took it and placed it on the bust of Augustus.

"Old Shakespeare," she said endearingly and patted the travesty of a bust on the cheek. "Stupid old fellow who didn't know what he was doing. Did he sit there dabbling in the ink — did he? And churn out a Hamlet bust without thinking about what he was doing? Is that what he did?" She lifted the hat from the bust and let her hand glide maternally over its forehead, as if she wanted to smooth back the hair from its eyes. "Lucky old fellow, in spite of it! Old, not unlucky poet! Because you *could* say that — couldn't you, Mr. Lyhne? — that he was no unlucky man of letters, that Shakespeare."

"Well, I have my own opinion about that man," replied Niels, somewhat offended, and blushed.

"Good Lord, you have your *own* opinion about Shake-speare! So what do you think? Are you with us or against us?" At once she positioned herself with a smile beside the bust and placed her hand around its neck.

"I couldn't say whether the opinion which it so astounds you that I possess is so fortunate as to have any significance by coinciding with yours, yet I believe it must be said to be *for* you and your protegé. At any rate, it's *my* opinion that he knew what he was doing, had weighed what he was doing, and dared to do it. Many times he dared with some doubt, so the doubt is still evident; many times he only dared halfway and then erased that with new lines, as if he didn't dare let it stand as it was . . ."

And he went on in this manner.

As he talked, Mrs. Boye began to grow restless; she looked nervously about, first to one side, then to the other, and tapped her fingers impatiently, while a worried and finally pained expression darkened her face more and more.

Finally she couldn't contain herself any longer.

"Don't forget what you were going to say!" she said. "But I beg you, Mr. Lyhne, do stop moving your hand like that— that gesture as if you were going to pull out teeth. Do stop it! Don't let me disturb you, now I'm listening again. And I quite agree with you."

"Then there's no need to say any more."

"Why not?"

"Since we agree."

"Yes, since we agree."

Neither one of them meant anything special by these last words, but they said them in a meaningful tone, as if there were a world of sophistication hidden behind them, and they looked at each other with a brilliant smile on their lips — the lingering shadow of the wit that had just been flashing — as each of them worried over what exactly it was the other one could have meant, rather annoyed at being so slow-witted.

Together they sauntered over to the others, and Mrs. Boye took her place again on the low chair.

Erik and Frithiof had almost exhausted their conversation and were glad to have the company of the others. Frithiof immediately approached Mrs. Boye and was very charming. With the modesty of a host, Erik stayed in the background.

"If I were a curious person," said Frithiof, "I would ask you what book had made you and Refstrup argue when we arrived."

"Are you asking me?" Mrs. Boye said.

"Yes, I am."

"Ergo?"

"Ergo," replied Frithiof with a humble, conciliatory bow.

Mrs. Boye held up the book and proclaimed solemnly, "*Helge.* Oehlenschläger's *Helge.* And which song was it? It was 'The Mermaid Visits King Helge.' And which verses? The ones where Tangkjær has lain down by Helge's side, and he can no longer control his curiosity but turns . . .

> ... and becomes aware
> Of arms swelling white.
> The greatest beauty the earth possesses,
> Slumbering by his side.
>
> The black caftan no longer swirls
> And hides the beauty of the girl,
> A delicate, fluttering, silver tulle
> Swathes the loveliest limbs.

And that is all we get to see of the loveliness of the mermaid, and that's what I was annoyed about. I want a lush, smoldering description here, I want to see something so dazzlingly beautiful that it takes my breath away. I want to be initiated into the extraordinary beauty of a mermaid's body, and now I ask you, what am I to do with white arms and lovely limbs with a piece of iridescent tulle on top? Good Lord! No, she should be naked like a wave, and the wild beauty of the sea must live in her. There should be some of the phosphorescent sheen of the summer sea on her skin, some of the black, tangled nightmare of the seaweed forest in her hair. Don't you think so? Yes, the water's thousand colors must come and go with a glittering interplay in her eyes; her pale breast must be cold with a voluptuously chilling coldness, the waves trickling their undulating way along all her curves; the suction of the maelstrom should be in her kiss and the breaking gentleness of the foam in her arms' embrace."

She had talked herself into a fervor, and she stood there now, still quite moved by her topic, and looked at her young listeners with the big, inquisitive eyes of a child.

But they said nothing. Niels was blushing quite red and Erik was very embarrassed. Frithiof was completely enraptured and stared at her with the most obvious admiration, and yet he was the one who was least aware of how captivatingly beautiful she was as she stood there before them, behind her words.

Not many weeks had passed before Niels and Frithiof were guests in Mrs. Boye's house just as regularly as Erik Refstrup was. In addition to Mrs. Boye's pale niece they met a number of young people there — promising poets, painters, actors, and architects — all artists by virtue of their youth more than their talent, all full of hope, courageous, eager to fight, and exceedingly easy to fill with enthusiasm. There were probably among them a few of those quiet dreamers who bleat sorrowfully for the bygone ideals of a bygone time, but most of them were filled with what was new at the time, intoxicated with the theories of the New, wild with the power of the New, and dazzled by its morning clarity. They were new, bitterly new, new to a fault, and perhaps not least because deep within there was a strange, powerfully instinctual yearning that had to be stifled, a yearning that the New could not suppress, even as universal as the New was: encompassing all, having power over all, enlightening all.

But that did not matter. There was a stormy rejoicing in these young souls, and there was faith in the starry light of great thoughts, and there was hope just as there are seas; enthusiasm bore them on the wings of eagles, and their hearts swelled with courage a thousandfold.

No doubt life scoured it out of them later on, hushed most of it away; common sense helped break it down, and cowardice easily carried off the remains, but what does that matter? The time that passes with goodness will not return with evil; and nothing experienced in life later on can make one day wither or erase one hour of the life that has been lived.

For Niels the world took on an entirely different appearance during those days. To hear his most secret and obscure thoughts clearly expressed by ten different voices, to see his eccentric, peculiar ideas (which for him lay like a hazy landscape with fog-shrouded features, with indeterminate depths, and with hushed tones), to see that landscape unveiled, in pure, sharp colors bright as day, revealed in all its details, furrowed with roads and with crowds of people on those roads — there was something strangely fantastical about the way fantasy had become so real.

He was no longer a lonely child-king who ruled over lands he had imagined; no, he was one of the crowd, a man of the crowd, a soldier in the pay of the New, of Ideas. There was a sword in his hand, and there was a banner for him too.

What a wonderful time that was, full of promise. How odd it was to hear with his own ears the indistinct, mysterious whispering of his soul ring forth in the air of reality like the wildly challenging tones of lur-horns, like the crash of bludgeons against the temple walls, like the whistle of David-stones in flight toward Goliath-brows, and like the fanfare confident of victory. It was like hearing himself speak in a foreign tongue with strange clarity and strange power about what was his deepest, innermost self.

The gospel of the New about disintegration and perfection rang not only from the lips of his peers; there were also older people, men with names of a certain influence, who had an eye for the New and its glory, and they possessed bolder words than the young. They had a much grander perspective, the names of bygone centuries accompanied them; they had history with them, the history of the human spirit, the odyssey of Ideas. They were men who, in their youth, had been gripped in the same way as those who were young now, and had testified to that spirit which gripped them now. But when they had heard in their own voices what you hear in a shout in the desert — that you are alone — then they were silenced. But the young only thought about the fact that these men had spoken out, not that they had fallen silent, and they were ready with laurel wreaths and martyrs' crowns, eager to admire them, happy to admire them. And the ones who were the object of that admiration did not reject this belated appreciation; in good faith they put on the crowns, regarded themselves highly and historically, wrote the less heroic out of their past — and their old convictions, which the misfortunes of time had cooled, they declaimed with ardor once again.

Niels Lyhne's relatives in Copenhagen, the old Councilor's family, were not at all pleased with the society that the young student had chosen. It wasn't so much the new ideas that caused them concern as the fact that some of the young people found long hair, big hunting boots, and a careless slovenliness to be of benefit to the ideas. Although Niels was not fanatical in that way, it was still uncomfortable for them to meet him and even more uncomfortable to have their acquaintances meet him in the company of youths of this persuasion. But this was merely a trifle compared with the fact that he visited Mrs. Boye so often and went to the theater with her and her pale niece.

It wasn't that you could say anything in particular against Mrs. Boye.

But people did talk about her.

In numerous ways.

She came from a good family; she was born a Konneroy, and the Konneroys were one of the oldest and finest patrician families in the whole city. And yet she had broken ties with them. Some people said it was because of a profligate brother who had been sent off to the colonies. But it was certain that the break was complete, and it had even been whispered that old Konneroy had cursed her and had then suffered a bad attack of his spring asthma.

All this had occurred after she became a widow.

Boye, her husband, had been a pharmacist, *Assessor pharmaciae,* and a knight. When he died he was sixty years old and the owner of one and a half barrels of gold. As far as anyone knew, they had had a good life together. In the beginning, the first three years, the elderly man had been very much in love. Later they lived mostly apart, he busy with his garden and with maintaining his reputation as a great man in gentlemen's company, she with the theater, romantic music, and German poetry.

Then he died.

When the year of mourning was over, the widow took a trip to Italy and lived down there for a few years, mostly in Rome. There was no more to the story that here she had

smoked opium in a French club than there was to the tale that
she had agreed to pose in the same way as Paolina Borghese;
and the little Russian prince who shot himself while she was in
Naples certainly did not shoot himself for her sake. But it *was*
true that the German artists tirelessly came to serenade her, and
it was also true that one morning, dressed in an Albanian
peasant girl's costume, she had sat down on some church steps
up in Via Sistina and had let herself be persuaded by a newly
arrived artist to pose with an urn balanced on her head and a
little brown boy holding her hand. Such a painting hung on her
wall, in any case.

On the journey home from Italy she met a fellow country-
man, a well-known, intelligent critic who would rather have
been a poet. He was said to have a negative, skeptical temperament and a sharp mind — a man who treated his fellow
human beings harshly and without mercy *because* he treated
himself harshly and without mercy, and thought his brutality
was justified by this "because." But he was not quite the man
people made him out to be; he was not cast so unpleasantly
solid nor so inconsiderately consistent as he appeared, for in
spite of the fact that he was always on the warpath against the
idealistic direction of the times and called it by other censori-
ous names, he still had empathy for the ideal, the dreaming, the
ethereal, that blue, blue mystical, that incomprehensible exaltation and vanished glow — an empathy he did not feel toward
the more earthbound direction for which he was fighting, and
in which he for the most part believed.

Against his will he fell in love with Mrs. Boye, but he did
not tell her about it, for this was no young and open love, full
of hope. He loved her as a creature of another, finer, and
happier race than his own, and thus there was a rancor to his
love, an instinctual bitterness toward this race in her.

With hostile, jealous eyes he gazed on her inclinations and
opinions, her tastes and her world-view; and fully armed, with
keen articulateness, with heartless logic and cruel authority and
derision cloaked in compassion, he fought his way to her, won

her over to him and to his point of view. But when truth was victorious and she had become like him, then he saw that he had won too much, and that he had loved her with her illusions and prejudices, her dreams and her faults, and not the way she was now.

Dissatisfied with himself, with her, and with everything at home, he went away and stayed away.

But she had just then begun to love him.

Naturally, people could make much of this relationship, and they did. The Councilor's wife told Niels about it, the way old virtue talks about young folly, but Niels took it in a way that both offended and disturbed the Councilor's wife; he contradicted her and began declaiming about the tyranny of society and the freedom of the individual, about the plebeian integrity of the masses and the nobility of passion.

From that day on he rarely visited his cautious relatives, but Mrs. Boye saw him all the more.

VII

I t was a spring evening; the sun shone so red into the parlor,
just about to set. The vanes of the mill up on the city ramparts drove their shadows across the windowpanes and the
walls of the room, appearing, disappearing, in a monotonous
alternation of shadow and light — one moment of shadow, two
moments of light.

Niels Lyhne sat at the window staring through the dark
bronze elms along the embankment toward the fire of the
clouds. He had been outside the city, beneath newly budding
beech trees, in the green fields of rye, through flower-sprinkled
meadows; everything had been so bright and carefree, the sky
so blue, the Sound so sparkling, and the promenading women
so unusually beautiful. Singing, he had walked along the forest
path; then the words vanished from his song, then the rhythm
faded, the notes died away, and silence came over him like a
dizziness. He closed his eyes but still could feel how the light
seemed to seep into him, flickering through every nerve, while
with every breath the cool, intoxicating air sent his oddly ex-
cited blood with wilder and wilder force through his veins,
quivering with powerlessness, and a feeling came over him as
though everything teeming, bursting, budding, multiplying in
the springtime nature around him was mystically trying to
gather inside him in one great big shout; and he thirsted after
that shout, listened until his listening took the form of a vague,
burgeoning longing.

Now, as he sat there at the window, the longing awoke
again.

He longed for thousands of trembling dreams, for images
of cool sensitivity: pastel colors, fleeting scents, and fine music

from tensely stretched, tautly stretched streams of silvery strings; and then silence, into the innermost heart of silence, where the waves of air never carried a single scrap of sound, where everything rested to death in the still glow of reddish colors and the expectant warmth of fiery fragrance. He did not long for this, but it emerged from the other and drowned it, until he turned away from it and recaptured his self.

He was weary of himself, of cold thoughts and intellectual dreams. Life a poem! Not when you perpetually went around inventing your life instead of living it. How meaningless it was, empty, empty, empty. This hunting for yourself, slyly observing your own tracks — in a circle, of course; this pretending to throw yourself into the stream of life and then at the same time sitting and angling for yourself and fishing yourself up in some peculiar disguise! If only it would seize him: life, love, passion — so that he wouldn't be able to invent it, but so that it would invent him.

Involuntarily he made a deprecating motion with his hand. Deep inside he was afraid of that mighty thing called passion. That windstorm that whirled away with everything established, everything authorized, everything acquired in a human being, as if it were all withered leaves! He did not like it. That thundering flame that spent itself in its own smoke — no, *he* would burn slowly.

And yet — this living at half force was so pathetic, living in still waters with the coast in sight; so if only it would come with currents and storms! If only he knew how: he would fly with all sails set, racing toward the Spanish sea of life. Farewell to the slowly dripping days, farewell to the happy small moments; farewell you dull moods that have to be polished up in poetry in order to shine, you lukewarm feelings that have to be dressed up in warm dreams and yet freeze to death — go on as you must! I am steering for a shore where emotions fling themselves like lush vines up every fiber of the heart — a primeval forest. For every withering vine there are twenty in bloom, for every blossoming vine there are a hundred buds.

If only I were there!

He was exhausted by his longing, he was sick of himself. He needed people. But of course Erik was not home, and he had been with Frithiof that morning, and it was too late to go to the theater.

He went out all the same, and wandered dejectedly through the streets.

Perhaps Mrs. Boye was home? This was not one of her regular evenings and it was rather late.

What if he tried anyway?

Mrs. Boye was home.

She was home alone; she had been too tired from the spring air to accompany her niece to a dinner party, preferring to lie on the sofa and drink strong tea and read Heine; but now she was weary of verse and felt like playing lotto.

So they played lotto.

Fifteen, twenty, seventy-seven, and a long column of figures, the rattling of the wooden tiles in the bag and an irritating roll of marbles across the floor in the apartment overhead.

"This is no fun," said Mrs. Boye after they had not filled up any cards for quite a while. "Is it? No," she answered herself, shaking her head despondently. "But what should we play?"

She folded her hands in front of her on top of the tiles and looked at Niels with a hopelessly searching gaze.

Niels really didn't know.

"And don't say music!"

She bowed her face over her hands and touched the clasped fingers with her lips, one knuckle after the other, down the whole row and back again.

"This is the most despicable existence of all," she said, looking up. "It's impossible to experience the slightest thing, and the little that life discards — how can that keep you in flight? Don't you feel the same way?"

"Well, yes. All I can think of is for us to act like the Caliph in *A Thousand and One Nights*. If you had a white kerchief on your head to go with that white dressing gown you're wearing

and I borrowed your big East Indian shawl, we could pass for
two merchants from Mossul."

"And what would we two unhappy merchants do then?"

"Go down to Storm Bridge and hire a boat for twenty
pieces of gold and then sail up the dark river."

"Past the sand sheds?"

"Yes, with colored lanterns on the mast."

"Like Ganem, the slave of love. I know it all so well, that
whole way of thinking; it's so typically male to be at once
so atrociously busy building up the scenery and the situation
and neglecting the main issue in deference to the extraneous.
Haven't you noticed that we women daydream infinitely less
than you men? We can't anticipate pleasure in our imagination
or keep suffering out of our lives with some imaginary consolation. Whatever is, is. Imagination! It's so paltry! Yes, when
you've grown older, as I have, you occasionally make do with
the poor comedy of the imagination. But one should never do
that, never!"

Listlessly she settled herself on the sofa, half reclining, half
sitting, with her hand under her chin and her elbow supported
by the sofa pillows.

Her eyes gazed dreamily out into the parlor, and she
seemed completely lost in sad thoughts.

Niels was silent too, and the room grew quite still. The
restless hopping of the canary became audible, the clock on the
mantelpiece ticked its way through the silence, louder and
louder, and a string in the open piano loosened with a sudden
little snap and resounded with a long, faint, dying note along
with the soft singing of the silence.

She looked so young as she lay there, directly beneath the
gentle yellow glow of the astral lamp, illuminated from head
to toe, and there was an enchanting disharmony between the
lovely, powerfully formed neck, the matronly Charlotte Cor-
day cap, and then the childishly trusting eyes and the little
open mouth with the milk-white teeth.

Niels looked at her with admiration.

"How strange it is to yearn for oneself!" she said, slowly letting go of her dreams and coming back with her gaze. "And I long so often, so very often for myself as a young girl, and I love her like someone I've been intimately close to and with whom I've shared life and happiness and everything, and then I lost her without being able to do the slightest thing about it. What a lovely time that was! You have no idea how delicate and tender a young girl's life is during the time of her first love. It can only be told in music, but imagine it like a party, a party in a fairy castle where the air glitters like blushing silver. It's full of cool flowers and they change their colors, slowly exchanging color with each other, everything is ringing inside, rejoicing but muted, and the dawning intimations gleam and glow like a mystical wine in fine, delicate dream-goblets, and it is ringing and fragrant: thousands of scents drift through the rooms. Oh, I could cry when I think about it and when I also realize that if I had it all again, by some miracle, the way it was, that that life wouldn't be able to bear me now, I would fall through like a cow that wanted to dance on a spider's web."

"No, not at all," said Niels earnestly, and his voice quavered when he continued. "No, you would be able to love far more sensitively and much more spiritually than that young girl."

"Spiritually! How I loathe this spiritual love. Nothing more than artificial flowers spring from the earth of that kind of love; they don't even grow, they're taken from the head and stuck into the heart, because the heart has no flowers of its own. That's exactly what I envy in that young girl — in her there is nothing false, she doesn't put the surrogate of the imagination into the goblet of her love. Don't think that because her love is interwoven with and overshadowed by fantasy images and pictures in one great, lush vagueness that this is because she cares more for the images than for the earth she walks on — it's just because all her senses and instincts and faculties reach for love everywhere, everywhere, and yet she does not tire. But it's not because she enjoys her fantasies or even simply dwells on them, no, she is real in quite a different way, so real that she often becomes innocently cynical in her own ignorant fashion. You have no idea, for example, what an intoxicating pleasure it can be for a young girl to inhale secretly the smell of cigar smoke from her beloved's suit — it means a thousand times more to her than a whole bonfire of the imagination. I despise imagination. What good is it when one's entire being yearns for a human heart, only to be locked into the cold chamber of fantasy? And how often it's like that! And how often we have to resign ourselves to having the one we love dress us up in his fantasy, put a halo in our hair, bind wings to our shoulders, and wrap us in star-strewn drapery, and not find us truly worth loving until we walk about in all that masquerade finery, in which none of us can really be ourselves because we are much too decorated, and because they confuse us by throwing themselves in the dust before us and worshipping us instead of taking us as we are and simply loving us."

Niels was quite bewildered; he had picked up the handkerchief she had dropped and was sitting there, intoxicating himself with her perfume, and he was not at all prepared for her to look at him so impatiently inquisitive, just now when he was so absorbed in looking at her hand; but he managed to reply that he thought it was the greatest proof of how deep a man's love was if, in order to justify it to himself, to love someone so inexpressibly much, he had to surround that person with an aura of godliness.

"Yes, that's exactly what is so insulting," said Mrs. Boye. "We are godly enough the way we are."

Niels smiled obligingly.

"No, you shouldn't smile, it wasn't meant as a joke. On the contrary, it was meant in all seriousness, because that adoration, in its fanaticism, is basically tyrannical. We are forced to fit into the man's ideal. Like Cinderella, chop off a heel and snip off a toe! Whatever in us does not match up with his ideal image has to be banished, if not by subjugation then by indifference, by systematic neglect, by denying all development;

and whatever is lacking in us or is not part of our nature must be driven to the wildest flowering by praising it to the skies, by always assuming that we possess it to the highest degree, and by making it the cornerstone upon which the man's love is built. I call that violence against our nature. I call that conditioning. The man's love is manipulative. And we bow under it, even those whom no one loves bow under it, disgustingly weak as we are!"

She sat up from her recumbent position and looked hostilely over at Niels.

"If only I were beautiful! Oh, seductively beautiful, lovelier than any other woman who has ever lived, so that everyone who saw me was gripped with an unquenchable, agonizing love, was struck as if by a magic spell; how I would use the power of my beauty to force them to worship me, not their conventional, bloodless Ideal, but *me* as I live and breathe, myself, every inch, every fold of *my* being, every glimmer of *my* nature."

She had now stood up, and Niels was also considering leaving, but he stood there turning over numerous bold phrases which he did not dare voice. Finally he gathered his courage, grabbed her hand and kissed it, but she gave him her other hand to kiss too, and then he couldn't manage to say anything except: Good night.

Niels Lyhne had fallen in love with Mrs. Boye, and he was happy.

As he walked home through the same streets where he had wandered dejectedly earlier in the evening, it seemed to him that it was a long, long time ago that he had walked here. And there was also such a confidence, such a calm dignity about his step and bearing, and when he meticulously buttoned up his gloves he did it with the sense that a great change had occurred in him, and with a half-conscious feeling that he owed it to this change to button his gloves — meticulously.

Much too preoccupied with his thoughts to sleep, he went up onto the ramparts.

His thoughts were so strangely calm, and he was surprised at the silence within him, but he didn't really believe that silence; it was as if what was in the very depths of his being were bubbling quite softly yet incessantly, welling up and fermenting and insistent, but far, far away. He felt as if he were waiting for something to come out of the distance, a far-off music that would approach little by little — resounding, rushing, seething, roaring — and resonantly whirl down around him, seize him, he didn't know how, carry him, he didn't know where, come like a river, fight like the surf, and then...

But now he was calm, there was only that quivering singing in the distance, and everything else was peace and clarity.

He was in love, he said it aloud to himself, repeatedly: he was in love. There was such a peculiar ring of dignity to those words, and they meant so much. They meant that he was no longer a prisoner in the power of all those fantastical childhood influences, that he was no longer a plaything for aimless yearnings and hazy dreams, that he had rescued himself from the fairyland that had grown up with him and around him and had entwined him in a hundred arms, covered his eyes with a hundred hands. He had wrenched himself out of its grasp and had won himself; though it might reach out for him, plead with the charm of its mute eyes for him to come down, and beckon with white robes, its power was dead, a dream killed by day, a sun-scattered fog. For wasn't it daylight and sunshine and the whole world — his young love? Hadn't he been strutting about before in a noble purple that was not spun, acting mighty on a throne that was not raised? But now: it was as if he were standing on a high mountain and looking out over the wide plains of the world, a world thirsty for song, where he did not exist, was not foreseen, was not expected. It was a jubilant thought to realize that not a single breath of his had shaken a leaf or rippled a wave in all this wide, alert infinity. All of it was his to conquer. And he knew he could do it, felt confident of

victory and strong, as only he can who has all of his songs
swelling unsung in his breast.

The mild spring air was full of fragrances, not sated with
them the way a summer night can be, but as if striped with
fragrance, with the spicy balsam scent of young poplars, the
cool breath of late violets, the mild almond smell of wild cherry
trees, and everything that came and blended together, left and
parted, flared up individually for an instant, was extinguished
all at once, or dissolved slowly in the night air. And like shadows of the capricious dance of fragrances, airy moods raced
through his soul. And just as his senses were teased by the
fragrances that ebbed and flowed as they pleased, his soul also
longed in vain to be borne away, softly resting, in silent flight
on the gentle, fluttering wings of a mood; but it was not a bird
with wings that could bear him, only feathers and down that
were carried before the wind, fell to the ground like snow, and
disappeared.

He tried to visualize her image, the way she had lain on the
sofa talking to him, but it would not appear. He saw her walking down a boulevard, saw her sitting and reading, wearing a
hat, holding one of the large white pages of the book between
her gloved fingers, just about to turn the page, and turning
page after page; he saw her getting into her carriage in the
evening after the theater, nodding to him from behind the
window, and then the carriage drove off; he stood gazing after
it, and it drove on, and he could still follow it with his eyes.
Meaningless faces came and spoke to him, figures he hadn't
seen for years walked down the street, turned around and
stared after him, and the carriage still drove on and kept driving
on, he couldn't free himself from that carriage, couldn't think
of any other image but that carriage. Then, just as he was
completely nervous with impatience, the image appeared: the
yellow light, the eyes, the mouth, the hand under her chin, as
clearly as if she were right there in front of him in the dark.

How lovely she was, how gentle, how pure! He loved her
in kneeling desire, at her feet he implored her for all this

enchanting beauty. Cast yourself down from your throne to me. Become my slave, place the chains of slavery around your neck, but not in play; I will pull on the chain, there must be obedience in all of your limbs, servitude in your glance. If only I could make you bow to me with a love potion, no, not a love potion, for that would be forcing you and you would passively obey its power, and I am the only one who should be master, and I would accept your will, lying broken in your humbly outstretched hands. You would be my queen and I your slave, but my slave's foot would be on your proud, queenly neck; what I desire is not madness, for is it not a woman's love to be proud and strong and to surrender? It is love, I know, to be weak and to rule.

He felt that the part of her soul that was the soul of the voluptuous, the blushing, and the sensually soft in her beauty would never allow itself to be drawn to him, it would never take him in its embrace with those dazzling Juno arms, never in all eternity, weak with passion, surrender that sensually fragrant neck to his kiss. He understood perfectly that he could win the young girl in her, he had already won her, and he was certain that the voluptuous woman had felt how the young beauty who had died within her was mysteriously stirring in her living grave, to embrace him with slender virgin arms and come to him with fearful virgin lips. But this was not his love. He loved only what was unattainable, loved the back of her neck with its warm blossom-whiteness and its sheen of dewy gold beneath the dark hair. He sobbed with the longing of love and twisted his hands in ardent impotence; he threw his arms around a tree, leaned his cheek against its bark, and wept.

VIII

There was a certain paralyzed levelheadedness about Niels Lyhne, child of an instinctive resistance to daring, grandchild of a vague feeling of lack of character, and he waged a constant battle with this levelheadedness, at times goading himself on against it by giving it base names, at times attempting to dress it up as a virtue that had the most intimate connection with what was natural in him, or even more: actually determined what he was and what he was capable of. But whatever he made it into, however he regarded it, he always hated it as a secret disability, which, no matter how well it might be hidden from the world, never could be hidden from himself but was always there to humiliate him every time he was truly alone with himself. And how he envied that self-confident recklessness that is so facile with the sort of words that prompt action and have consequences — consequences to which a man doesn't give a thought until they are at his heels. People like that seemed to him like centaurs, man and horse cast in one piece, one in thought and action, all one, while he was divided into rider and horse, his thoughts one thing, action something else entirely.

When he imagined confessing his love to Mrs. Boye (and he always had to imagine everything), he would visualize himself so clearly in that situation, his bearing, every movement, his entire figure, from the front, from the side, and even from the rear. He pictured himself made uncertain by the fear of action that always paralyzed him and robbed him of all composure, so that he would stand there and accept an answer as if it were a blow that would knock him to his knees, instead of receiving it like a shuttlecock that could be thrown back, in who knows how many different ways, to be returned in who knows how many other different ways.

He thought about speaking to her and he thought about writing, but he never did manage to tell her anything. It was never spoken of except in enigmatic declarations or when he, in a semi-feigned lyrical ardor, could pretend that he let himself be swept along to amorous words and romantic yearnings. And yet, gradually, a relationship did develop between them, an odd relationship, born of a young man's humble love, a fantast's dream-feverish lust, and a woman's wish to be desired in romantic inaccessibility. And the relationship found its form in a myth that came into existence for them — neither of them knew how — a quiet, pallid myth about a beautiful woman who in her early youth had loved one of the great men of the time, who had gone away to die in a faraway land, forgotten and forsaken. And the beautiful woman grieved for many years, but no one knew of her sorrow, only loneliness was sacred enough to perceive her grief. Then a young man appeared who called the great, impetuous man his master and who was filled with his spirit and enthralled by his works. And he loved the grieving woman. For her it was as if those happy, dead days rose up from their grave and lived again, so all that was strangely sweet merged together, and past and present melted into a silver-veiled, dawning daydream in which she loved the young man, partially as himself, partially as the shadow of another, and completely gave him half her soul. But he had to tread softly so the dream would not shatter, sternly he had to lock out the hot earthly desires so they would not disperse the gentle dawn and she would not awaken to sorrow again.

Little by little, sheltered by this myth, their relationship took on a more definite shape. They used the intimate form of address and they called each other by their first names when they were alone, Niels and Tema, and the presence of the niece was limited as much as possible. It is true that Niels did try occasionally to break through the boundaries as first prescribed, but Mrs. Boye was so much his superior that she could easily and gently crush these attempts at revolt, and Niels would soon give up and resign himself once more, for a while, to that love fantasy with real-life tableaux. Nor did the relationship blur into platonic insipidness, just as it did not slip into the monotonous calm of a relationship of habit. Calm was what there was least of. Niels Lyhne's hope never tired, and if it was gently pushed back each time it flared up insistently, in hiding it would only smolder even hotter than before; and wasn't his hope also kept alive by Mrs. Boye's innumerable flirtations, her provocative naiveté, and her naked courage to speak of the most difficult subjects? And besides, the game was not totally in her control either, for once in a while, in its idleness, her blood would dream of rewarding this partially tamed love, of lavishly overwhelming it with all the richest delights of passion, in order to rejoice in its astonished happiness. But it was difficult to extinguish such a dream, and when Niels would arrive, there would be the nervousness of a sinner about her, the modesty of someone conscious of her guilt, a charming shamefulness, which made the atmosphere strangely wary of love.

There was one other thing that gave the relationship a unique resilience: the fact that there was so much virility in Niels Lyhne's love that he chivalrously declined in his fantasy to take what reality had refused him, and even there, in that other world where everything obeyed his command, he respected Mrs. Boye as if she were actually present.

In this way the relationship was well supported by both sides and there was no impending danger of it falling apart. It also seemed custom-made for a nature like Niels Lyhne's, dreamy and yet thirsty for life, and even if it was just a game, it was still a game in reality and enough to give him a basis of passion to build on.

And that is what he needed.

A poet was what Niels Lyhne was to become, and there had been much in the outward conditions of his life to lead his inclinations in this direction, much to make his talents aware of this vocation. But up until now he hadn't had much of any-thing except his dreams to use as a poet, and nothing is more monotonous and dull than fantasies, for in the apparently infi-nite and eternally changing lands of dreams, there are in fact certain short, well-worn paths which everyone takes and from which no one strays. People can be very different from each other, but their dreams are not, because in their dreams they award themselves the three or four things they desire, sooner or later, to a greater or lesser extent, but they always get them, everyone does; there is no one who seriously dreams himself empty-handed. That's why no one discovers himself in his dreams, never becomes conscious of his uniqueness, for dreams know nothing about *how* to be satisfied with winning the treasure, how to let go of it when it is lost, how to be satiated with pleasure, or what road to take when you yearn for something.

Niels Lyhne had thus composed poems from an aesthetic persona in general, someone who found the spring voluptuous, the sea enormous, love erotic, and death melancholy. He had not put himself into this poetry, he merely composed the verses. But now things began to change. Now when he courted a woman's love and wished for her to love him, Niels Lyhne from Lønborggaard—who was twenty-three years old, walked slightly stooped over, with beautiful hands and small ears, and who was a little disheartened about himself—he wanted her to love *him* and not the idealized Nicolaus of his dreams with his proud stride, his confident bearing, and who was somewhat older; now he began to take a lively interest in this Niels whom he had walked around with as if he were a less presentable friend. He had been much too busy dressing himself up with the things he lacked to have time to notice what he did possess, but now with the passion of an explorer he started to piece himself together from his childhood memories and childhood impressions, from the moments of experience in his life, and with joyous wonder he saw how it all fit together, piece by piece, and was welded together into a differently familiar person from the one he had run after in his dreams. And differently genuine too, and strong and talented. This was not a dead lump of an ideal; the wondrous, authentic nuances of life itself played inside him in shifting eternity, behind thousandfold unity. Good Lord, he *did* have powers that could be used just as they were, he *was* Aladdin; there was nothing he had reached toward the sky for that had not fallen into his turban.

And now came a joyous time for Niels — that joyous time when the mighty swing of development sends you cheering beyond the dead points in your nature, when everything in you grows and is filled so that, with the excess of your strength, you press your shoulder against mountains if required and bravely build up that Tower of Babel which is supposed to reach to heaven, but which only becomes a pitiful stump of a colossus you build onto for your whole life with abject spires and curious oriels.

Everything seemed changed; his nature and abilities and work meshed with each other like cogs in a wheel. There was no question of stopping to enjoy his art, for whatever was finished was also rejected. He had grown beyond it as he worked; it became merely a step that lifted him up toward the ever elusive goal, step by step, abandoned roads that were forgotten even as they resounded beneath his feet.

But as he was carried forward in this way by new forces and new thoughts to greater maturity and broader views, he also became more alone, as one after the other his acquaintances and colleagues slipped away and were gone. He gradually could no longer retain interest in them, since day by day it grew more difficult for him to see any visible difference between these men of the opposition and the majority to which they were opposed. It all merged for him into one great inimical mass of boredom. What did they write when they were on the attack? Pessimistic poems about dogs being more faithful than people, and prisoners who were often more honest than those who walked free, eloquent odes about the green forest and the benefit of the brown heath as opposed to the dusty cities, stories about the virtues of peasants and the vices of the rich, about the blood of nature and the anemia of civilization, comedies about their elders' lack of understanding and the superior right of youth. How easily satisfied they were when they wrote! They were much better, however, when they talked within the safety of four walls.

No, when he was done someday, there would be music — with fanfares . . .

Things were not the same with his old friends either. Especially with Frithiof. The fact of the matter was that Frithiof, who was of an optimistic nature and had a good head for systems and a broad back for dogmas, had been reading rather too much Heiberg and had accepted all of it as gospel, not realizing that the inventors of systems are clever people who create their systems according to their works and not their works according to their systems. And the truth is that young people who have fallen under the power of a system easily become great dogmatists at once because of the commendable love that youth usually feels for the established conditions, the proven, and the absolute. And when you have thus become the possessor of the whole truth — the one, genuine truth — wouldn't it be unforgivable if you kept it all to yourself and let your fellow human beings, less fortunately situated, go their own crooked way instead of leading and teaching them, instead of grabbing at their wild tendrils with loving ruthlessness and with kind force pressing them against the wall and showing them in what foolish ways their development might lead? So that someday, however late, they will come as true and artistic espaliers to thank you for all the trouble you took with them.

It is true that Niels often said that there was nothing he valued more than criticism, but he was still more fond of admiration, and now he could not tolerate being criticized by Frithiof, whom he had always regarded as his subordinate and who had always been delighted to wear the livery of Niels' opinions and convictions. And now here he was wanting to play Niels' equal in his self-selected masquerade costume of robes! This had to be rejected, of course, and Niels tried, at first with arrogant friendliness, to make Frithiof seem ridiculous to himself, but when this did not succeed he took refuge in shameless paradoxes which he scornfully refused to discuss; he simply presented them in all their baroque repulsiveness and then retreated into teasing silence.

That is how they drifted apart.

Things went better with Erik. There had always been a kind of reserve about their boyhood friendship, a certain spiritual modesty, and in this way they had avoided any great intimacy between them, which is so exceedingly dangerous to a friendship; they had been enraptured with each other in the banquet room of their souls, they had talked together, familiarly and contentedly in the parlor, but they had not gone in and out of each others' bedrooms, bathrooms, and other obscure rooms like these in the apartment of their souls.

It was no different now — the reserve was perhaps even somewhat stronger, at any rate in Niels, but the friendship had not diminished because of it, and its cornerstone was, now as always, Niels Lyhne's admiration for Erik's dauntlessness and joie de vivre, the way in which he was so at ease in life and so ready to grab hold and take what he wanted. But Niels could not hide from himself that the friendship was very one-sided, not because there was any lack of true friendliness on Erik's part, or because he had no faith in Niels. On the contrary, no one had more regard for Niels than Erik; he perceived him as being so absolutely superior in intelligence that there could never be any thought of criticism, but at the same time, with this blind acknowledgment, he also regarded Niels' work and what attracted his thoughts as completely removed from the horizon that he could reach with his own eyes. He was confident that Niels would master the path he had set himself, but he was just as certain that *his* feet had no business on that road, nor did he attempt to set them there.

This was rather hard for Niels, because even though Erik's ideals were not his own, and what Erik expressed in his art —

the romantic or perhaps the sentimental-romantic — did not appeal to him, he could nevertheless sustain a broader, more encompassing empathy and thus faithfully follow his friend's development, rejoice with him when he made progress, and help him regain hope when he stood still.

In this way the friendship was one-sided, and it was not so strange that during this time when so many new things were happening to Niels and the need for communication and sensitive understanding was so great, that precisely at this time Niels should become aware of the inadequacy of this friendship, and in bitterness begin to look a little closer at this hitherto so leniently judged friend. And this gave him a sad feeling of loneliness; it was as if everything he had brought from home, from the old days, fell away and abandoned him, he felt forgotten and forsaken. The door back to the old was locked and he stood outside, empty-handed and alone; whatever he longed for and desired he would have to win for himself: new friends and new comforts, new space in his heart and new memories.

For well over a year Mrs. Boye had been Niels' only true companion. Then a letter from his mother, in which she told him that his father was mortally ill, called him back to Lønborggaard.

When he arrived his father was dead.

The fact that in recent years Niels had longed so little for his home weighed heavily on him, almost like guilt; he had sought it out in his thoughts often enough, but he had only been there as a guest, with the dust of other regions on his clothes and memories of other places in his heart. He had not, with unnamable homesickness, yearned for it as if for the bright sanctuary of his life, longing to kiss its earth and to rest beneath its roof. Now he regretted that he had been unfaithful to his home, and oppressed as he was by grief he felt his remorse darkened by a mysterious sense of collaboration in what had happened, as if his faithlessness had drawn death in. And he wondered how he could have lived peacefully away from this home, for now it pulled him with a strange power; and with every fold of his being he clung to it with an endless longing, heavy with loss, uneasy that he could not become one with it no matter how ardently he wanted to, unhappy that the thousands of memories calling from every corner, every bush, from sounds and the play of light, from a thousand fragrances and from the silence itself, that all of this called to him with much too distant voices which would not let themselves be captured in all the fullness and clarity he needed, but only whispered to his soul with the sound of leaves that *have* fallen to earth, with the murmur of waves, ebbing away and ebbing away...

Happy is the person who, in his grief, when one of his loved ones is gone, can weep all his tears at the emptiness, abandonment, and loss; for they are heavier, more bitter tears that must atone for what bygone days have seen of lack of love for the one who is now dead, toward whom no offense can be expiated again. For now they come back: not only the harsh words, meticulously poisoned replies, intolerant censure, and thoughtless anger, but also caustic thoughts that were never voiced, hasty judgments that raced through your mind, lonely shrugs of the shoulder and unseen smiles, full of scorn and impatience; they all come back like evil arrows and sink their shafts deep in your own breast, their shafts blunt because the points have broken off in the heart that is no more. It is no more, there is nothing you can make good again, nothing. Now there is plenty of love in your heart, but now it is too late; go on up to the cold grave with your full heart! Can you get any closer? Plant flowers and weave wreaths — do you get any closer?

At Lønborggaard they also wove wreaths. Bitter memories of hours when love kept silent in favor of harsher voices came back to them too, and for them as well there was enough remorse to be read in the stern lines around the closed mouth of the grave.

It was a dark and heavy time, but there was one bright spot, in that it brought mother and son closer to each other than they had been in many, many years; for even though they felt great love for one another, they still were on their guard, and there had been a reserve in their give and take, ever since that time when Niels had gotten too big to sit on his mother's knee, since *he* had grown afraid of the intense and high-strung side of her nature, while *she* had felt herself alienated by what was dispirited and hesitant in him; but now life with its give and take, its stimulation and its restraint, had made their hearts ready and would soon give them completely to each other.

Scarcely two months after the funeral Mrs. Lyhne fell gravely ill, and for a long time her life was in danger. The anxiety that filled these weeks pushed the earlier sorrow into the background, and when Mrs. Lyhne began to recover, for both Niels and herself it seemed as if years had come between them and the fresh grave. It seemed especially long ago to Mrs. Lyhne, for during her whole illness she had been convinced that she was going to die and she had been very frightened. Even now, when she had begun to recover and the doctor had declared all danger past, she could not escape these gloomy thoughts.

It was also a very melancholy convalescence, in which her strength returned drop by drop, as if against its will, and there was no gentle, soothing somnolence about her; on the contrary, there was an uneasy feebleness with a depressing feeling of powerlessness, an eternal, despondent yearning for strength.

After a while there was a change in that too: things progressed more quickly, her strength returned, but the thought that she and life would soon part did not diminish but lay like a shadow over her and held her captive in a restless sadness filled with longing.

One evening during this time she was sitting alone in the conservatory staring out through the open French doors.

The golden glow of the sunset was hidden by the trees in the garden; only in one place did a fiery-red spot open among the trees and let a sun of deep golden, flashing rays awaken green colors and bronze-brown reflections in the dark foliage.

Up above the restless treetops the clouds chased darkly across the smoke-red sky and in their haste left little bits of cloud behind, small thin strips of loose cloud, which the gleam of the sun then sated with a wine-red glow.

Mrs. Lyhne sat listening to the sighing of the wind and with little movements of her head she followed the irregular swelling and sinking of the gusts, as they rustled louder and still louder and then died away. But her gaze was far away, much farther away than the clouds she was staring at. She sat there, pale in her widow's black dress, with an expression of painful restlessness about her faintly colored lips, and her hands were restless too, as they turned over the thick little book on her lap. It was Rousseau's *Héloïse*. Around her lay other books: Schiller, Staffeldt, Ewald, and Novalis, and heavy volumes with copperplates of old churches, ruins, and mountain lakes.

Now the door opened inside, searching steps were heard from the room beyond, and Niels came in. He had been on a long walk along the fjord. His cheeks were colored by the fresh air and the wind was still in his hair.

Up there in the sky, blue-gray colors had won out, and a few heavy drops of rain beat against the windowpanes.

Niels told her about how high the waves had washed up, about the seaweed they had carried to shore, about what he had seen and who he had met, and as he talked he gathered up the books, closed the conservatory door, and fastened the hasps on the windows. Then he sat down on the footstool at his mother's feet, took her hand in his, and leaned his cheek against her knee.

Outside everything had grown dark and the rain hailed down in sheets, washing over the windowsills and panes.

"Do you remember," said Niels when they had been sitting quietly for a while, "do you remember how often we sat like this in the twilight and set off on adventures while Father was talking to Foreman Jens in his office and Miss Duysen was rattling the tea service in the dining room? And then when the lamp was brought in we would both wake up from the strange fairy tales to the comfort around us, but I remember very well how I always thought the fairy tale didn't stop because of that but would keep on going all by itself over there at the foot of the hills toward Ringkøbing."

He didn't see his mother's sad smile, he only felt her hand gently stroking his hair.

"Do you remember," she said a little while later, "how you promised me that when you grew up you would sail away in a great ship and bring back all the delights of the world to me?"

"Of course I remember! There were going to be hyacinths because you were so fond of hyacinths, and a palm like the one that withered, and pillars of gold and marble. There were always so many pillars in your stories. Do you remember?"

"I've been waiting for that ship — no, be still, my son, you misunderstand me — it wasn't for myself, it was the ship of your happiness . . . I had hoped that life would be great and rich for you, that you would have traveled the glorious path — fame . . . Everything — no, not that, just that you would be involved in the struggle for Greatness, I don't know how. But I was so tired of ordinary happiness and ordinary goals. Can you understand that?"

"You wanted me to be born under a lucky star, Mother, someone who doesn't bear the yoke like the others, someone who has his own heaven where he is blessed and who has his own personal place of damnation. Isn't that true? There were supposed to be flowers on board, lush flowers to scatter across the poor world, but the ship kept us waiting, and they just turned into poor birds, Niels and his mother, didn't they?"

"Have I hurt you, my boy? They were only dreams; pay no attention to them."

Niels was silent for a long time, he was so shy about what he wanted to say.

"Mother," he said, "we're not as poor as you think. Someday the ship will come after all . . . If you'll just believe in it or believe in me... Mother, I am a poet — truly — in my very soul. Don't think these are childish dreams or dreams of vanity. If only you could feel how much grateful pride I feel at the best in me and what a humble joy it is to say this, so impersonally and without arrogance, then you would believe it, the way I so fervently wish that you would. Dearest, dearest! I *will* join in the fight for Greatness, and I promise you that I will never falter, always be faithful to myself and what I possess; only the best will be good enough for me and nothing more, no compromises, Mother. Let me promise that if what I have created is not pure, or if I can hear that it has faults or cracks, then into the crucible with it again: always the utmost I am capable of each time. Do you understand that I need to promise? It is gratitude for all my wealth that drives me to promises, and you must accept them, and it will be a sin against you and against Greatness if I fail, for aren't you the one I am indebted to for the height of my soul, isn't it your longings and dreams that have driven my talents to develop, and isn't it through your sympathies and your never satisfied yearning for beauty that I have been initiated into what will be my work?"

Mrs. Lyhne wept silently. She felt pale with joy.

She placed both her hands on her son's head, and he tenderly pulled them down to his lips and kissed them.

"You have made me so happy, Niels... now my life hasn't been one long, useless sigh since it has carried you forward the way I had so fervently hoped and dreamed, good Lord, dreamed so often. And yet there is so much sadness mixed with the joy; for Niels, now that I am about to have my dearest wish fulfilled, my wish down through so many years... it comes only when life has so little time left."

"You mustn't talk like that, you mustn't. Everything is going so well; you're getting stronger day by day, aren't you, Mother?"

"Oh, I'm so reluctant to die," she sighed to herself. "Do you know what I thought about during those long, sleepless nights when death seemed so terribly near?... what seemed to me the most difficult to bear was that there were so many great and beautiful things out there in the world, and I was going to die and leave them behind without seeing them. I thought about the way the world had fulfilled, elevated to happiness, and lent stature to thousands and thousands of souls, but it had not existed for me, and when my soul departed, impoverished and on listless wings, it would not take along in rich memories a golden reflection of the glory of its homeland; it had merely sat by the hearth and listened to fairy tales about the wonderful earth. Niels, no one can understand what an unspeakable misery that was, to lie imprisoned in the suffocating gloom of that sickroom, fighting in my feverish imagination to call forth the beauty of unseen regions. I remember snow-capped alpine peaks above dark blue lakes, shining rivers between vine-covered hills and long-ridged mountains where ruins were visible above the woods, and high-ceilinged halls too, and marble gods — and then never to be capable of seeing it, always having to give up, only to begin all over again because it was so infinitely sad to say farewell without having had the slightest share in it... Oh God, Niels, to long for it with all your soul while you feel yourself being slowly led closer to the threshold of another world, to stand on the threshold and look wistfully back, as you are continually forced through the door to a place where none of your longings lead, none of them... Niels, take me along in your thoughts, my son, when someday you take part in all that glory I will never, ever see."

She wept.

Niels tried to comfort her. He made bold plans about how they would travel together just as soon as she was completely well, in a very short time. He would go into town to talk with the doctor about their trip, and he was certain the doctor would agree with him that it was the best thing to do — so-and-so had taken a journey like that and he had recovered from his illness just from the change, change alone could do so much good. He proceeded to go over the route of their journey in great detail, talked about how well he would bundle her up, what short excursions they would take at first, what a priceless diary they would keep, how they would notice even the most insignificant things, what fun it would be to eat the strangest things in the loveliest places, and what shocking errors in grammar they would make in the beginning.

He kept on in this manner day and night and never tired, and she would smile at one thing and agree to another as if in an enjoyable fantasy, but it was quite obvious that she was convinced the journey would never take place.

On the doctor's advice, however, Niels continued to make all the necessary preparations, and she let him do as he wished, set the day for the departure and everything, certain as she was that something would happen which would make all the plans come to naught. But when finally there were only a few days left and her youngest brother, who was to manage the farm in her absence, had actually arrived, she began to grow uncertain and was suddenly the one who was the most eager to leave, because there was still some fear remaining that an obstacle would arise and appear right at the very last minute.

And then they departed.

The first day she was still uneasy and nervous because of the last remnants of fear, and only when the day had successfully been brought to an end was it possible for her to feel and realize that she was really on her way toward all the glory she had so sadly longed for. Then an almost feverish joy came over her, and an overwrought anticipation marked all her thoughts and words, which perpetually concerned what the days would bring, one after the other.

And all of it did come about, all of it, but it did not fulfill or enthrall her with either the power or the intensity she had anticipated. She had expected it to be quite different, but she had also expected herself to be quite different. In dreams and in poetry it had always somehow been on the other side of the lake; the mist of distance, full of presentiment, had veiled the turbulent throngs of details and gathered the shapes in broad outlines into a completed whole, and the silence of distance had spread its festive mood over it, and it had been so easy to grasp in its beauty; but now, when she was in the midst of it and every little feature stood out with the many voices of reality, and beauty was scattered like the light from a prism, now she couldn't gather it together, couldn't pull it over to the other side of the lake, and with a deep sense of dejection she had to admit to herself that she felt impoverished in the midst of all this wealth over which she had no power.

She pushed on, ever onward. Wasn't there at least one place in existence that she would recognize as a corner of the dreamed world, which seemed, with each step she had taken to approach it, to extinguish the magical glow in which it had shone until now, and to her disappointed eye revealed itself prosaically illuminated by the ordinary sun and the ordinary moon? But her search was not rewarded, and when it was late in the year they hastened to Clarens, where the doctor had advised them to spend the winter and to which one last faintly shining hope still beckoned to her weary, dream-possessed soul; for wasn't it Rousseau's Clarens, Julie's idyllic Clarens?

And there they stayed, but it was in vain that the winter was mild and withheld its cold breath from her — it could not protect her from the affliction in her blood. And spring, when it arrived in its triumphal procession through the valley with the portent of germination and the gospel of budding leaves, had to leave her standing there, withering in all that lushness of renewal; and its strength, which swelled toward her from the light and air and earth, was unable to become strength in her, so that her blood, drunk with health, might also rejoice in the great jubilation over the omnipotence of spring. No, she had to wither; for the last dream that had revealed itself to her in the secret recesses of home as a new dawn, the dream of the glory of the distant world, had not brought the day with it, its colors were faded the closer she came to it, and she felt that they faded just for her because she had longed for colors that life did not possess, for a beauty that the earth could not ripen. But her longing was not extinguished; silent and strong it burned in her heart, hotter in its loss, hot and consuming.

And all around her the festival of spring, pregnant with beauty, was celebrated, surrounded by the white bells of snow-drops, joyously greeted by the veined goblets of crocus blossoms. Hundreds of small mountain streams plunged head over heels down toward the valley to announce that spring had arrived, and they all came too late, for wherever they flowed between green banks, yellow primroses and blue violets stood nodding: we know, we know, we noticed it before you did. Willows hoisted their yellow banners, and curling ferns and velvet-soft moss hung green garlands on the naked vineyard walls, as thousands of nettles hid the base of the walls in long borders of brown and green and soft purple. The grass spread out its green cape so far and wide, and many decorative weeds were scattered over it: hyacinths with blossoms like stars and flowers like pearls, daisies by the thousands, gentians, anemo-nes, dandelions, and hundreds of other flowers. And above the flowers on the earth, held aloft by the hundred-year-old trunks of the cherry trees, nearly a thousand shining islands of blos-soms swayed in the air, with the light foaming against the white coasts, which butterflies speckled with red and blue as they brought word from the continent of flowers below.

Each day that came brought new blossoms; it drove them in multicolored patterns up out of the earth in the gardens by the lake, it dumped them onto the branches of the trees down there, giant violets on the royal pawlonia tree, and great purple-splashed tulips on the magnolia. The flowers thronged along the pathways in blue and white rows, they filled the meadows with yellow hordes, but nowhere was as covered with flowers as up among the heights in sheltered, secret val-leys, where the larch stood with sparkling ruby cones in the bright needles, for there the narcissus bloomed in dazzling myriads and filled the air all around with a deafening scent from their white orgies.

In the midst of all this beauty she sat with unanswered longings for beauty in her heart, and only on an occasional evening — when the sun sank behind elegantly sloping heights of the Savoy and the mountains beyond the lake seemed made of brownish, opaque glass with the light practically drowning in their steep sides — would nature capture her senses, for that was the time when yellow-lit evening mists hid the distant Jura Mountains, and the lake, red as a copper mirror with golden flames scalloped by the sun-red glow, seemed to merge with the radiance of the heavens into one vast, brilliant sea of infinity, then once in a great while it was as if her longing were silenced and her soul had found the land that it sought.

The more the spring progressed, the weaker she became, and soon she left her bed no more; but now she was not afraid of death, she longed for it, because she had the hope, on the other side of the grave, of finding herself face to face with that glory, soul in soul with that abundance of beauty which here on earth had filled her with prescient longings that were now distilled and clarified through the growing yearning of long years of life, and now they would finally embrace their goal. And she dreamed many a gentle, melancholy dream about how she would return in memory to what the earth had given her, would return to it out there in the land of immortality where all earthly beauty, all time, would be on the other side of the lake.

And so she died, and Niels buried her in the pleasant cemetery in Clarens, where the brown mulch of the vineyards protects the children of so many lands and where the broken pillars and veil-shrouded urns repeat the same words of sorrow in so many languages.

They gleam white through the dark cypresses and winter-blooming viburnum; early roses sprinkle their petals over many of them, and the earth is often blue with violets at their feet, but around every mound and every stone twine the shiny-leaved vines of the gentle periwinkle, Rousseau's favorite flower, sky-blue the way no sky is ever blue.

I X

Niels Lyhne hurried home; he couldn't stand the loneliness among all those foreigners, but the closer he came to Copenhagen, the more often he asked himself why he was really going there, and the more strongly he regretted not having stayed away. Who did he have in Copenhagen anyway? Not Frithiof. Erik was on a grant in Italy, so he wasn't there either. And Mrs. Boye? That was such an odd relationship, the one with Mrs. Boye. Now, as he came straight from his mother's grave, it seemed to him not exactly profane or anything like that, but he couldn't get it to harmonize with the tone in which his emotions now vibrated. There was a dissonance to it. If he had been going to meet his fiancée, a blushing young girl, now that his soul had been turned for so long toward fulfilling his filial duties, it would not have been in conflict with his feelings. And it was no help that he tried to justify it to himself by calling this change in his attitude toward his relationship with Mrs. Boye philistine and narrow-minded. The word "gypsy-like" came into his mind almost unconsciously to express the aversion he could not rationalize away, and it was also a kind of extension of the same mood that, as soon as he had secured his old rooms up near the city walls, he went first to the Councilor's apartment and not Mrs. Boye's.

He went there the following day but did not find her at home. The doorman told him that she had rented a villa close to Emiliekilde, which surprised Niels since he knew that her father's estate was right nearby.

Someday he would have to go out there.

But the very next day he received a note from Mrs. Boye

asking him to meet her at her apartment in town. The pale
niece had seen him on the street. At 12:15 he should come, he
had to come. She would tell him why, *if he didn't know why
already*. Did he know why? He must not judge her unfairly or
be unreasonable. He knew her, after all. Why should he take it
the way plebeian types probably would? He wouldn't, would
he? The two of them weren't like other people. If only he
would *understand* her. Niels, Niels!

This letter threw him into a state of tension; suddenly he
recalled uneasily that the Councilor's wife had looked at him
half mockingly, half sympathetically the other day, smiling and
silent, so unusually silent. What could it be, what in the world
could it be?

The mood that had kept him away from Mrs. Boye had
vanished. He didn't even understand it anymore, he was so
frightened. If only they had written to each other like other
sensible people. Why hadn't they done that? He hadn't really
been *that* busy. The way he was acting was remarkable too, the
way he let himself be taken over by the place where he was at
the moment. And forgot about everything distant. Not forgot,
but pushed it so far back, let it be buried by what was close at
hand. As if underneath mountains. You wouldn't think he had
any imagination at all.

Finally, Mrs. Boye opened the door to the foyer herself,
even before he had rung the bell. She said nothing but clasped
his hand in a long, condoling handshake; the newspapers had
reported his bereavement. Niels didn't say a word either, and
silently they walked through the front room, between two
rows of chairs with red-striped upholstery. The chandelier in
there was wrapped in tissue and the windows were whitewashed. In the parlor everything was the same as usual, except
that the blinds were pulled down in front of the open windows
and they were moving in the gentle breeze, rattling with little
uniform taps against the window frame. The light reflecting off
the sunlit canal filtered in, muted, between the yellow slats,

sketching a restless, curving slate of wavy lines up on the ceiling,
quivering the way the waves quivered outside; everything else
was so soft and quiet, gently waiting with subdued breath . . .

Mrs. Boye could not decide where she wanted to sit. Finally
she decided on the rocking chair, energetically wiping the dust
off it with her handkerchief, but then she placed herself behind
the chair with her hands on its back. She still had her gloves on
and she had only pulled one arm out of the sleeve of the short
black cape she wore over her Scottish plaid silk dress, with its
tiny plaid checks just like on the wide ribbon of her big round
Pamela hat, whose light straw half hid her face, especially as
she stood there now, looking down, while she rocked the chair
hard, back and forth.

Niels sat down on the stool by the piano, far away from
her, as if he expected to hear something unpleasant.

"Do you know about it, Niels?"

"No, what is it I don't know?"

The rocking chair stopped. "I'm engaged."

"Mrs. Boye is engaged? But why? And how?"

"Oh, don't be so formal. Don't be unreasonable right from
the start!" A little defiantly she leaned on the rocking chair.
"You can imagine that it's not particularly pleasant for me to
stand here and explain everything to you. I will, but you have
to cooperate."

"That's a lot of nonsense. Are you engaged or aren't you?"

"I told you that I am," she said with tender impatience and
looked up.

"Well, then permit me to congratulate you, Mrs. Boye, and
thank you very much for the time we have known each other."
He stood up and bowed sarcastically several times.

"So that's the way you part with me, quite calmly like this:
I'm engaged and so we're through, everything there has been
between the two of us is an old, stupid story, not to be thought
about anymore. What's over is over. Just like that. Niels, all
those sweet days, will their memories be silent from now on,
will you never, ever think about me, never miss me? Won't you

often, on a quiet evening, dream the dream alive again and give it colors it could have blazed with? In your thoughts can you totally avoid loving it all again and letting it mature to the fullness it could have attained? Can you? Can you place your foot on it and stomp it out, every bit of it, stomp it out of the world? Niels!"

"I hope so; you have shown me, after all, that it can be done. Oh, but that's nonsense, all of it, stupid nonsense from start to finish; why have you set up this comedy? I don't have the shadow of a right to reproach you. You have never loved me, never said that you did, you have given me permission to love you, you have, and now you're taking away your permission; or may I continue to do so now that you've given yourself to another? I don't understand you; did you think *that* was possible? We aren't children, after all. Or are you afraid that I'll forget you too quickly? Don't worry. You aren't someone a man can erase from his life. But take care; a woman won't find a love like mine twice in her lifetime, take care it doesn't bring you unhappiness, the fact that you've rejected me. I don't wish you anything bad, no, no, I wish all illness and need would keep away from you, I wish you all the happiness that wealth, admiration, and society can bring, I wish that you find it in full measure, the fullest measure, that is my wish. I hope the entire world will be open to you, except for one little door, one single little door, no matter how hard you knock, how often you try, but otherwise everything, everything as far and wide as could be desired."

He said this slowly, almost dejectedly, not at all bitterly, but with a strangely quivering resonance to his voice, a sound that she did not recognize and that made an impression on her. She had turned slightly pale, and was standing stiffly, supported by the chair. "Niels," she said, "don't predict anything bad for me, remember that you weren't here and I didn't know how real my love was, it was more as though it just intrigued me; it echoed through my life like a lovely, spiritual poem, it never took me with strong arms, it had wings — only wings. That's what I thought, I didn't know anything else before now or until the moment I did it, until I said yes. And it was so difficult too, there was so much involved in it, so many people to take into consideration... It started with my brother — Hardenskjold, you know, the one who went to the West Indies. He'd been a little wild here at home, but over there he became staid and sensible and went into partnership with someone and made a lot of money and married a rich widow too, a sweet little woman, I assure you, and then he came home and he was reconciled with my father, for Hatte was completely changed, oh, he's so respectable, there's no end to it, so sensitive to what people say: oh, shockingly narrow-minded! So of course he thought I should be on speaking terms with the family again, and he preached and begged and babbled every time he came to visit, and Father is an old man, after all, and so I did it, and it was just like in the old days again."

She paused for a moment, proceeded to take off her cape, her hat and gloves too, and preoccupied with all of this she turned away from Niels as she continued speaking.

"And Hatte had a friend who is well regarded, enormously well regarded, and they all thought I should, and wanted me to so badly, and you see, then I could take my proper place among people again, the way I had before, actually even better because he is so highly regarded, in every way, and I had been longing for this for such a long time. You can't understand that, can you? You never thought I was like that? Quite the opposite. Because I always ridiculed society and all their conventional stupidity and their patent morality, their virtue thermometers and femininity compasses, you remember how witty we were? It's enough to make you cry, you know, it wasn't true, at least not always, because I have to tell you that we women, Niels, we can tear ourselves away for a while when there is something in our lives that has opened our eyes to that urge for freedom which we do possess, but we can't hold out, we have a passion in our blood for the most correct of the correct, all the way up to the most prudish point of propriety. We can't hold out waging a battle against what is accepted by all those ordinary people; deep inside we think that they are right because they are the ones who judge, and in our hearts we bow to their judgments and suffer under them, however bravely we may pose. It's not for us women to be exceptions, it doesn't work, Niels, it makes us so strange, perhaps more interesting, but otherwise... Can you understand that? Don't you think it's pitiful? But you can see that it had to make a strange impression on me to go back to the old surroundings; so many memories came back — and the memory of my mother, her way of thinking. I thought I had returned to safe harbor, everything was so peaceful and right, and I only needed to bind myself to it in order to be nicely content all of my days. And so I let them bind me, Niels."

Niels couldn't help smiling, he felt himself so superior and he felt so sorry for her as she stood there, so youthfully unhappy over all that self-confession. He felt so tender and could not find any harsh words.

Then he went to her.

In the meantime she had turned the chair around and let herself sink down into it, and now she sat there quite faint, forsaken by the world, cast back with her arms hanging, with her face lifted and her eyes half closed, gazing out through the darkened front room with the two rows of chairs, out into the dim foyer.

Niels placed his arm across the back of the chair and leaned down over her, his hand supported on the chair's arm: "And you had forgotten all about me," he whispered.

It was as if she didn't hear him, she didn't even lift her eyes; then she finally shook her head, just a little, and then quite a while later, once again, just a little.

It was so silent around them at first; then a maid could be heard out on the landing, humming and polishing the locks, and the creaking of the door handles brutally broke the silence and made it seem even greater when it suddenly returned. Then the noise stopped, now there was only the gentle, sleepy, steady tapping of the venetian blinds.

It robbed them of words, this silence, almost of thoughts as well, and she remained sitting there as before, with her gaze toward the darkness of the foyer, and he remained standing there, leaning over her, staring down at the plaid of her silk lap, and unconsciously, seduced by the gentle silence, he began to rock her in the chair, very gently, very gently...

She slowly raised her eyelids to look at his softly shadowed profile, and let them close completely in quiet pleasure. It was like a long embrace, it was like surrendering to his arms when the chair tilted back, and when it rocked forward so her feet touched the ground, then there was something of him in the floor's light pressure against her foot. He felt it too, the rocking began to interest him, and little by little he rocked harder, it was as if he were getting closer and closer to possessing her, the farther back he brought the chair, and there was a kind of anticipation in that second when it was just about to tilt forward again; and then when it came down there was a strange satisfaction in that little slap when her unresisting feet struck the floor, and there was complete possession in it when he forced the chair farther forward to press the soles of her feet gently against the floor so that her knees lifted just a little.

"Let's not dream," said Niels then with a sigh and let go of the chair in resignation.

"Oh yes," she said almost pleadingly and looked at him innocently with big eyes drowning in sorrow.

Slowly she stood up.

"No, no dreams," said Niels nervously and put his arm around her waist. "There have been enough dreams between the two of us, haven't you ever noticed that? Haven't they ever touched you like fleeting breaths of air across your cheek or through your hair? Is it possible, has the night never quivered with sigh after sigh that drifted, dying, down onto your lips?"

He kissed her, and it seemed to him that she became less

young under his kiss, less young but more lovely, more radiantly beautiful, more captivating.

"I must tell you," he said, "you don't know how much I love you, how I have suffered and missed you. If only my rooms near the city walls could talk, Tema."

He kissed her again and again, and she wrapped her arms tightly around his neck so her wide sleeves slid all the way back, up past the billowing white undersleeves, past the gray elastic that held them tight above the elbow.

"What would your rooms say, Niels?"

"They would say 'Tema' ten thousand times and more; they would pray with that name, rage with that name, sigh and sob with it. Tema, they would threaten too."

"Would they?"

From down on the street there came a conversation through the open windows, complete and uncut, the most irrelevant wisdom of the world in shabby, everyday words, drawled and kneaded into each other by two emotionless conversing voices. All of that prose came in to them and made it even more wonderful to be standing there, breast to breast, caressed by the soft, subdued light.

"How I love you, my sweet, my sweet—you feel so good in my arms; are you so good, so good? And your hair . . . I can hardly speak, and all my memories . . . so good . . . all the memories of when I cried and was unhappy and longed so inexpressibly are coming back as if they want to be happy with me now in my happiness—can you understand that? Do you remember, Tema, do you remember the moonlight last year? Are you fond of it? Oh, you don't know how cruel it can be. Such a clear moonlit night when the air is frozen in cool light and the clouds are stretched so long—Tema, the flowers and leaves hold their scent so closely as if a frost of scent lies on them, all sounds grow so faint and vanish so suddenly, do not linger at all—it is so merciless, that night, for in it the yearning becomes so peculiarly strong, the night forces it out of every corner in your soul, sucks it out with hard lips, and no hope shines, no promise slumbers in all that cold, staring clarity. Oh, I wept, Tema! Tema, haven't you ever cried through a moonlit night? My sweet, it would be a shame for you to cry; you *mustn't* cry, there will always be sunlight around you and rose-colored nights — a rose-colored night . . ."

She had completely sunk into his embrace, and with her gaze lost in his, her lips murmured, as if in dreams, strangely sweet words of love, almost smothered by her breathing, and she repeated words, his words, as if she were whispering them to her heart.

Outside, the voices moved away up the street and made her uneasy. Then they came back, rhythmically accompanied by the curt ring of a cane against the pavement; moved away once more to the other side, lingering for a long time, muted in the distance, then disappeared, died away.

And the silence swelled up again around them, flared up around them, heartpounding, heavy with breath, betraying. The words had withered between them and the kisses fell heavy from their lips, like hesitant questions, but containing no re-lease, no enjoyment of the moment. They did not dare release each other's eyes and yet did not dare put speech into their gaze, but rather veiled it, as if hiding themselves from one another behind it, silent, brooding over secret dreams.

Suddenly there was a trembling in his embrace that awak-ened her, and she pressed her hands against his chest and tore herself away.

"Go, Niels, go, you must not be here; you must not, do you hear!"

He tried to pull her to him but she stepped back, wild and pale. She was shaking from head to toe, standing with her arms away from her body, as if she did not dare touch herself.

Niels tried to kneel and grasp her hand.

"You mustn't touch me." There was despair in her glance. "Why won't you go when I ask you to? My God, won't you leave! No, no, you mustn't speak, go away. Can't you see how I tremble for you? Look, look, look! Oh, it's wrong of you, the way you defy me. When I beg you to go!"

It was impossible to utter a single word, she wouldn't listen. She was in a terrible state: the tears were streaming from her eyes, her face was almost distorted and seemed to shine with pallor. What should he do?

"*Won't* you please leave? Can't you see how you're humiliating me by staying, you're mistreating me, you are. What have I done to you that you can be so mean. Oh, go! Have you no pity?"

Pity? He was cold with anger. This was insane. There was nothing to do but leave. So he left. He despised the two rows of chairs, but he walked slowly between them, with a stern glance at them, as if in defiance.

"Exit Niels Lyhne," he said when he heard the click of the lock in the foyer door behind him.

Thoughtfully he went down the stairs with his hat in his hand; on the landing he paused, gesticulating to himself: damned if he could understand any of it! Why *that*, and again why that? Then he walked on. There were the open windows. He almost felt like splintering that nauseating silence up there with a screeching howl, or finding someone to talk with here, talk for hours — mercilessly — penetrate that silence with babble, bathe it in babble. He couldn't get it out of his blood; he could see it, taste it, he walked in it. Suddenly he stopped and turned blazing red with embittered shame. Had she been trying to tempt herself with him?

Up there Mrs. Boye still stood weeping. She had stepped in front of the mirror and stood with both hands leaning on the table, and wept so the tears dripped from her cheeks into the rose-colored interior of a large conch shell. She gazed at her contorted face as it appeared above the hazy spot that her breath made on the mirror, and she followed her tears as they welled up out of her eyes and rolled down. How they kept coming! She had never cried like this before; oh yes, once in Frascati when her horses had bolted.

Little by little her tears came more slowly, but a nervous trembling still sporadically rippled through her from head to foot.

The sun grew stronger; the quivering reflection from the waves stretched diagonally up across the ceiling, and at the sides of the venetian blinds whole rows of parallel rays came in, entire shelves of yellowish light. The heat increased, and through the ripe smell of heated wood and sun-warmed dust, other scents swelled forth; from the variegated flowers of the sofa cushions, from the silk curve of the chair backs, from books and folded blankets the heat released hundreds of forgotten perfumes that moved through the air, ephemeral as ghosts.

Very slowly the trembling diminished, leaving a strange dizziness behind, in which fantastical feelings, partial sensations, whirled in the tracks of her astonished thoughts. And she closed her eyes but remained standing with her face turned toward the mirror.

How odd! The way it had come over her, so shrilly frightening. Had she screamed? A scream lingered in her ears and she felt a weariness in her throat, as if after a long, terror-stricken shout. What if he had grabbed her? She felt herself being grabbed, and hugged her arms defensively to her breast. She struggled, but still — now it was as if she were sinking naked through the air, blushing, burning with shame, shamelessly caressed by all the winds. He would not leave, and it would soon be too late, all her strength left her like bubbles bursting; bubble after bubble that pushed through her lips and burst, unceasingly; in a second it would be too late. Had she begged him on her knees? Too late! She was lifted irresistibly toward his embrace like a bubble rising up through the water — quivering; that is how her soul rose up naked toward him, with every desire exposed to his gaze, every secret dream, every hidden surrender unveiled before his possessing eyes. Again in his embrace, lingering, sweetly trembling. There was an alabaster statue in the midst of the flames, which turned glowingly transparent in the heat of the fire, little by little losing more and more of its dark core, until everything at last was shining bright.

Slowly she opened her eyes and looked at her reflection with a discreet smile as if to a confidante with whom she did not want to become too familiar; then she walked around the parlor and collected her gloves, hat, and cape.

The dizziness had completely vanished.

She liked the feeling of weakness she could still feel in her legs, and she kept walking about in order to experience it more fully. Secretly, almost accidentally, she gave the rocking chair a little intimate push with her elbow.

She was rather fond of scenes.

With a glance she took her leave of something invisible in the room, then she rolled up the blinds, and it became an entirely different place.

Three weeks later Mrs. Boye was married, and now Niels Lyhne was all alone with himself.

He couldn't quite rid himself of his indignation that she had so shamelessly thrown herself into the arms of the society she had so often ridiculed. It had simply opened the door and beckoned, and she had gone. But was it right for him to throw stones, hadn't he himself felt the magnetic attraction of respectable philistinism? It was only this final meeting (if it *was* the last) he condemned her for, if it was supposed to have been a flippant farewell to the old life, one last folly before she retreated to the most proper of the proper. Was that possible? Such a boundless self-contempt, such a cynical scorn for herself which dragged him under her scorn as well, him and everything they had had together of memories and hope, enthusiasm and sacred ideas. It made him blush and it made him rage. But was he being fair? Because, on the other hand, she had really done nothing but tell him, openly and honestly: such and such is pulling me to the other side, pulling me strongly, but I recognize your right, more than you yourself demand, and here I am; if you can take me, then take me, if you can't, then I'll go where the power is the strongest. And if that was the way things were, then wasn't she within her rights? He had not been able to take her . . . the whole decision could have depended on so little: the shadow of a thought, the nuance of a mood.

If only he knew what she *must* have known for a moment, but perhaps no longer knew. He was so reluctant to believe what he couldn't help accusing her of. Not only for her sake, least of all for her sake, but because he felt that it left a mark on his banner. Not in any logical sense, of course, but still . . .

No matter why she had rejected him, one thing was certain: now he was alone, and he felt it as a loss, but also, a little later, as a relief. There was so much awaiting him; the year at Lønborggaard and abroad had been an involuntary hiatus, in spite of how deeply it had involved him, and the fact that during that year he had in so many ways become more aware of his good points and his shortcomings only increased his thirst to make use of his powers, working undisturbed and in peace. Not to create, there was no rush for that, but to collect; there was so much he had to make his own, such an overwhelming amount that he began to measure the brevity of life with despairing eyes. He had not been wasting his time before, but it is not easy to free yourself from the ancestral bookcase, and it is so easy to make your way along the same paths that have led others to their goal, and that is why he had not sought his own Vinland in the wide world of books but had followed the way his forefathers had gone. Obedient to authority, he had closed his eyes to much that beckoned, the better to see in the great night of the Eddas and the sagas, and he had closed his ears to so much that called, the better to hear the mystical, natural sounds of the folk songs. Now he had finally realized that it was not a necessity of nature to be either a Viking or a Romantic, and that it was simpler to speak his own doubt than to place it in the mouth of Gorm the Loke-worshipper, more reasonable to find the sound for the mystery of his own being than to shout against the cloister walls of the Middle Ages and receive the same words back, a weakened echo that he himself had shouted.

He had had an eye for what was new for the times, but he had been more preoccupied with listening to the way the New was obscurely expressed in the Old, rather than hearing what the New itself was saying to him, clearly and distinctly; and there was nothing remarkable in this, for no new gospel has ever been preached here on earth without the whole world suddenly becoming preoccupied with the old prophecies.

But something else was required, and Niels threw himself with enthusiasm into his new work; he had been seized with that desire to conquer, that thirst for the power of knowledge, which every servant of a spirit, no matter how humbly he may later come to perform his task, at one time has felt, even if it was only for one single, pitiful hour at the end. Who among us — positioned by a kind fate in such a way that we could tend to the development of our own spirit — who among us has not stared out over the mighty sea of knowledge with an enthusiastic gaze, and who has not been pulled down toward its clear, cool waters, to begin scooping it up in the hollow of our hands with the gullible arrogance of youth, just like the child in St. Augustine's legend? Do you remember how the sun would laugh over the fair summer land? You saw neither flower nor cloud nor spring, life's celebrations would pass by, arousing not even dreams in your young blood, even your home was far away. Do you remember? And do you remember the way it built up in your thoughts from the yellowing pages of the books, final and complete, resting in itself like a work of art, and it was yours in every detail, and your spirit lived in all of it? When the pillars rose up slender into the air, their strong curves confident in their power to bear, that bold thrust was from you, that proud stature was in you, and when the vault seemed to hover because it had gathered all its gravity, stone by stone, and in a mighty flow of weight confidently settled down on the shoulders of the pillars, then it was yours, this dream of weightless hovering, because that confidence with which the vault descended, that was you, placing your foot on solid ground.

Yes, that's the way it was, that's the way your being grows with your knowledge, is clarified by it, unified by it. It is as wonderful to learn as it is to live. Don't be afraid of losing yourself in larger spirits than your own. Don't sit there anxiously brooding about the uniqueness of your soul, don't cut yourself off from what has power, out of fear that it will carry you off with it and drown your beloved, most intimate character in its mighty surge. Be confident: the uniqueness that is lost in the disassembling and recreating during a vigorous development has only been an imperfection, merely a shoot sprouting in darkness that was unique only as long as it was sick with pallor, shunning the light. And it is the healthy part of you that you must live on, the healthy part that will become great.

Niels Lyhne was quite astonished to find that it was already Christmas Eve.

For half a year he had gone nowhere, except occasionally to visit the Councilor and his family, and he had an invitation to spend the evening with them; but last Christmas had been the Christmas in Clarens, and so he wanted to be alone. A few hours after dark, he went out.

It was windy. A thin layer of snow, not yet stamped down, lay on the streets, making them wider, and the white snow on the roofs and along the windowsills lent the buildings a decorative, but also more lonesome appearance. The gas streetlamps, fluttering in the wind, shot their light as if in distraction up along the walls, so that here and there a sign would start up from its dreams and stare straight ahead with a grandiose vacancy of thought. Even the shop windows, which were only partially lit, and whose displays had fallen into disarray during the bustle of the day, looked different than usual; something strangely introspective had come over them.

He turned down side streets, and here Christmas seemed already in full swing, for music came to him constantly from the cellars and ground-floor apartments, sometimes from a violin, but most often from concertinas which, undaunted, whined their way through popular dance tunes, and with the plodding way in which the songs were rendered, they gave an impression more of the joyous work of dancing than of any real festivity. But there was a certain illusion about it of shuffling steps and steamy air — it seemed to him, standing outside — and in his loneliness he grew polemical toward all that celebration. He had much more sympathy with the workman who was standing outside the dimly lit window of a little shop, discussing with his child one of the cheap treasures inside, seeming so eager to establish firmly what they would select before they ventured into the cave of temptations. And with those shabby old women who continued to appear, one by one, almost every hundred paces; all wearing the most peculiar capes and wraps from times long since past, and all with meek, shy movements in their old throats, like mistrustful birds, and with something uncertain and reclusive in their bearing, as if day in and day out they had sat forgotten up on the uppermost floors of the remoteness of the back buildings, and only on that one evening of the year were taken down and remembered. He grew sad thinking about them, and his heart moved inside him with a sick feeling when, daydreaming, he imagined himself in the slowly ebbing existence of one of these old, lonely women, and he could hear in his own ears, so painfully rhythmic, the slow now-again now-again dripping of a parlor clock into the bowl of the day, full of meaningless seconds.

He had to see about getting that Christmas dinner over with, and he walked back the same way he had come, with a half-conscious fear that in the other streets new kinds of loneliness were stirring and other forms of desolation were gathering dew, different from the loneliness that had struck him and lain so bitterly upon his lips.

Out on the main streets he breathed more freely, he walked faster, with a certain defiance in his step, and divorced himself from all connection with what he had just left behind, with the thought that *his* solitude he had chosen himself.

Then he went into one of the larger restaurants.

While he sat waiting for the food, from behind an old newspaper supplement he observed the people coming in. They were almost exclusively young people; some of them came alone, some a little aggressive in their bearing, as if they wanted to forbid those present from counting them as fellow sufferers. Others couldn't hide that they were embarrassed at not being invited out on a night like this, but all of them had a strongly pronounced taste for secret corners and out-of-the-way tables. Many came in pairs, and it was obvious from looking at most of these pairs that they were brothers; Niels had never seen so many brothers at one time. They were often quite dissimilar in their clothing and bearing, and their hands bore even clearer witness to how different their positions in life often were. It was seldom that you noticed any real intimacy between them, either when they arrived or later when they sat talking with each other; here one of them was the superior, the other the admiring one, over there one of them was affable, the other on the retreat, and over here there was a cautious vigilance on both sides, or, even worse, an unspoken condemnation of the other's goals and hopes and means. For most of them it was apparently necessary to have a holiday evening, and in connection with this a certain feeling of loneliness, in order to make them remember their common roots and bring them together.

As Niels sat thinking about this and about the patience with which all these people waited, neither ringing nor shouting for the waiters — as if they had all tacitly agreed to keep out as much of a restaurant atmosphere as possible — as he sat thinking about this he noticed one of his acquaintances come in, and this sudden view of a familiar face after all those strangers was so unexpected that he could not help standing up and greeting the new arrival with a glad and astonished "Good evening."

"Are you waiting for someone?" said the other man, looking for a hook for his overcoat.

"No, solo."

"That's just fine, then."

The new arrival was a Dr. Hjerrild, a young man whom Niels had met a couple of times at the Councilor's apartment, and he knew, not from conversation but because of some teasing remarks by the Councilor's wife, that Hjerrild was an extreme freethinker in religious matters; from conversation, on the other hand, he knew that in political matters Hjerrild was quite the opposite. You didn't usually meet people like that at the home of the Councilor, who was both religious and liberal. Because of his views and because of his deceased mother, the doctor belonged to one of those circles, so numerous at that time, where they regarded the new freedom with partially skeptical, partially hostile eyes, and where in religious matters they were more than rationalistic, less than atheistic, when they were not either indifferent or mystical, which also did occur. In these circles (which, by the way, were quite varied) they found that Holstein was at least as dear to their hearts as Jutland was, they felt no kinship whatsoever with Sweden, and they did not unconditionally love Danishness in its neo-Danish forms. Finally, they knew their Molière better than their Holberg, Baggesen better than Oehlenschläger, and were perhaps somewhat sentimental in their taste in art.

It was under the influence of these kinds of views and sympathies, or at least related ones, that Hjerrild had developed.

He sat gazing at Niels with an uncertain expression while Niels told him about his observations of the other guests, dwelling particularly on the way they seemed practically ashamed that there was no home or familiar place that had drawn them in on this evening.

"Yes, I understand that so well," he said coldly and almost disapprovingly. "You don't come here on Christmas Eve of your own free will, and then you have the humiliating feeling of being set outside, whether it's other people or yourself who are responsible. Do you want to tell me why you're here? If you don't want to, just say no."

Niels told him no more than that he had spent the last Christmas Eve with his late mother.

"I beg your pardon," said Hjerrild. "It was very kind of you to answer me, but you must forgive me for being so mistrustful. I have to tell you that it's possible that some people come here to give Christmas a youthful kick, and, you see, I am here out of respect for other people's Christmas celebration. This is the first Christmas I've been here in the city and not with a dear family that I know from my home town, but I've had the feeling that I was in the way when they sang their Christmas hymns. Not so much that they were embarrassed, they were much too polite for that, but I do think it made them uneasy to have someone sitting there for whom the songs were sung into the clear blue sky, with no conviction."

They ate their dinner in almost complete silence, then lit their cigars and agreed to go somewhere else to drink their toddies. On this evening neither of them felt like looking at the gilt frames on the mirrors or at the red sofas which they saw so regularly on other evenings of the year, so they sought out a little café that they usually never frequented.

They saw at once that this was no place for them to stay.

The owner, the waiters, and a couple of friends were sitting in the back of the room playing three-card with two trumps. The owner's wife and daughters were watching and serving at the table, but not for Niels and Hjerrild; one of the waiters brought them their drinks. They hastened to drink up when they noticed that they were intruding, for the others immediately started talking more quietly, and the owner, who had been sitting in his shirtsleeves, could not persuade himself to remain seated but had rushed to put on his coat.

"We certainly seem to be homeless tonight," said Niels as they walked down the street.

"Yes, that's as it should be," was Hjerrild's rather pathetic reply.

They began to talk about Christianity. It was as if the subject was in the air.

Niels spoke fervently but rather superficially against Christianity.

Hjerrild was tired of retracing the threads of conversations that were old for him, and he said suddenly, without any real connection to the preceding: "Be careful, Mr. Lyhne; Christianity has power. It's stupid to quarrel with the ruling truth by agitating for the truth of the crown prince."

"Stupid or not, that's not a consideration."

"Don't say that so lightly. It was not my intention to tell you the obvious thing, that in material respects it is stupid; it is stupid in terms of ideas, it is stupid and even more than that. Be careful; if it isn't unavoidably necessary for your temperament, then don't bind yourself too strongly to *that* right now. As a poet you have so many other interests."

"I probably don't understand you, but I can't treat myself like an organ grinder who takes out a less popular tune and puts a different one in, one that everybody is going around whistling."

"You can't? There are those who can. But you could say: we don't play that tune. Usually you can do a lot more in that way than you think. People aren't that consistent. When you keep on energetically using your right arm, an excess of blood rushes to it, and it increases in size at the cost of the other limbs, while the legs that you use only when necessary grow rather thin, all by themselves. Do you get the picture? Look at the way most, and also probably the best, intellectual forces here in Denmark have turned exclusively toward political freedom. Look at that and let it be a lesson to you. Believe me, there is a redeeming joy for a person in fighting for an idea that is popular, while it is so demoralizing to belong to the losing minority which life, in the course that it takes, proves wrong, point by point and step by step. It could not be any different, for it is so bitterly discouraging to see that what you are convinced, from the innermost silence of your soul, is true and right, to see this truth ridiculed and struck in the face by even the lowliest believer in the victorious army, to hear it slandered with obscene names, and then not be able to do anything, nothing but love it even more faithfully, kneel before it in your heart with even deeper reverence. And to see its beautiful countenance just as radiantly beautiful, just as full of the sublime and the immortal light, no matter how much dust is whirled at its white forehead, or how close a poisonous fog thickens around its halo. It *is* bitterly discouraging, it cannot be avoided — your soul will be hurt by this, for it's so easy to hate so that your heart grows weary, to call up the cold shadows of contempt around you, and, apathetic with pain, let the world pass by. Of course, if you have it in you, if instead of choosing the easier way, instead of taking yourself out of all connection with the whole, you can stand erect and with all your talents alert, all your sympathies awake, you can receive the many-thorned lashes as they fall, lash after lash, and still keep your bloody head from drooping, as you listen for the dull sounds prophesying change in your time, and search for the faint, distant gleam which is a day — a time — perhaps; if you have *that* in you! But do not try it, Lyhne. Think what such a man's life would be like, if he is to do his utmost. Unable to speak without boos and hisses foaming up in the footsteps of his speech. To have all his words distorted, besmirched, twisted out of joint, twined into cunning snares, thrown at his feet, and then before he has even gathered them up out of the dirt and untangled them from one another, suddenly to discover that the whole world is deaf. And then to start all over again from another point, with the same results, over and over. And then perhaps the most painful of all, to see himself misunderstood and scorned by noble men and women, whom he, in spite of his different beliefs, regards with admiration and respect. And that's the way it *has* to be, it *cannot* be any different. The opposition *cannot* expect to be attacked for what it actually is and wants, but for what those in power *want to believe* it is and intends. And besides, power used upon the weak and misuse of power: how can they be two different things? And certainly no one will demand that those in power ought to make themselves weak in order to fight with equal weapons against the opposition. But that is why the struggle of the opposition is so painful, so agonizing. And do you really think, Lyhne, that a man can fight that battle, with all those vulture beaks sunk into him, without the invincible, blind enthusiasm that is fanaticism? And how in the world can he be fanatical about something negative? Fanatical about the idea that there is *no* God!—and without fanaticism, no victory. Hush, listen!"

They stopped outside a high-ceilinged apartment on the ground floor where the blinds were pulled up on one of the windows, and through the open ventilation window a song reached them, borne by the clear voices of women and children:

> A child is born in Bethlehem,
> Bethlehem!
> For Jerusalem rejoices.
> Hallelujah, hallelujah!

They walked on in silence. The melody, or rather the notes from the piano, followed them down the quiet street.

"Did you hear," said Hjerrild, "did you hear the excitement in that old Hebraic cry of victory? And those two Jewish city names! Jerusalem, it was not merely symbolic: the whole city — Copenhagen, Denmark. It was us, the Christian people among the people."

"There is no God, and the human being is His prophet!" said Niels bitterly, but also with despair.

"Yes, that's right!" ridiculed Hjerrild. A little later he added: "But atheism is so boundlessly pedestrian, and its goal, in the long run, is nothing less than a disillusioned humanity. Belief in a ruling, judgmental God, that is the last great illusion of humanity, and what then, when that is gone? Then people will be wiser; but richer, happier? I can't see it."

"But don't you see," exclaimed Niels, "that the day humanity can freely cry: there is no God, on that day a new heaven and a new earth will be created as if by magic. Only then will heaven become the free, infinite place instead of a threatening, watchful eye. Only then will the earth belong to us and we to the earth, when the dim world of salvation and condemnation out there has burst like a bubble. The earth will be our proper fatherland, the home of our heart where we do not dwell as foreign guests for a paltry time but for all our days. And what intensity it will give life when everything must be contained in life and nothing is placed outside of it. That enormous stream of love, which now rises up toward that God who is believed in, will bend back over the earth when heaven is empty, with loving steps toward all the beautiful, human traits and talents with which we have empowered and adorned God in order to make God worthy of our love. Goodness, justice, wisdom, who can name them all? Don't you realize what nobility would spread over humanity if people could live their lives freely and meet their deaths without fear of hell or hope of heaven, but fearing themselves and with hope for themselves? How our conscience would grow, and what stability it would bring if passive remorse and humility could no longer atone for anything, and no forgiveness was possible except to use goodness to redeem the evil you committed with evil."

"You must have an amazing faith in humanity; atheism will make greater demands on people than Christianity does."

"Of course."

"Of course; but where will you find all the strong individuals you will need to put together your atheistic humanity?"

"Little by little, atheism itself will teach them; not this generation or the next one or the next one after that — they will not be able to bear atheism, I realize that, but in every generation there will always be a few who will honestly fight for a life in it and a death in it, and over the course of time they will acquire a number of spiritual ancestors whom their descendants can look back on with pride and gain strength by observing them. In the beginning the conditions will make things the most difficult, most will fall in the struggle, and those who are victorious will win only with tattered banners, for their inner-most marrow will still be steeped in tradition, and because there is so much else in a human being than just the brain that must be convinced: blood and nerves, hopes and longings, yes, and if there are dreams they must be convinced too. But it doesn't matter, someday it will come, and the few will become the many."

"Do you think so? I'm searching for a name; couldn't you call it 'pietistic atheism'?"

"All true atheism..." began Niels, but Hjerrild quickly interrupted him.

"Of course!" he said. "Of course; by all means let us have only a single gate, one single eye of a needle for all the camels in the kingdom of the earth!"

X

Early in the summer Erik Refstrup came home after a two-year stay in Italy. He had left as a sculptor but returned as a painter, and he had already enjoyed some success, sold his paintings, and obtained commissions for more.

The fact that success had come as if on his first attempt was due to the steady self-knowledge with which he wrapped his talent around him. He was not one of those great, promising talents whose hands are so close to all the laurels, whose passage over the earth is like a Bacchic procession, jubilantly marching through every region, sowing golden seed in all directions, and with guardian spirits on all their panthers. He was one of those in whom a dream is buried which spreads holiness and peace around a little place in their souls, where they are most themselves and least themselves. And what *they* create in the art they possess always rings with the same yearning refrain, and every one of their works always bears the same anxiously narrow mark of kinship, as if they were images from the same small homeland, the same little corner hidden deep in the mountains. It was like this with Erik — no matter where he dove down into the sea of beauty, he always brought up the same pearl into the light.

His paintings were small: in the foreground a single figure, clay-blue from its own shadow; behind, the heather-covered earth, heath, or countryside; on the horizon the reddish-gold glow left behind by the setting sun. One of them is of a young girl who is telling her own fortune in the Italian manner. She has knelt down at a spot where the earth shows brownish through the short grass; she has taken off a heart, a cross, and an anchor of beaten silver from her necklace and has flung them to the ground. Now she is on her knees, her eyes faithfully closed, with one hand covering them, the other stretched out, searching for inexpressible happiness in love or bitter sorrow, which the cross will soothe, or the hopeful everyday fate of hope. She has not dared touch the ground yet, her hand is so afraid in that cold, secretive shadow; her cheeks are burning and her mouth is midway between prayer and tears. The atmosphere is so solemn, the glow of the sun threatens, so wild and hot out there, coming as softly as sorrow across the heather. If she only knew: happiness in love, inexpressible — bitter sorrow, which the cross will soothe, or the hopeful everyday fate of hope?

There is another painting in which she stands upright, longingly, on the brown heath with her cheek brought to rest on her folded hands, so sweet in her naive yearning, so infinitesimally unhappy with the awful life that is passing her by. Why doesn't Eros come with kissing roses, does he think she is too young? He should just feel her heart, how it's pounding; just come with his hand, oh, there's a world inside there, a world of a world, if only it would awaken. And why doesn't it call? It's lying in there like a bud, folded around all its sweetness and beauty, existing only for itself and oppressed by itself. For it knows that Eros exists, but not what it is. Hasn't it felt warm around the sheltering leaves, hasn't Eros come down around it, so the bud has grown light inside, right into the innermost, reddest darkness where the fragrance, sensing itself, lies without scent, pressed together in one quivering tear? Will it never come? Will the bud never breathe out what it perceives it possesses, be rich in its wealth? Will it never, will it ever unfold and blush awake as the rays of the sun rush shining in under all its petals? She really has no more patience with Eros, already her lips are beginning to quiver with the impending tears; hopelessly challenging, her eyes gaze out into space and her little head sinks, more and more despondent, slowly turning her fine profile into the painting, where a gentle breeze sails with reddish dust across the dark green deerweed, in toward the sherry-golden sky.

This is how Erik painted, and what he wanted to present always found its expression in paintings like these. He could probably imagine others, might long to escape the narrow confines in which he conjured them up, but if he stepped outside and tried other styles, he would soon have a chilling, dejected feeling that he was borrowing from others and that what he was doing was not his own. If he then returned from this kind of unsuccessful excursion, which each time taught him more than he realized, then he would become even more Erik Refstrup-ish than before, he would surrender himself even more courageously, and with an almost painful intensity, to his own individuality, and wherever he went he maintained a mood of celebration full of piety which marked even his least action, revealing itself in the entire manner in which he regarded himself. It was as though the beautiful shapes that stirred within him, younger sisters of Parmigianino's slender-limbed women with the long necks and the long, slim princess hands, sat down at the table with him and tasted his goblet before presenting it with gestures full of nobility and grace, and held him in the power of their radiant dreams with the mysterious, introspective smile of Luini, so enigmatically elegant in its secretive sweetness.

But when he had served his god faithfully for eleven days, other forces would sometimes take control of him, and he would be gripped by a raging need for the coarse desires of coarse pleasures and would throw himself into them, feverish with the human desire for self-annihilation which (while the blood burns the way blood can burn) yearns for degradation, corruption, dirt, and filth with the very same measure of power possessed by that other, equally human desire: the desire to preserve oneself greater, and purer, than oneself.

At such moments almost nothing was raw or violent enough for him, and it took him a long time to regain his equilibrium when they had passed, for in a certain way they were unnatural to him. He was too healthy, too little poisoned by dreams, and those moments would come almost like a swing in the opposite direction from his surrender to the higher forces of art, almost resembling revenge, as if his nature felt offended by his choice of that higher, more ideal goal in life, which circumstance had prompted him to pursue.

Now this struggle in two directions was not, however, so pronounced in Erik Refstrup that it found outward expression in him or made him feel the need to use it to explain himself to those around him. No, he was the same simple, cheerful fellow as before, somewhat awkward because of his shyness about feelings that mattered, somewhat of a buccaneer with his ability to grab hold and take what he wanted. And yet this struggle *was* inside of him and might appear in quiet hours, like the bells that ring in the sunken city on the bottom of the sea. He and Niels had never understood each other as well as they did now; they both felt it, and silently each of them struck up a new friendship with the other. And when vacation time arrived and Niels finally had to carry out his intention of visiting his Aunt Rosalie, who was married to Consul Claudi in Fjordby, Erik went along.

The main road, which comes from the richest area surrounding Fjordby, arrives at the town through two mighty hawthorn thickets that form the hedge of Consul Claudi's vegetable patch and his large seaside garden. What happens to the road then — whether it stops right at the Consul's farm entrance, which is as big as a town square, or whether it is the road that turns and continues on past his barn and lumberyard up through the town to become a street — that is all a matter of opinion; because many travelers make the turn and continue on, but there are also many who stop and consider their goal reached when they enter the Consul's tarred portal, which always stands wide open, with the doors thrown back and with skins spread out to dry above the doors.

The farm buildings were all old, with the exception of the tall storehouse, whose dreary, dead slate roof was the latest thing in Fjordby in terms of architecture. The long, low front building looked as though it had been brought to its knees by three large garret windows, and it was joined at a dark angle to the wing containing the brewery and stable, at a brighter angle to the storehouse. In the dark corner was the back door to the shop, which along with the peasants' room, the office, and the servants' quarters formed a gloomy little world all its own where the blended smell of ordinary tobacco and earthen floors, of spices and rancid dried fish and wet homespun, made the air heavy and almost thick enough to taste. But if you went through the office, with its penetrating reek of sealing wax, and made your way into the corridor that formed the boundary between commerce and family, then the overpowering scent of new feminine finery would prepare you for the mild flowery scent of the rooms. It was not the fragrance of a bouquet, not of a real flower; it was the mysterious, memory-provoking atmosphere that lingers over every home, and no one can say with certainty where it comes from. Every home has its own; it may remind you of a thousand things, of the smell of old gloves, of new playing cards or open pianos, but it is always different. It may be masked with incense, perfumes, or cigar smoke, but it cannot be killed; it always comes back and is present again, unchanged as before. Here it was like flowers, not roses or stocks, not any flower that really exists, but the sort of fragrance you might imagine from those fantastical, dull sapphire rows of lilies that twine and bloom around vases of old porcelain. And how it suited those big, low-ceilinged rooms with their heirloom furniture and old-fashioned prim-ness! The floors were so white, the way only Grandmother's floors were, the walls were all the same color, with a simple, bright garland stencil beneath the molding; there was a plaster rose in the middle of the ceiling, and the doors were ridged and had shiny brass handles in the shape of dolphins. At the leaded-glass windows hung airy net curtains, white as snow, flowing and coquettishly caught up with bows of colored ribbon, like the canopy on a bridal bed for Corydon and Phyllis; and on the windowsill in variegated green pots, old-fashioned flowers bloomed: blue agapanthus, blue pyramid bells, finely leaved myrtle, fiery-red verbena, and geraniums, colorful as butter-flies. But it was the furniture in particular that gave everything its character; those immovable tables with extended leaves of darkened mahogany, chairs whose backs curved like the fluke of an anchor around you, chests of drawers in every conceiv-able shape, gigantic buffets inlaid with mythological scenes in light yellow wood — Daphne, Arachne, and Narcissus — and small writing desks as well, on thin, curving legs, every little drawer with a mosaic of dendritic marble depicting desolate, rectangular buildings with a tree nearby, all of it from long before Napoleon. There are also mirrors with flowers in white and bronze painted on the glass — rushes and lotuses floating on the smooth lake — and then there is the sofa, not one of those trifles on four legs with room for two, no; solid and massive, it rises from the floor, a whole spacious terrace, on each side joined to a chest-high cupboard, on top of which there is a smaller cupboard architectonically rising up to a man's height, lifting a precious old vase out of the reach of children. It was no wonder that there were so many old things in the Consul's home, for his father and his grandfather before him had relaxed and rested within these walls when there was respite from the work at the lumberyard and office.

The grandfather, Berendt Berendtsen Claudi, whose name the business still bore, had built the farm and had been most interested in the shop and the salvage business. The father had built up the lumber business, bought acreage for the farm, built the barn, and put in two gardens. The present Claudi had gone in for grain, had built up the storehouse, and had combined his role as English and Hanoverian Vice-Consul and as an agent for Lloyds with his occupation of merchant. And the grain and the North Sea took so much of his attention that he could only manage a dilettantish supervision of the other branches of his business, which were divided between a bankrupt cousin and an intractable old farm hand who was constantly issuing ultimatums to the Consul by declaring that no matter how things were going with the shop, the land had to be taken care of, and when it was time for him to plow they would have to get horses somewhere else for moving the lumber — they wouldn't get his, may the devil take him. Since the farm hand was good at his job, however, there was nothing to be done about it.

Consul Claudi was in his early fifties, a rather stately man with heavy, regular features bordering on coarseness, which just as easily took on an expression of energy and tepid shrewdness or relaxed into an almost raffish expression of amorous, pungent pleasure. And he also felt just as much in his proper element whether he was coaxing through a deal with sly farmers or negotiating with a crowd of stubborn salvage men, or whether, with one last bottle of port, he listened among grizzled sinners to stories that were more than obscene, or told them himself in that explicit, colorful way for which he was famous.

However, this was not the whole man.

The result of the education he had received was that, except in matters of a purely practical nature, he found himself on foreign ground. Nevertheless he did not ignore what he didn't understand, nor did he hide the fact that he didn't understand, and it would have been even further from his mind to carry on a discussion and demand that his arguments be respected just because he was an elderly, highly esteemed citizen with much practical experience. On the contrary, with an almost touching devotion he would sit and listen to the conversations of women and young people on such topics and now and then, with an effusive apology, pose a modest question, which almost always was answered with the greatest attentiveness; then he would thank them for the answer with all the courtesy that an older person can put so gracefully into his thank-you to a younger one.

On the whole, at certain fortuitous moments, there could be something surprisingly sensitive about Consul Claudi, an expression of longing in his clear brown eyes, a melancholy smile on his strong lips, a searching, nostalgic tone to his voice, as if he yearned for a better world, in his eyes, than the one his friends and acquaintances thought he was so wholeheartedly caught up in.

His wife was the messenger between him and this better world. She was one of those pale, gentle, virginal natures who do not have the courage or perhaps the instinct to love so strongly that there is nothing of themselves left in the deepest depths of their souls. Not even for the most fleeting instant can they be gripped in this way so that in blind enchantment they would throw themselves beneath the wheels of the carriage of their idol. They cannot do this, but otherwise they will do everything for the one they love, they will fulfill the heaviest obligations, they are prepared for the most painful sacrifices, and there is no humiliation they are afraid to bear. The best of them are like this.

There weren't *that* many demands made on Mrs. Claudi, but neither had her marriage proceeded completely without sorrow. It was, you see, a public secret in Fjordby that the Consul was not, or at any rate had not been up until a few years ago, the most faithful husband, and that he had numerous illegitimate children both in town and in the countryside. Naturally this was a great sorrow for her, and it had not been easy for her to force her heart to hold on tight and not let go, in that revolt of jealousy, contempt, and anger, shame and languishing disgust, which had then made her feel that all firm ground had vanished from beneath her feet. But she fought against it. Not one reproachful word passed her lips, but she prevented any confession on her husband's part, any obvious plea for forgiveness, and everything that might look like a remorseful promise. She felt that if it came to words, they would sweep her away with them, away from him. It had to be borne in silence, and in silence she sought to assume complicity in her husband's guilt by condemning herself for that self-entrenchment which her love had not been strong enough to make her relinquish. She succeeded in making this sin so great that she would feel an obscure need for forgiveness, and in the course of time she reached such a stage that rumors began to spread about the girls Consul Claudi had seduced, that they and their children were looked after in ways other than with money — there must have been the hidden hand of a woman protecting them, keeping evil things away from them, supporting and guiding them.

In this way sins were transformed into goodness, and a sinner and a saint happened to make each other better.

The Claudis had two children, a son who was in a merchant's office in Hamburg, and a nineteen-year-old daughter named Fennimore after the heroine in *St. Roche,* one of Mrs. von Palzow's novels that had been very popular in Mrs. Claudi's childhood.

Fennimore and the Consul went down to meet the steamer on the day it brought Niels and Erik to Fjordby, and Niels was pleasantly surprised to see that his cousin was beautiful, for up until then he had only known her from a terrible old family daguerrotype, in which she formed a group along with her brother and her parents in a steam-filled atmosphere, all of them with feverish carmine on their cheeks and with heavy gilding on their golden finery. And now she was so lovely as she stood there in her pastel morning dress with slim bandolier slippers and black cross-bands around the white instep of her stockings. She stood there with one foot up on the beam at the edge of the wharf and leaned over, smiling, to give him the handle of her parasol as a hello and a welcome before the steamer had actually docked. How red her lips were and how white her teeth, and how elegant her forehead and temples beneath the wide Eugénie hat, through the long black lace of the brim, heavy with shiny, jet-black beads. Finally the gangway was lowered and the Consul went off with Erik, to whom he had already introduced himself while there was still twelve feet of water between them; shouting, he had at once involved him in banter about the torments of seasickness with a wizened hatmaker's widow who was on board the steamer, and now he was in the process of directing Erik's admiration toward the great linden trees outside the house of the district revenue officer and toward the new schooner standing in drydock at Thomas Rasmussen's shipyard.

Niels accompanied Fennimore. She pointed out to him that the flag was flying at Strandhaven in honor of him and his friend, and then they began to talk about the Councilor and his wife in Copenhagen. They agreed at once that the Councilor's wife was a little — just a bit — they didn't want to say the word, but Fennimore put on a tight-lipped smile as she made a catlike movement with her hand, and that was apparently significant enough for both of them, the way they smiled and then immediately looked so serious. Silently they went on, keenly absorbed in thought about how they must appear in each other's eyes.

Fennimore had imagined Niels Lyhne more stately, more distinctive in his bearing, more firmly defined, like a word underlined in black. But Niels, on the other hand, had found so much more than he expected, he found her enchanting, almost captivating, in spite of her dress that had so much of the provincial lady's oversophistication about it. When they entered the Consul's foyer and she took off her hat and, preoccupied, looked down as she smoothed her hair with such wonderfully graceful, indolent, gentle movements of her hand and wrist, he felt so grateful for these gestures — as if they had been caresses. Neither the following day nor the next could he escape from that gratitude, rather puzzling even to himself, which at times surged so strangely that he thought it would be the greatest happiness to dare thank her in words for being so beautiful and so sweet.

Soon Erik, as well as Niels, felt at home in the Consul's hospitable house, and after a few days' time he was completely absorbed by the comfortably ordered idleness which is a true vacation and which is so difficult to protect against the friendly interference of well-meaning people. They had to call up all of their diplomatic skills in order to avoid all the stuffy evening parties, great sea excursions, summer dances, and amateur performances that continued to threaten their peace. They were on the verge of wishing that the Consul's farm and gardens were located on some desert island; and Robinson was not seized by any greater fear when he found the footprints in the sand than they were when they saw the greatcoats of strangers hanging in the foyer, or discovered unfamiliar reticules on the parlor table. They would much rather have been alone, for they had not even reached the middle of the first week before they were both in love with Fennimore. Not with that fully mature love which must and will know its destiny, which longs to possess and embrace and feel secure — not yet that kind of love — but the first dawning of love that lies like a strange springtime in the air, and swells with a yearning that is melancholy, with a restlessness that is a gently pulsating joy. The mind is so tenderly and easily moved, so ready to surrender. A light over the lake, a rustling in the leaves, yes even a flower that opens its petals, they have all acquired such an extraordinary power. And vague, nameless hopes suddenly burst forth and spread sunshine over everything in the world, and just as suddenly there is no more sun: a gentle despondency sails, wide as a cloud, over the radiance and churns the sparks of hope down into the grayness of its wake. So dispirited, meltingly dispirited, and in sweet pain surrendering to his fate, with his heart full of self-pity, and a despondency in love with itself and reflecting itself in quiet elegies, and swooning in a sigh that is half feigned . . . and then all over again, then it rustles with roses: the dreamland emerges from the fog with golden mist above the soft crowns of beech trees, and summer darkness, rich with fragrance, beneath the leaves that arch over pathways — no one knows where they end.

One evening after teatime they were all gathered in the parlor. There could be no question of sitting in the garden or anywhere else outdoors, for the rain was pouring down. They were shut inside but were not at all unhappy because of it. There was something of a winter evening's coziness over the room — to be shut inside four walls — and besides, it was so good to have rain, everything needed water so badly, and when it really pelted down and drummed with heavy drops on the casing of the gossip mirror, the sound called up fleeting, blurred images of lush green fields and fresh leaves, and someone would exclaim to himself: "Look how it's raining!" and gaze at the windowpanes with a feeling of contentedness and with a little spark of pleasure, in a half-conscious communion with what was outside.

Erik had taken out a mandolin he had brought with him from Italy and had sung about Naples and shining stars, and now a young woman who was there for tea sat at the piano, accompanying herself to "My Little Hideaway in the Hills," putting an "ah" at the end of all the words so it would sound really Swedish.

Niels, who was not particularly musical, let the music make him gently melancholy and fell into a reverie, until Fennimore began to sing.

That woke him up.

But not pleasantly; her song filled him with uneasiness. She was no longer the same little provincial girl when she gave herself up to the sound of her voice. How she let herself be taken by those notes, how she breathed into them, so unreserved and free — yes, he almost felt it was indecent, it was as though she were singing herself naked before him. His heart grew so hot, his temples were pounding, and he cast down his eyes. Was there no one else who noticed it? No, they hadn't noticed. She was removed from herself, far away from Fjordby, from Fjordby poetry and Fjordby feelings. She was taken away to another, more daring world where passions grew wild on great mountains and surrendered the red blossoms to the storm.

Could it be because he had so little understanding of music that he found so much in her song? He couldn't quite believe that, but he hoped it was true. He was fond of her in quite a different way; he was fond of her the way she usually was. When she sat with her sewing and spoke in that gentle, calm voice, looking up with those clear, faithful eyes, then his entire being would be drawn to her with the irresistible power of a strong and quiet homesickness. He needed to humble himself before her, bend his knee and call her holy. He always had such a strange yearning for her, not just as she was, but for her childhood and all the days he had not known her; and when they were alone, he would constantly bring the past into their conversation and get her to tell him about her little troubles, little follies, little idiosyncrasies that every childhood is filled with. And he lived in these memories, leaned toward them with a restless, jealous longing, a vague desire to grasp, share, become one with these fine, faintly colored shadows of a life which *had* flared up to richer and more mature hues. But now suddenly this song that was so strong, that came upon him so surprisingly, as a wide horizon can come upon you at a bend in the path and transform the cozy forest nook, which was the whole world to you, into a corner of a landscape, and make its elegant, sinuous lines grow small and insignificant in comparison with the grand contours of the hills and the distant marshes. Oh, but it was only a *fata morgana*, that landscape, only a fantasy, all that he had felt from the song, for now she was speaking the way she always spoke, and she was so lovely and herself again. And he also knew in hundreds of ways what a still water she was, without storm and without waves, mirroring the sky, blue with stars.

This is the way he loved Fennimore, this is the way he saw her, and this is the way she gradually began to behave with him. Not with any conscious pretense, for in a way there was so much that was true about it, and it was so natural since his every word and expression, each and every dream and thought, was accompanied by wishes, prayers, and homage to precisely that side of her personality — then it was so natural for her to be herself in the guise that he forced on her. And how could she make sure that everyone had a completely accurate impression of her as she really was, now that her thoughts were full of only one man? — Erik, the only one, her love-chosen master, the one whom she loved with a wildness that was not part of herself, and with an idolatrous adoration that shocked her. She had believed that love was a sweet dignity, not this consuming restlessness, full of fear and humiliation and doubt. Many times, when she thought she saw a confession working its way toward Erik's lips, the feeling would seize her that it was her duty to place her hand over his mouth, to warn him against speaking, and to condemn herself and tell him that she was betraying him, tell him how unworthy she was of his love, how earthbound and small, how girlish she was, so far from sublime, oh so wretchedly low and plainly ugly. She felt herself so false under his admiring glances, so calculating whenever she refrained from avoiding him, and so guilty whenever she could not persuade her heart, in her evening prayers, to ask God to turn his soul away from her so that there might be nothing but sunshine in his destiny, and nobility and glory. For she would drag him down with her lowborn love.

It was almost against his will that Erik loved her. His ideal had always been refined, great, and proud, with a quiet melancholy over pale features and temple-cool air around the strict folds of the drapery; but Fennimore's sweetness had conquered him. He could not resist her beauty. There was such a fresh, unconscious sensuality about her entire figure; even her walk whispered of her body, there was a nakedness about her movements, a dreamy eloquence about her repose, neither of which she could help, and which it would have been beyond her power to hide or to silence if she had had any inkling of it. No one realized this better than Erik, and he was fully aware of how great a role her purely physical beauty played in his affection; that is why he fought against it, for there were noble, romantic ideas about love in his soul, ideas that he possessed, perhaps, not just from tradition and poetry, but from deeper layers of his nature than those which normally won expression in his being. No matter where they came from, they had to retreat.

He had still not confessed his love to Fennimore, but then *Berendt Claudi's Minde* arrived and was lying there at anchor out in the bay. It was going to take on cargo farther up the fjord, so it did not come into the harbor, and since the Consul was very proud of his schooner and wanted to show it to his guests, they rowed out to it one evening to have tea.

The weather was lovely, perfectly calm, and they were all in the mood to enjoy themselves. And they did have a good time; they drank English porter, bit into English biscuits as big as the moon, and ate smoked mackerel that had been caught on the journey across the North Sea. They worked the ship's pump until it foamed, tilted the compass back and forth, hoisted water up out of the water barrels with the big tin siphon, and listened to the first mate playing an octagonal concertina.

It was completely dark when they were ready to go home.

They rowed away in two groups: Erik, Fennimore, and a couple of elderly people in the ship's dinghy; the others in the Consul's own boat. The first boat was supposed to row on ahead and make a swing away from land, while the other one would make straight for the shore; the reason for this arrangement was that they wanted to hear how the song would sound across the water on a still evening like this. So Erik and Fennimore sat together on the thwart in the stern of the first boat and took the mandolin along. But the song was long forgotten, for when the oars came up, it became apparent that there was an unusually large amount of phosphorescence in the water, and this completely preoccupied them. Gently the boat glided forward, and the dull, smooth surface was rippled into receding lines and circles by a faint white light that barely illuminated the path it took, and only where it was strongest did it send a fine, dim glow, like a cloud of light, out over its surroundings. It gleamed white around the oars and glided backward in quivering circles that grew fainter and fainter, and in light drops it dripped from the blades of the oars in a phosphorescent rain that was extinguished in the air but ignited the water, drop by drop. It was so quiet on the fjord, and the rhythm of the oars merely seemed to measure off the silence in pauses of equal length. Hushed and soft lay the gray twilight over the silent deep, and the boat and the people were gathered into a dim unity from which the faint phosphorescent sheen limned only the racing oars, and once in a while a rope that dragged, or the calm brown face of a sailor. No one spoke; Fennimore cooled her hand in the water, and she and Erik sat there, facing backwards, and stared at the phosphorescent net that moved soundlessly after the boat, catching their thoughts in its bright mesh.

A shout from the land for a song awoke them, and they sang a couple of Italian romances together, to the accompaniment of the mandolin.

Then they fell silent once more.

Finally they put in at the little dock that jutted out from the seaside garden. The Consul's boat lay empty at the pier, and everyone had gone up to the house. The aunt and the other person also started up after them, but Erik and Fennimore stood there and watched the boat being rowed back to the ship. The latch on the garden gate up the slope fell into place, the sound of the oars grew fainter and fainter, and the movement of the water around the dock died away. Then a gust of wind rustled through the dark foliage around them, like a sigh that had been hiding and now quite gently lifted the leaves up and flew away, leaving them completely alone.

At the exact same moment they turned toward each other, away from the water. He grabbed her hand, pulling her slowly, almost inquiringly, toward him, and then kissed her. "Fenni-more," he whispered, and they moved through the dark garden.

"You've known it for so long," he said. She said yes. Then they walked on, and then the latch fell into place again.

Erik couldn't sleep when he finally got to his room after drinking coffee with the others and saying good night to them at the front door.

There was no air in there. He threw open the windows; then he flung himself onto the sofa and listened.

He wanted to go out again.

He could hear every sound in the house! He could hear the Consul's slippers, and now Mrs. Claudi was opening the kitchen door to see whether the fire was out. What could Niels be doing with his suitcase at that time of night! Well. There was a mouse behind the paneling. Now someone was walking in stocking feet across the attic. Now there were two people. Finally! He opened the door to the guest room next door and listened; then he quietly opened the window and climbed over the windowsill and then into the courtyard. Through the laun-dry room he would be able to get out to the seaside garden. If anyone saw him, he would say that he had left his mandolin down at the dock and wanted to rescue it from the dew. That's why he had it with him on his back.

The garden was lighter now; there was a slight breeze and a bit of moon, which drew a quivering silver stripe from the pier out to *Berendt Claudi's Minde.*

He walked around out to the breakwater which protected the garden, and which then stretched in sharp angles around a large dammed-up area and all the way out to the end of the harbor's jetty. The whole way, he kept balancing on the big, uneven, sloping rocks.

A little out of breath, he reached the end of the breakwater and sat down on the bench there.

High above his head the red lantern of the lighthouse rocked gently with the sighing sound of iron, and the rope of the flag flapped softly against the flagpole.

The moon had grown a little brighter, but not much, casting a cautious, gray-white light over the quiet vessels in the harbor and over the town's jumble of rectangular roofs and white, dark-eyed gables. And beyond, above everything, the church tower loomed, bright and tranquil.

He leaned back, dreamily, and a wave of infinite joy and jubilation swelled up in his heart and made him feel so rich and full of power and the warmth of life. It was as if Fennimore could hear every thought of love that sprang from his happiness, vine after vine and flower upon flower, and he stood up, strumming briskly on the mandolin, and sang in triumph to the slumbering town:

> My maiden she lies there awake,
> Listening to my song!
> My maiden she lies there awake,
> Listening to my song!

Again and again, when his breast felt too full, he repeated the words of the old folk ballad.

Gradually he grew calmer; memories of those hours in bygone days when he had felt himself weakest, most wretched, and most forsaken broke forth with a quiet, intense pain, the kind of pain that brings the first tears to your eyes. He sat down on the bench, and as his hand lay damping the strings of the mandolin, he stared out across the vast surface of the blue-gray fjord, where the glittering moon bridge stretched past the dark ship over to the fine, melancholy silhouette of the Morsø Hills, drawn by cloud-blue land through a haze of white.

And the memories fled, more and more gently, lifting themselves up to brighter lands, as if illuminated by an aurora of roses.

"My maiden she lies there awake . . ." he sang to himself.

> My maiden she lies there awake,
> Listening to my song!

X I

Three years have passed; Erik and Fennimore have been married for two, and they live in a little village near Mariager Fjord. Niels has not seen Fennimore since that summer in Fjordby. He lives in Copenhagen and does a great deal of socializing with people but has no intimate relationship with anyone, except for Dr. Hjerrild, who calls himself old because streaks of gray are starting to appear in his dark hair.

It was a hard blow for Niels, that unexpected engagement, and he has grown a little lethargic because of it, also a little more bitter and a little less trusting; and he no longer has so much enthusiasm to counter Hjerrild's despondency. He is still involved in his studies, but they are more haphazard, and the idea of finishing in order to step forth and get started has only an uncertain, flickering life to it. He lives a great deal among people, but he does not live with them; he is interested enough in them, but he does not care in the least whether they are interested in him, and he notices that the power within him is growing weaker and weaker, the power that was supposed to drive him forward to do his work, either with the others or against them. He can wait, he says, even if he has to wait until it's too late. "He that believeth shall not make haste," that is his excuse. For he has faith enough, he feels, if he were really to delve into himself, faith enough to move mountains, but he cannot manage to put his back into it. Once in a while the need to create wells up in him, the longing to see a part of himself set free in a work by him, and for days at a time his being can be tensed with joyous, titanic efforts to mold the clay into his Adam. But he is never able to shape him into a semblance of his image; he does not have enough stamina to maintain the self-discipline that it demands. It may take weeks for him to give up the work, but he does give it up, and irritably asks himself why he should keep on: what more does he have to gain? He has enjoyed the pleasure of creation; the tedium of upbringing remains, to nurse, nurture, and support entirely — why? For whom? He is no pelican, he says. But whatever he says, he is still ill at ease and feels that he has not done justice to the expectations he has of himself. It doesn't help him to confront these expectations and try to doubt that their demands on him are justified. He is faced with a choice, and he must choose; for life is such that when the first youth is gone, sooner or later — depending on the natural disposition of a person — sooner or later a day dawns when resignation comes to you like a seducer and tempts you, and you have to say farewell to the impossible and accept it. And resignation has so much on its side; haven't the idealistic demands of youth often been rejected, its enthusiasm humiliated, and its hope destroyed? The ideals, so bright, so brave, have not yet lost any of their luster, but they no longer wander the earth in our midst, as in the first days of our youth. Up the broad-based stairs of the world's wisdom they have been led, step by step, back to that heaven from which our simple faith had taken them down, and there they sit, radiant but distant, smiling but weary, in divine idleness, while the incense of an inert homage fitfully coils up toward their throne in grand swirls.

Niels Lyhne was tired; these perpetual attempts at a leap that was never leaped had exhausted him, everything was empty and worthless for him, distorted and confused, and so trivial as well. It seemed most natural to him to close his ears and shut his mouth and then sink down into studies that had nothing to do with the nausea of the world, but were like the quiet, isolated ocean deep, with peaceful forests of seaweed and peculiar animals.

He was tired, and it was from his aborted hope of love that

the root of his weariness issued, it was from there that it had swiftly and confidently spread through all his being, all his talents, and all his thoughts. Now he was cold and passionless enough, but in that first period, when the blow had struck him, his love had grown day by day with a fever's incessant power, and there had been times when his soul, urged by insane passion, had swollen up like a wave with infinite longing and foaming need, had risen up and kept on climbing and climbing until every fiber of his brain, every string of his heart had been stretched taut to the very limits of tension. That is when the weariness had come, dulling and healing, and had made his nerves deaf to the pain, made his blood too cold for enthusiasm, his pulse too weak for action. And more than that, it had prevented him from falling back by giving him all the caution and egoism of a convalescent. Now, when he thinks back to the days in Fjordby, he has the same feeling of security as someone who has survived a terrible illness and thinks that now, after he has endured the suffering and the fever has burned itself to ashes in his body, now he will be safe for a long, long time.

So one summer day, after Erik and Fennimore had been married for two years, Niels received a partly miserable, partly boasting letter from Erik in which Erik accused himself of wasting his time recently, but he didn't know why, he didn't have any more ideas. The people he associated with in the region were very lively and merry, not at all prudish or foolish, but the most shocking oafs about art. There wasn't a single person he could have a sensible conversation with, and he had fallen into a stupor of laziness and low spirits that he couldn't shake because he never saw an idea or mood the way he had before, or felt inspired, so he was often both anxious and afraid that he was finished and that he would never do anything again. But this couldn't possibly keep on forever, it had to come back, he had been much too talented for it to end like this, and then he would show them what art was, those others who painted away as if it were something they had learned by rote. For the time being, however, there seemed to be a spell over him, and it would be a demonstration of friendship if Niels would come to Mariager Fjord; he would be treated as well as circumstances allowed, and he might just as well spend his summer there as anywhere else. Fennimore sent her greetings and would be very happy if he came.

That letter sounded so unlike Erik that there really must have been something seriously wrong for him to complain like that. Niels saw this at once, and he also knew how feeble was the source of Erik's production — only a meager stream which unfavorable conditions might easily dry up. He would leave immediately; whatever had happened, Erik would find him a completely loyal friend, and whatever bonds the years had loosened, whatever illusions they had uprooted, he would still, at the very least, safeguard that friendship from their childhood days. He had supported Erik before, he would support him now. An obsessive feeling of friendship seized him. He would renounce the future, fame, ambitious dreams, everything for Erik's sake. All that he possessed of smoldering enthusiasm and of fermenting creativity he would concentrate on Erik; he would devote himself to Erik, to his self and his ideas. Everything was ready, nothing would be his own, and he dreamed that the one who had intervened so roughly in his life would be great, and he himself would be obliterated, overlooked, impoverished, with no spiritual heritage, and he dreamed further that what Erik had been given would gradually no longer be borrowed, but truly his own, with the stamp he gave it by minting it out of deeds and work. Erik would be ennobled and honored, and Niels simply one of the many, many ordinary people, really nothing more; forced into poverty in the end, not voluntarily; a true beggar and not a prince in rags . . . and it was sweet to dream himself so bitterly insignificant.

But dreams are dreams, and he laughed at himself and thought that people who neglect their own selves can always afford to devote an infinite amount of attention to other people's work; and he also thought about the fact that Erik, when they stood face to face, would naturally deny his letter, shrug it off as a joke, and find it enormously funny if Niels actually went there and announced himself ready to help him find his talent again. But Niels went all the same; deep in his heart he thought that he could be of some use, and no matter how he tried to explain it away and cast doubt upon it, he nevertheless could not free himself from the feeling that it really was the old boyhood friendship which had been reawakened in all its naiveté and all its warmth, in spite of the years and what they had brought.

The estate near Mariager Fjord belonged to an elderly couple who for health reasons had found it necessary to take up residence in the south of Europe for an indefinite time. They had not expected to rent the place out since they thought, when they left, that they would only be gone for half a year, and so they had left everything as it was. When Erik rented the house fully furnished, this was so literally the case that he acquired it with knickknacks, family portraits, and everything else, yes, even down to a cupboard full of junk and old letters in the desk drawers.

Erik had discovered the place when he left Fjordby after his engagement, and since it had everything they needed and more, and since he was thinking of taking up residence in Rome for a while in a couple of years, he had persuaded the Consul to postpone buying furnishings and they had gone to Marianelund as if it were a hotel, except that they had a few more suitcases than travelers usually do.

The façade of the estate faced the fjord, not ten yards from the water. It was quite ordinary in appearance, with a balcony above and a terrace below, and it had a new garden in back whose trees were not much thicker than a walking stick; on the other hand, you could walk from the garden straight into a magnificent beech forest with open patches of heather and low, damp ravines between hills of white clay.

This was Fennimore's new home, and for a while it was as bright as happiness could make it, for they were young and in love, after all, healthy and energetic and with no worries about their livelihood, either spiritual or material.

But every palace of happiness that rises up has sand mixed into the foundation on which it rests, and the sand collects and runs out beneath the walls, slowly perhaps, imperceptibly perhaps, but it keeps running, grain after grain . . . And love? Love is no rock either, no matter how much we want to believe it is.

She loved him with all her soul, with the ferocity and trembling ardor of fear; and he was more than a god to her, much closer to an idol whom she worshipped, without restraint and beyond all measure.

His love was as strong as hers but it lacked the delicate, manly tenderness which protects the beloved woman from herself and keeps vigil over her dignity. It was like the memory of some dim obligation, calling like a soft voice, but he did not want to listen, for she was so enchanting in her blind love; and her beauty, which had the loveliness of a slave's unguarded voluptuousness and humble grace, urged and drove him toward a passion without limits and without mercy.

In the old myth about Amor, doesn't it say somewhere that he places his hand over Psyche's eyes before, in sweet intoxication, they soar off into the smoldering night?

Poor Fennimore! If she could have been consumed by the fire in her own heart, he who should have protected her would have fed the flame, because he was like that drunken ruler who, with the torch of murderous arson in his hand, rejoiced at seeing the capital of his empire burn because his drunkenness grew at the sight of the flickering flames, until the ashes made him sober.

Poor Fennimore! She didn't know that the swelling hymns of happiness can be sung so often that neither melody nor words remain, but only a babble of triviality; she didn't know that the intoxication which uplifts today, takes its power from the wings of tomorrow; and when sobriety finally, heavily, started to dawn, then she began to understand, trembling, that they had loved themselves down into a sweet contempt for themselves and each other, a sweet contempt whose sweetness grew weaker day by day, and finally became bitter. They turned as far away as possible from each other, he to dream about a betrayed ideal of scornful nobility and cool grace, she to gaze with despairing longing toward the pale, still, now so infinitely distant coast of her girlhood. Day by day it grew more difficult for her, shame burned wildly in her veins, and a nauseating loathing for herself made everything miserable and hopeless for her. There was a desolate little room where there was nothing but the suitcases she had brought from home, and there she would often sit, hour after hour, until the sun sank over the world and filled the room with reddish light. There she would martyr herself with thoughts stiffer than thorns and lash herself with words more biting than whips until she would be confused by torment and pain and seek a deadening solace by throwing herself to the floor like an inanimate object, too full of hideous rottenness and dregs, a carcass of herself, too repulsive to be the seat of a soul. Her husband's whore — that thought was never absent from her heart; with that thought she threw herself contemptuously into the dust beneath her feet, with that thought she locked out any hope of resurrection and petrified every memory of happiness.

Gradually a harsh, brutal indifference came over her, and she stopped despairing just as she had stopped hoping. Her heaven had collapsed, and she felt no need to dream it into a high vault again, she made no demands for blessedness, she was not too good for this earth nor the earth too good for her — they were worthy of each other. She cast no hatred onto Erik, nor did she withdraw in horror from him. On the contrary, she accepted his kisses because she had far too much contempt for herself to avoid them; she was his wife, after all, a man's wife!

For Erik, too, it was bitter to awaken, although with a man's prosaic foresightedness he had told himself that it had to happen eventually. But when it did, when love was no longer a

salve for every yearning and when the scintillating golden veil
in which it had descended to earth to him was waved away,
then he experienced it as a release of all life's spirits, a sinking of
all his abilities which made him afraid and full of regret, so that
with a feverish eagerness he turned to his art to seek assurance
that there was not something else he had squandered besides
happiness. But he did not receive the reply he had hoped for,
he fell prey to several unfortunate ideas that led nowhere, but
that he could not bring himself to give up. He couldn't really
make anything out of them, but they continued to preoccupy
him and prevented other ideas from emerging and attracting
him, and he grew despondent and dissatisfied and fell into a
brooding idleness because his work was so deathly recalcitrant
and because he thought that he only needed to wait and the
spirit would certainly come over him again. But it dragged on
and on, his talent continued to be barren, and here by the quiet
fjord there was nothing in his social life that might have a
stimulating effect on him, nor were there any artistic colleagues,
the sight of whose triumphs might spur him on, either to competition or to creative opposition. This inactivity became intolerable to him, and he longed intensely to find himself, no
matter how or in what. When nothing else presented itself, he
began to seek out the company of a circle of older and younger
farmers who, under the leadership of a sixty-year-old squire,
eased the dullness of country life with whatever excesses their
none-too-lively imaginations could come up with, greatly limited as they were by their rather narrow-minded taste. The real
core of their dissipation was drinking and card games, which
were all more or less the same, whether the pretense was a
hunting expedition or a trip to the fair. And it made no significant difference if, once in a while, they moved the scene to one
of the nearby towns and there, in the course of an afternoon,
conducted real or imaginary business with the merchants, because the crux of the expedition was always in the evening at
the inn, whose owner, with great discretion, would show all
those of the right persuasion in to them in a private room. If

there were traveling actors in town, they would ignore the merchants, for actors were much more companionable, not so restrained about liquor, and in general willing to subject themselves to that miracle cure (unfortunately seldom experienced with complete success) of drinking themselves sober—with gin, that is—after they were drunk on champagne.

The mainstays of the group were landowners and farmers of all ages, but there was also an enormous young dandy of a distiller and a pale-necked tutor, who had not been a tutor for at least the past twenty years but who had made the rounds as a guest together with his sealskin portmanteau and a gray nag, and the joke was that he had stolen it from a horse butcher. He was a silent drinker, a great virtuoso on the flute, and was presumed to know Arabic. An attorney, who was always telling new stories, and a doctor, who knew only one—from 1806 about the siege of Lübeck—also belonged to what the squire called his staff.

This group was spread over a wide area, and it almost never happened that they were all together at the same time. But if anyone neglected the company for too long and stayed at home, the squire would issue a call to all the faithful to go over and have a look at the recreant's bulls, which was understood to mean that for two or three days they would take up lodging at the unfortunate man's farm, and turn it upside down with boozing and card-playing and any other country highjinks that the season might offer. During one such visitation the whole party had been snowed in for so long that the host had gradually run out of coffee, rum, and sugar, and they finally had to settle for a coffee punch brewed from chicory, sweetened with syrup, and spiked with aquavit.

It was on the whole a terribly coarse bunch that Erik fell in with, but people with such an enormous life-force apparently felt stifled by more civilized amusements, and their indestructible humor and their broad, teddy-bear kind of camaraderie actually tempered much of the rawness. If only Erik's talent had been of the same kind as Brouwer's or Ostade's, this select group of boozing guests would have been an absolute gold mine for him; but such as it was, the only profit for him, as for the others, was that he enjoyed himself immensely. Too much so, for soon this wanton revelry became indispensable to him, and little by little it took up almost all of his time. If he now and then reproached himself for his inactivity and promised himself that it would end, he was, however, driven back to the old life by the emptiness and the spiritual impotence he felt every time he tried to work.

The letter he wrote to Niels one day when he had been struck by the impression that his perpetual barrenness was like a consumption which had attacked his talent — that letter he had regretted as soon as it was sent off, and he hoped that Niels would let his complaints go in one ear and out the other.

But Niels came — friendship's knight errant personified — and received that half repudiating, half pathetic welcome that wandering knights have always received from those for whom they have taken Rozinante out of her warm stable. But since Niels was cautious and patient, Erik soon thawed out, and the old intimacy between them was again brought to life. And Erik needed to talk, to complain, and to confess — he needed to, with an almost physical need.

One evening when it was past bedtime and Fennimore had retired, they were sitting with their cognac and water in the dark parlor. Only the glow of their cigars indicated where they were sitting, and then once in a while when Niels leaned all the way back in his chair, his upward-staring profile would be silhouetted against the dim windowpanes. They had drunk a great deal, especially Erik, while they talked about the old days at Lønborggaard when they were boys. Now, after Fennimore's departure, there came a pause which neither of them seemed to have any desire to break, for their thoughts came rolling with such comfortable gentleness as they sleepily listened to their blood, warm from the dawning intoxication, singing in their ears.

"What fools we were when we were twenty!" Erik said

from the darkness. "God only knows what I was looking for and where I got it into my head that something like that even existed. No doubt we gave it the same names that it possesses in reality, but what we meant was something so utterly superior in comparison with the tame benediction from God that we received. There isn't much to life, actually. What do you think?"

"Oh, I don't know, I take it as it comes. Generally, people don't really live. Most of the time people just exist. If only we could have life in one big, appetizing cake that we could chop away at . . . but in pieces like this! That's no fun at all."

"Tell me, Niels — you're the only one I ever talk to about peculiar things like this, but I don't know, you're so strange about it all. Tell me — do you have anything in your glass? — Good! — Have you ever thought about death?"

"Me? Well, yes, have you?"

"I don't mean at funerals or when I'm sick, but at other times, just when things are going well, it can come over me, like a . . . almost like a kind of despair. I sit here and mope and don't get anything done, *can't* get anything done, and then I start to notice how time is slipping away from me, hours, weeks, months! With nothing in them they rush past me, and I can't nail them to the spot with work. I don't know if you can understand what I mean, it's just a kind of feeling I have, but I want to take hold of time with something that I've created. You see: when I paint a picture, the time it takes will always be mine, or I get something out of it; time doesn't end because it has passed. I feel sick when I think about the days that are passing — interminably. And I don't *have* anything, or I can't get at it. It's torture; I can get so furious that I have to pace the floor and sing something idiotic so that I won't start crying with rage, and then I almost go crazy when I stop again and realize that meanwhile time has been passing, and is passing while I'm thinking, and keeps on passing and passing. There is nothing so wretched as being an artist: here I stand strong and healthy; I can see; my blood is rich and warm; my heart is beating; there's nothing wrong with my mind and I *want* to work, but I just can't. I'm struggling for and grasping at something that can't be grasped, and no amount of effort will help me reach it even if I slaved so that the blood burst from my fingertips. What do I have to do for inspiration, to get an idea? I can pull myself together as much as I like, I can try to ignore it and go out and look around, without searching, but no! Never, never anything at all, only the awareness that now time is standing out there in eternity up to its waist and hauling in the hours so that they race past, twelve white and twelve black, without stopping, without stopping. What should I do? There must be something I can do, when things get like this; I couldn't be the first one, could I? Can't you think of anything?"

"Travel."

"No, not that, how can you think of that? You don't think I'm finished, do you?"

"Finished! No, but I meant with new impressions . . ."

"New impressions! That's the whole point. Haven't you ever heard about people who were full of talent as long as they were in their youth and they were fresh and full of hope and plans, but then, when these were gone, their talent disappeared too — and never came back."

He was silent for a long time.

"*They* traveled, Niels, looking for new impressions. That was their obsession. The South, the Orient, it was all in vain, it all glanced off them like off a mirror. I've seen their graves in Rome. Two of them, but there are many, many of them. One of them went mad."

"I've never heard that about painters before."

"Oh yes — and what do you think it might be? A secret nerve that is severed? Or is the person himself the cause of it? Something he has betrayed or offended, perhaps — who knows? A soul is such a fragile thing, and no one knows *how deep* a soul goes in a human being. You should be good to yourself — Niels!" His voice had grown soft and gentle. "Sometimes I have that yearning to travel because I feel so empty; you have no idea how strong it is, but I don't dare travel, I think, because what if it didn't help and I was one of those I told you about? What then? Just imagine if I came to stand face to face with the knowledge that I was finished, didn't have the slightest bit left, nothing, couldn't do anything, just imagine: couldn't do a thing; a rag of a man, the damnedest dog of a cripple, a miserable eunuch! Where do you think I would sink? And you see, that wouldn't be impossible; my first youth has gone, and I don't have many illusions or anything like that. It's incredible how many of them a man squanders, and I have never been the sort of person who is happy to get rid of them, I wasn't like the rest of you who visited Mrs. Boye, you were all so busy plucking the elegant feathers off each other, and the balder you got, the more self-confident you were. But it's all irrelevant anyway, sooner or later everyone loses his feathers."

Then they were silent. The air was acrid with cigar smoke, cloying with cognac, and they sighed heavily from the nauseating atmosphere in there, and then from their very heavy hearts.

There he sat: Niels, who had traveled three hundred miles to help, sat there feeling ashamed at the colder part of his nature. Because what could he do, when it came right down to it? Should he start to talk artistically with Erik, lots of words full of purple and ultramarine, dripping with light and wading in shadow? There had been a dream about something like that in his mind when he left home. How ridiculous it was! Help? Perhaps you could chase away Penia, the goddess with the closed hands, from an artist's door, but that was really all you could do; you could no more help him to create than you could help him to lift his little finger by himself if he were paralyzed. No matter how full you were of heart and sympathy and the willingness to sacrifice and everything else that is generous. Mind your own business, that's what you had to do; it was healthy and it was useful, but it was certainly much easier to be a man of heart out into the clear blue sky, all the way up to the highest heavens. The only thing was that it was so boundlessly impractical and so miserably unproductive. Mind your own business, and do it well; there wasn't any salvation in that, but you wouldn't need to lower your eyes for anyone, not for God or for other people.

Niels had many opportunities to indulge in despondent reflections on the impotence of the goodhearted, because the only purpose he served was to keep Erik at home more than usual for about a month or so. At the same time he had no desire to return to Copenhagen right in the middle of the warm season, nor did he wish to continue to be a guest indefinitely, so he rented a room with a family who did not belong to the peasant class over on the other side of the fjord, only so far away that it was possible for him to row across to Marianelund in a quarter of an hour. He might just as well stay here as anywhere else, and besides, now he was familiar with the area, and he was the kind of person who becomes easily attached to his surroundings, and he did have his friend here, after all, and his cousin Fennimore; there were plenty of reasons, especially since there was no one in the world who was waiting for him anywhere else.

When Niels decided to come over here, he had carefully thought about what his attitude would be toward Fennimore; that is, how he should show that he had so completely forgotten, that he didn't even remember that there was anything to forget. Above all else: no coldness, a hearty indifference, a superficial courtesy, a polite sympathy, that's the way it would be.

All of this, however, turned out to be irrelevant.

The Fennimore he encountered was a completely different one from the one he had left. She was still beautiful, her figure was as voluptuous and lovely as ever, and she had the same indolent, lingering gestures that he had admired in the past; but there was a sad emptiness in the expression of her mouth, as in a person who has thought too much, and there was a pathetic, miserable, tormented cruelty in her gentle eyes. He did not understand it at all, but it *was* clear to him that she had had

other things to do than think about him and that she was
entirely numb to the memories that he might awaken. She
looked exactly like someone who had taken her stand and made
the worst out of it that she could.

Little by little he started to put two and two together, and
one day as they were walking together along the shore he began
to understand.

Erik was busy cleaning up his studio, and as they were
walking along the water, the maid came down with a whole
apronful of junk and threw it onto the beach. There were old
paintbrushes, pieces of castings, broken palette knives, chipped
linseed oil bottles, and empty tubes of paint — a big heap.
Niels poked around in it with his foot, and Fennimore watched
with that vague eagerness for discovery that people always feel
about junk. Suddenly Niels pulled back his foot as if he had
burned himself, recovered at once, and quickly stirred up the
heap again.

"Oh, let me see it," said Fennimore and put her hand on his
arm, as if to stop him.

He bent down and pulled out a plaster casting, a hand that
was holding an egg. "It must be a mistake," he said.

"No, it's broken, you see," she said calmly, taking it out of
his hand. "See, the index finger is gone," she showed him, but
when all at once she realized that the plaster egg was cut open
and that a yolk had been painted inside it with yellow paint,
she blushed a little, and she leaned forward and quite slowly
and meticulously broke the hand into small pieces with a rock.

"Do you remember when it was cast?" asked Niels just for
something to say.

"I remember that I was coated with green soap so the plaster wouldn't stick to my hand. Is that what you mean?"

"No, I mean the time that Erik passed around the cast of
your hand at the tea table, don't you remember? And when it
came to your old aunt, how she had tears in her eyes, and with
the deepest sympathy for you she hugged you and kissed you
on the forehead, as if someone had hurt you."

"Yes, people are so emotional."

"Oh no, we all laughed at her all right, but there was still something fine about it, even though it was so meaningless."

"Yes, there's a lot that is meaningless but fine."

"I think you want to quarrel with me."

"No, I don't, there's just something that I want to say to you. You won't be angry at a little honesty, will you? Well, then tell me, don't you think that when a man wants to say something that's a little vulgar in front of his wife, for example, or is otherwise rather inconsiderate toward her, in your opin-ion—don't you think it's superfluous for you to protest by behaving with exaggerated delicacy and quite dreadful gallan-try? One has to assume that the husband knows his own wife best and realizes that it won't harm her or offend her; other-wise he wouldn't do it, would he? Isn't that true?"

"No, that's not true, in general; but in this case and by your authority I am willing to say yes."

"Yes, do that, you can be certain that women are not such ethereal creatures as many a good youth dreams of; they are really no more delicate than men, and they are no different than men at all. Believe me, the clay that they were both made from was a little dirty."

"My dear Fennimore, thank God you don't know what you're talking about, but you are being very unfair toward women, toward yourself; *I* believe in the purity of woman."

"The purity of woman, what do you mean by the purity of woman?"

"I mean . . . well . . ."

"You mean—I'll tell you what you mean: nothing, because that's one of those fine, meaningless things too. A woman *cannot* be pure, she mustn't be pure, how could she? What kind of unnatural thing is that? Is she destined to be pure from the Lord's hand? Answer me! No, and ten thousand times no. Then what sort of madness is this? Why do you cast us up toward the stars with one hand when you have to pull us down with the other? Can't you just let us walk on the earth beside you, as a human being, and not a bit more? It's impossible for us to take firm control in prose when you blind us with your will-o'-the-wisps of poetry. Leave us alone, just leave us alone, for God's sake!"

She sat down and wept.

Niels understood a great deal; Fennimore would have been unhappy to know just how much. It was partly the old story about the banquet of love that would not become daily bread, but continued to be a banquet, only more insipid, day by day more nauseating, less and less nourishing. And one person cannot perform a miracle, nor can the other, and there they still sit in their fancy clothes, careful to keep smiling at each other and use festive words, but inside there is a torment of hunger and thirst and their eyes begin to be afraid of each other's, for rancor is sprouting in their hearts. Wasn't this the first story, and wasn't the second story just as sad? About a woman's despair that she cannot reclaim herself after she discovers that the demigod, whose bride she had so gladly become, is nothing more than an ordinary mortal. First the despair, the futile despair, and then the useful inertia — wasn't that it? He thought that was it, and he understood all of it, the coldness in her, the bitter humility and her coarseness, which for her was the most bitter drop in the whole goblet. Gradually he also began to comprehend how his consideration, his respectful homage, must be a burden to her and annoy her, because it is natural for a woman who has been tossed from the purple bed of her dreams out onto the cobblestones to hate anyone, almost, who wants to place carpets over the stones, because in the first bitterness she *wants* to feel the harshness in all its power, she doesn't want to settle for treading the path with her feet, she wants to crawl along it on her knees, and especially there where the path is the steepest and the rocks the sharpest. She wants no helping hand or assistance, refuses to lift her head, lets it be weighed down by whatever will weigh it down, she wants her face to be all the way down in the dirt and wants to taste it with her tongue.

Niels felt so sorry for her, but he left her alone, as she wished.

It was so hard to see her suffering, not allowed to help, to sit far off and dream about her happy in stupid dreams, or with the cool shrewdness of a doctor to wait and calculate, telling himself, so sadly and so wisely, that there would be no relief before her old hope about the beautiful, glittering richness of life had bled itself to death and a more lethargic stream of life had gained passage through all the veins of her being and made her dull enough to forget, heavy enough to resign herself, and finally, finally coarse enough to rejoice at the blessedness of a thick atmosphere many heavens below the one she had anticipated and which she had prayed, so imploringly and so afraid, to have wings to reach. He was so full of revulsion toward everything when he thought about her, before whom he had once in his heart knelt so humbly and adoringly — that she should be forced down so far, consigned to slavery, standing by the gate and shivering as he rode past her, up on his horse, with the great coins of life jingling in his pocket.

One Sunday afternoon in late August Niels rowed across the fjord. He found Fennimore at home alone. She was lying on a sofa when he arrived, in the corner parlor, and she complained at every breath with the short, regular gasping that seems to lessen the pain for someone who is ill. She had such a terrible headache, she said, and there was no one at home to help her. The maid had been given permission to go home to Hadssund, and a little while after she left, someone had come to get Erik; she couldn't understand where they had driven off to in this rain. She had been lying here now for a couple of hours, trying to sleep, but that was quite unthinkable because of the pain. She had never had this before, and it had come so suddenly — there had been nothing wrong with her at dinner — first in her temples and then deeper and deeper inside, as if it were behind her eyes; she hoped it was nothing serious. She was not at all used to being sick, and she was very frightened and unhappy.

Niels comforted her as best he could, told her to lie still, close her eyes, and keep quiet; he found a thick shawl to wrap around her feet, got the vinegar from the sideboard, and made a damp compress which he put on her forehead. Then he sat down quietly near the window and looked out at the rain.

From time to time he would tiptoe over to her and change the compress without speaking, just nodding to her when she gratefully looked up at him between his hands. Occasionally she tried to speak, but he prevented any words with a hushing gesture, shaking his head. Then he went back to his place again.

Finally she fell asleep.

An hour passed, and then another, and she continued to sleep. One quarter of an hour slipped slowly into the next as the melancholy daylight gradually diminished and little by little the shadows in the room grew, stretching out from the furniture and the walls. And it kept on raining outside, constant and regular, muting every living sound with its pelting torrent.

She kept on sleeping.

The fumes from the vinegar and the vanilla scent from the heliotropes on the windowsill blended into a tart aroma of wine, filling the air — warmed by their breath alone, it spread a denser and denser dew across the grayish windowpanes as the coolness of evening increased.

He was far away now in memories and dreams, although part of his consciousness kept watch over the sleeping woman the whole time and followed her sleep. Little by little, as the darkness advanced, his imagination tired of nourishing the dreams that were constantly flaring up and constantly dying away, just as the soil tires of perpetually bringing forth the same crop. And the dreams became duller, more barren, stiff and without lush details; they lost their far-reaching, oddly twisted vines. And his mind let go of it all, of everything distant, and returned home. How quiet it was! Weren't they both here, he and she, as if on an island of silence that rose up above the rain's monotonous ocean of sound? And their souls were silent, so silent and safe, while the future seemed to sleep in a cradle of peace.

If only it would never awaken and everything would stay like this, not a bit more happiness than what was to be found in peace, but no anguish either, no rolling unrest. If only it could close up, this moment in life, like a bud is closed around itself, so that no spring would ever come!

Fennimore was calling; she had been lying awake for a while, so happy to find herself free of pain that she hadn't thought of talking. Now she wanted to get up and light the lamp, but Niels continued to play the doctor and persuaded her to remain lying down. It would not be good for her to get up yet; he had matches and would find the lamp himself.

After he had lit it, he placed the lamp on the tiered flower stand in the corner, so that the bright white globe was partly hidden by the delicate, slumbering leaves of an acacia, and there was just enough light in the room so they could see each other's faces.

He sat down in front of her, and they talked about the rain, about how good it was that Erik had taken his raincoat along, and about how wet poor Trine would get. Then the conversation came to a halt.

Fennimore's thoughts were still a little sleepy, and the lethargy she felt made it so comfortable to lie there like that, only half thinking, without speaking, and Niels was not in the mood to talk either; he was still under the influence of the long silence of the afternoon.

"Do you like this house?" asked Fennimore at last.

Oh yes, he did.

"You do? Do you remember the furniture at home?"

"In Fjordby? Quite clearly."

"How I love that furniture, and how I long for it sometimes! The furniture we have here doesn't belong to us, after all, it's only rented and has no relationship to us, it holds no memories for us about anything and we won't live with it any longer than our stay here, either. You probably think it's strange, but I can assure you that I often feel so lonely among all this unfamiliar furniture that stands here, so indifferent and so stupid, and lets me pass for the person I am without caring about me in the least. And since it won't go with me but will only stay here until others come to rent it, I can't get attached to it either, or take an interest in it the way I could if I knew that my home would always be its home, and that whatever might happen, good or bad, it would happen to me in the midst of this furniture. Do you find that childish? Perhaps it is, but I can't help it."

"I don't know what it is, but I know the feeling myself from the time I was alone abroad. My watch had stopped, and when I got it back from the watchmaker and it was running again, it was like... what you said. I was pleased, there was something peculiar about that feeling — something truly good."

"Yes, that's so true. Oh, I would have kissed that watch if I were you."

"You would?"

"Tell me," she said suddenly, "you've never told me anything about Erik as a boy. What was he really like?"

"Everything that was good and beautiful, Fennimore. Magnificent, noble, a boy's ideal of a boy in every respect; not just a mother's or a teacher's ideal, but a boy's ideal, which is so much better."

"How did you two get along? Were you very fond of each other?"

"Well, you see, I was completely in love with him, and he didn't have anything against that, that's just the way it was; we were so different, let me tell you. I always wanted to become a poet and be famous, but do you know what he said he most wanted to be when I asked him one day? An Indian, a genuine red Indian with warpaint and everything! I remember that I couldn't understand it at all, I couldn't comprehend why anyone would wish to be a savage, I was so civilized myself."

"But then wasn't it strange that he wanted to be an artist?" asked Fennimore, and there was something cold and hostile in the tone of her question.

Niels noticed this and was surprised. "Oh, no," he said

then, "it's actually seldom that people become artists on the basis of their whole personality. And those types of intrepid, experienced people like Erik are just the kind who often have an endless longing for what is delicate and fine: the beautiful, virginally cold, the sweet heights, I don't know what I should call it. Outwardly they can be robust and vigorous enough; yes, they can even be vulgar, and no one realizes what strange, romantic, and sensitive secrets they have inside, because they're so modest — spiritually modest, I mean — those great, hard-stomping men, so that no pale little maiden could be more modest about her soul than they are. Do you understand, Fennimore, that such a secret, which cannot be revealed with mundane words in the common, ordinary air, might predispose someone to be an artist? And they can't talk about it, you see, they can't. You have to believe that it exists and is living quietly within, like a flower bulb down in the ground, because every so often it does send its fragrant, delicately colored treasure of a flower up into the light. You see, you mustn't demand any of the flower's might for yourself; believe in it, rejoice in nourishing it and in knowing that it exists. Don't be angry, Fennimore, but I'm afraid that you and Erik are not very good to each other. Couldn't things be different? Don't think about who's right or about the amount of the injustice. You shouldn't act righteous toward him, because how far would the best of us get with righteousness? No, think about him instead as he was in that hour when you loved him most; believe me, he's worth it. You shouldn't measure or judge; I know there are moments in love full of a bright, magnificent ecstasy when you would give your life for your beloved if it were required. Isn't that true? Remember that now, Fennimore, don't forget it, both for his sake and for your own."

He stopped speaking.

She didn't speak either; she lay there in silence with a heavy smile on her lips, pale as a flower.

Then she sat up a little and stretched out her hand to Niels.

"Will you be my friend?" she asked.

"I *am* your friend, Fennimore," and he took her hand.

"Will you, Niels?"

"Always," he replied, and reverently drew her hand to his lips.

Then he stood up — straighter, it seemed to Fennimore, than she had ever seen him before.

A little later Trine came in and announced that she was home, and then there was tea, and finally the rowing home through the sad rain.

Erik did not come home until after dawn, and when Fennimore, in the cold, sober light of day, saw him getting ready for bed, heavy and unsteady from drink, glassy-eyed from card games, with a dirty pallor from the wakeful night, then all the fair words that Niels had spoken seemed completely fantastical to her, and the bright promises she had made in the quietness of her soul blanched and swooned in the growing daylight. It was all dream buffoonery and futile thoughts: a noble flock of lies.

What good would it do to fight back, with the hopeless weight that hung over them both? It was so pointless to lessen the weight with lies; their life would never walk on feathers again. The frost had been there; the rustle of vines and creepers, with clusters of roses and even more beautiful flowers, which had twisted around them and bound them to each other, had dropped every little leaf and lost every blossom, all that remained were the naked, tough osiers that held them together in an indissoluble lattice. What good was it if, in the warmth of memories, she awakened feelings from bygone days to an artificial life and put her idol up on his pedestal again, and found the glitter of admiration in her eyes, the words of adoration on her lips, and the blush of happiness on her cheeks; what good was it if *he* wouldn't take it upon himself to be the idol's priest and help *her* with a pious deception! He! He didn't even recognize her love, not a single one of her words was left in his ears, not one day of their days was hidden in his soul.

No, silent and dead was the swelling passion of their hearts; the fragrance, the light, and the quivering tones had all floated away, and there they sat, out of old habit, he with his arm around her waist, she with her head resting on his shoulder. They sat like that, sinking heavily into silence, forgetting each other—she to remember the glorious being that he had never been, he to dream of her as that ideal which he always saw shining in the clouds, high above her head. That was their life together, and the days came and went, bringing no change, and day after day they stared out over the desert of life and told themselves that it *was* a desert, that no flowers existed, nor any prospect of flowers, of oases, or of green palms.

The more autumn progressed, the more frequent became Erik's binges. What use was it, he told Niels, for him to sit at home and wait for ideas that never came, until his thoughts turned to stone in his head. For that matter, he had little comfort from Niels' company; he needed people with vitality, people who were roaring flesh and blood, not music boxes of delicate nerves. So Niels and Fennimore often sat alone with each other, because Niels came over to Marianelund every day.

The pact of friendship they had made with each other, and the words that had been spoken between them on that Sunday evening, had made them more relaxed and completely secure in their relationship. And they joined forces, lonely as they both were, in a warm and intimate friendship which soon assumed great power over them and occupied their minds in such a way that their thoughts, whether they were together or apart, were always turned toward this friendship, like birds that build the same nest and look at everything—both what they collect and what they reject—with a single, intimate goal in mind: to make the nest truly warm and soft for each other and for themselves.

If Niels came over and Erik was out, they would almost always take long walks in the woods adjacent to the garden, even if it was raining or windy. They had fallen in love with these woods, which became more and more dear to them as the

life of summer was gradually extinguished. There were a thousand things to look at. First the way the foliage turned yellow
and red and brown, then the way it fell one windy day, drifting
in yellow shoals when it stopped blowing, leaf upon leaf upon
leaf, faintly rustling down between the stiff branches and the
pliant brown twigs. And as the leaves fell from the trees and the
small branches, didn't the most rewarding of the summer's
secrets become visible in nest after nest? And all around there
was an abundance of prim seeds and colorful berries, brown
nuts, shiny acorns and lovely acorn caps, tufts of coral bells on
barberry bushes, shiny black buckthorn and the scarlet urns of
the rosehip. The leafless beeches were dotted with spiny beech-
nuts, and the rowan trees drooped heavily with red clusters,
tart with a scent like apple cider. Late blackberries lay black
and brown in the damp leaves by the side of the road, there
were cranberries in the heather, and wild raspberry bushes
bore their dull-red fruit for the second time. The ferns had
hundreds of colors as they withered, and the moss was an
entire discovery in itself: not just the ground moss, which
almost looked like firs or palms or ostrich feathers, in the
ravines and on the slopes, but also the delicate moss on the tree
trunks, the way you might imagine the grain fields of the elves
would look, as they shot up in such fine wisps, with dark
brown buds like ears of corn at the tips.

They crisscrossed their way through the woods, as eager as
children to discover its treasures and peculiarities, and they had
divided up the forest between them the way children do, so
that whatever was on one side of the road belonged to Fennimore and whatever was on the other side belonged to Niels,
and they would often compare their riches and argue about
whose were the most glorious. And everything in the woods
had a name, the cliffs and hills, the pathways and stiles, the
ditches and ponds; and if there was an especially large or magnificent tree, then it had a name too. Thus they had taken
possession of the woods in every possible way, and thus they
had created a little world for themselves that no one else knew

about and that no one could walk through as they did, and yet they did not share a single secret that the rest of the world could not have heard.

Not yet, anyway.

But love was in their hearts and yet was not really there — just as crystals exist in a supersaturated solution and yet do not exist, not until a splinter or simply a speck of the right substance sinks into the liquid and as if by magic instantly precipitates out the slumbering atoms so that they race to meet each other, wedging themselves together, rivet upon rivet, according to unfathomable laws, and become all of a sudden a crystal . . . crystal.

In just this way it was also something insignificant that made them feel they were in love.

There is nothing to tell — it was a day like any other, they were alone in the parlor as they had been hundreds of times before, and their conversation had been quite unimportant, and what happened outwardly was as common and ordinary as possible. It was nothing more than that Niels was standing at the window, looking out, and Fennimore went over and looked out too; that was all, but that was enough, for, as if with a bolt of lightning, the past and the present and the future were changed for Niels Lyhne with the consciousness that he loved this woman who was standing at his side, not as something bright and sweet and happy and fair that would lift him up to bliss and ecstasy — his love was not like that. He loved her as something as impossible to live without as the breath of life, and he reached out the way someone who is about to drown reaches out, and pressed her hand to his heart.

And she understood him. Almost with a scream and in a tone full of fear and despair, she called to him, in reply and confession: "Oh *yes*, Niels!" and pulled her hand back at once.

Then she stood there, pale and fleeing, for a moment, and then sank down on one knee on an upholstered chair, hid her face against the prickly plush of its back, and sobbed aloud.

Niels was practically blind for a few seconds and his hand fumbled among the flower pots for support.

It was only for a few seconds, then he strode over to the chair where she lay, and leaned over without touching her, with one of his hands resting against the back of the chair.

"Don't be so unhappy, Fennimore, look at me and let's talk. You will, won't you? You mustn't be afraid, let us bear this together, my own beloved! Let us. Try, if you can."

She raised her head a little, then she looked up at him. "Oh God, what shall we do? Isn't it terrible, Niels? Why should this happen to me here in this world? And how lovely it might have been — so happy!" and she sobbed again.

"Should I have kept quiet?" he lamented. "Poor Fennimore, do you wish that you had never found out?"

She raised her head again and grabbed his hand. "I wish I knew about it and was dead; I wish I lay in my grave and knew about it, that would be so good, oh, so good!"

"It's a bitter thing for us, Fennimore, that the first thing our love brings to us is nothing but anguish and tears. Don't you think?"

"You mustn't be cruel to me, Niels, there's nothing else I can do. You can't see it the way I do. I'm the one who should be strong, because I'm the one who is bound. If only I could take my love by force and lock it in the most secret depths of my soul and be deaf to all of its moaning and pleading, and then tell you to go far, far away. But I can't, I've suffered so much, I can't endure that too, I can't, Niels. I can't live without you, you see. Can I? Do you think I could?"

She stood up and pressed herself to his chest.

"Here I am, and I won't let you go, I *refuse* to let you go and be left behind, sitting in the old darkness. It's like a bottomless pit of suffering and torment, I *refuse* to throw myself into it, I would sooner jump into the sea, Niels; and even if the new life brings pain, at least it will be a new kind of pain that won't have the dull thorns of the old pain and won't be able to strike me as surely as the old one, which knows my heart so hideously well. Am I talking wildly? Yes, I am, but it's so good to be able to speak to you without restraint, without needing to stop myself anymore from saying everything it wasn't right to tell you. But now you have the right above all others! If only you could take me whole, so that I was completely yours, and I didn't belong to anyone else in the slightest, if only you could lift me out of every other relationship that is fencing me in."

"We must break through them, Fennimore. I'll arrange it so well, just don't be afraid, and one day, before anyone has the slightest suspicion, we'll be far away."

"No, no, we can't run away, not that, anything else would be better than for my parents to hear that their daughter had run off. That's impossible and I'll never do that, by God in heaven, Niels, I'll never do that."

"Oh, but you have to, my dear, you have to. Can't you see all the ugliness and meanness that will rise up around us on all sides if we stay, all the disgusting cunning and pretense and sham that will trap us and weigh us down and make us miserable! I won't have you besmirched by all that, it mustn't eat its way into our love like a corrosive rust."

But she was immovable.

"You don't know what you're condemning us to," he said in dismay. "It would be much better if we strode forth with iron heels instead of trying to be gentle. Believe me, Fennimore, if we don't let our love be everything for us — the first and the only thing in the world, the thing that must be saved above all else, so that we have to strike when we would rather soothe, and cause sorrow when we would much rather keep any trace of sorrow away — if we don't do this, then you will see how everything that we bow to will weigh heavily on our shoulders and force us to our knees, so mercilessly and inexorably. You have no idea how difficult it is to fight a battle on your knees. Don't cry. We'll fight it all the same, my dear, side by side, against everything."

During those first days, Niels continued his attempts to persuade her to flee; then he began to visualize what a heavy blow
it would be for Erik if he came home one day and found that
his friend and his wife had vanished together, and little by little
it took on an unnatural, tragic character of impossibility in his
eyes, and he got used to not thinking about it, as he had with so
many other things he wished would have been different, and he
threw himself with all his soul into the relationships as they
were, with no conscious attempt to rewrite them or, with fantastical festoons and garlands, to mask their shortcomings with
lies. But how sweet it was to love, to love for once with the
passion of real life; because what he had thought was love
before was not love, not the heavy, swelling longing of the
lonely man, nor the smoldering yearning of the fantast, nor the
prescient nervousness of the child. They were currents in the
great ocean of love, single reflections of its full light, splinters
of love, just as meteors that race through the air are splinters of
a planet, because that's what love was: a world that was *whole*,
something complete, vast, and orderly. It was not a disheveled,
meaningless rush of emotions and moods; love was like nature,
eternally changing and eternally giving birth, and no mood
died away, no feelings withered except to give life to the seed-
ling that they bore within, to something even more perfect.
Calm, healthy, and breathing deeply — that's how beautiful it
was to love, love with all your soul. And the days fell new and
glistening from heaven itself now, not dragging by as a matter
of course, one after the other like the worn-out pictures in a
stereoscope: every one of them was a revelation, for on each
day he found himself greater and stronger and more distinguished. He had never known the intensity and vastness of this
kind of feeling before, and there were moments when he felt
himself a titan, much more than a human being; he sensed such
an inexhaustibility within him, such a wingspan of tenderness
swelled from his heart, so wide was his vision, so enormously
mild were his judgments.

This was in the beginning, when they were happy, and they were happy for a long time.

The daily pretense and dissimulation, the air of dishonesty in which they moved, all of this had no power yet, it could not reach them at the ecstatic heights to which Niels had elevated their relationship and them along with it, because he was not merely a man who was seducing his friend's wife — or rather he was, he said defiantly, he was — but he was also the one who had rescued an innocent woman whom life had wounded, stoned, and sullied, a woman who had lain down to let her soul die. He had given her faith in life again and made her trust in its best powers once more, lifted her spirit to nobility and to greatness, given her happiness. So which was better: innocent wretchedness, or what he had won for her? He didn't ask; he had made his choice, after all.

He didn't entirely mean this. Human beings so often build up theories that they do not wish to reside in, and ideas so often go much further than the sense of right or wrong cares to follow. But this idea *did* exist for him and removed much of the persistent, corrosive venom from the guile, dishonesty, baseness, and ugliness that were still necessary.

Gradually it became apparent, however, that it was eating away at so many delicate nerves that eventually it had to do harm and cause pain, and this moment was hastened considerably when, shortly after New Year's, Erik felt that he had found an idea, something about a green dress, he told Niels, and a threatening pose. Did he remember the green in Salvator Rosa's painting of Jonah? Something along that line . . .

Even though Erik's work now consisted mainly of lying on the sofa in his studio, smoking tobacco and reading Frederick Marryat, it did keep him home for a time, forcing them into a new caution and making new deceptions and new lies necessary.

The fact that Fennimore was so inventive in this area caused the first cloud in the sky. It meant nothing in the beginning, nothing more than a transient, fleeting doubt in Niels, that his love might be nobler than the woman he loved. But this thought was not pure and clear, only an indistinct feeling that pointed the way, a vague weakening in his soul, listing to that side.

But it came again, and with more in tow, at first obscure and unclear, then sharper and sharper each time. And it was astonishing at what a rapid pace it could undermine, demean, and detract from the luster. Their love did not diminish, on the contrary, as it was sinking it grew more passionate and smoldering, but those handclasps stolen under blankets, those kisses in the entryways and behind doors, those long looks right under the nose of the betrayed, all robbed it of its grand style. Happiness no longer hovered silently over their heads, they had to steal its smile and its light wherever they could, and guile and cunning were no longer sad necessities but enjoyable triumphs, deception became their natural element and made them so base and so small. There were also degrading secrets which earlier they had worried about separately, keeping themselves ignorant in each other's eyes; these they now had to share, for Erik was not bashful and would often caress his wife in Niels' presence, kissing her and taking her on his lap and embracing her, and Fennimore did not dare object and did not have the authority to reject these caresses, as she had before; the consciousness of her guilt made her uncertain and afraid.

In this manner the lofty palace of their love sank and sank, the palace from whose pinnacles they had surveyed the world so proudly and where they had felt so strong and so great.

But they were happy amidst its ruins.

Now when they strolled in the woods, it was mostly on dark days when the fog hung in the brown branches and thickened among the damp tree trunks so that no one could see them when they kissed and embraced here and there, and no one could hear them when their lighthearted talk would ring out in giddy fanfares of laughter.

That hint of the melancholy of eternity which had marked their passion was now erased; now there was nothing but smiles and teasing between them, and there was such a feverish haste about them, a greediness for the racing seconds of happiness, as if they had to rush to love and did not have a whole lifetime before them.

Things did not change when Erik, after a month's time, grew tired of his idea and again began his escapades, so zealously that he was seldom home two days in a row. Niels and Fennimore remained where they had fallen. Every now and then, perhaps, in lonely hours, they might look back with regret at the heights from which they had fallen; perhaps they would merely wonder at the exertion it must have required to keep themselves up there, and they would feel more comfortably situated where they were now. No change occurred. There was no return to the old days, at any rate, even though that lax baseness which resulted from living the way they did and still not running away together became more and more apparent to them, linking them together, tighter and lowlier, in a mutual feeling of guilt; because neither of them wished anything to be different than it was. They did not hide this from each other either, because a cynical intimacy had developed between them, the kind that tends to form between two accomplices, and there was nothing about their relationship that they were afraid to touch with words. With a sad confidence they would call things by their real names and look them in the eyes and see them, they said, for what they were.

In February it had looked as if winter were over, but then came March in its white cape with the loose lining, and snowfall after snowfall covered the earth with a thick layer. Later on everything grew so still with a piercing frost, and the fjord froze over with six inches of ice that remained for a long time.

Toward the end of the month, one night after tea, Fennimore was alone in the parlor, waiting.

The room was brightly lit. The piano stood open with its candles burning, and the shade had been removed from the lamp so that the gilt moldings and everything hanging on the walls stood out distinct and clear. The hyacinths had been moved from the windows and placed on the desk, and they stood there now, a cluster of glowing colors, filling the air with their pure, strong, almost cool scent. In the tile stove the fire was burning with a muted, contented crackle.

Fennimore was pacing up and down, practically balancing on one of the dark red stripes of the carpet. She was wearing a somewhat old-fashioned black silk dress, which, weighted down with flounces, trailed after her, swaying from side to side as she walked.

She was humming, and both her hands were holding on to the pale yellow necklace of large amber beads around her neck, and whenever she lost her balance on the red stripe, she would stop humming but continue to hold on to the necklace. Perhaps she was making a charm out of her steps, so that if she could just walk so and so many times across the floor without stepping off the stripe and without releasing her grip, then Niels would come.

He had been there that morning when Erik left and had stayed until nearly evening, but he had promised to look in again as soon as the moon came out and it was light enough for him to avoid the holes out on the fjord.

Fennimore had finished her ritual, whatever the result might be, and had stepped over to the window.

It didn't look as if there would be any moon at all tonight, the sky was so black, and it was much darker out on the gray-blue ice than on land where the snow lay. It would probably be best if he didn't come. And she sat down at the piano with a sigh of resignation, but stood up again to look at the mantelpiece clock. Then she came back and resolutely set a big, thick book of music in front of her, but she still did not play; distracted, she paged through the book and fell into a reverie.

What if he was standing over on the other shore right now, strapping on his skates, and would be here at any moment! She could see him so clearly: he was breathing a little hard from the exertion and blinking his eyes at the light in the room after all that darkness. He brought in such a chill with him, and his beard was quite full of tiny, glittering drops. Then he would say — what would he say?

She smiled and lowered her eyes.

And there was still no moon.

She went over to the window again and stood there gazing out into the darkness until it became full of little white sparks before her eyes, and rainbow-colored rings. But they were so indistinct. She wished there were fireworks out there, rockets that shot up in the air in long, long streaks and then turned into little snakes that bored their way through the sky and disappeared with a pop; or else a great big dull sphere that quivered up in the air and then slowly floated down in a rain of thousand-colored stars: look! look! as soft and round as a curtsy, like a golden shower that curtsied. Farewell! Farewell! That was the last one. Dear God, maybe he isn't coming! And she didn't want to play. And with that she turned to the piano, harshly struck an octave, and kept holding the keys down until the chord had died away completely, completely, and again, again and again. She didn't want to play. Didn't want to play, didn't want to. But dance, on the other hand! For a moment she closed her eyes and in her imagination swept through an enormous hall of red and white and gold. How lovely it would be to have danced, to feel hot and thirsty and drink champagne! Then she happened to think about the time when she was in school and with a girlfriend had made champagne out of soda water and eau de cologne, and got so sick from drinking it.

She drew herself up and crossed the room, instinctually straightening her dress after the dance.

"Now let's see about being sensible!" she said half aloud, picking up her needlework and settling herself in a big armchair next to the lamp.

But she was not very diligent; her hands soon dropped to her lap, and little by little, with slight movements, she hid herself cozily in the big chair, curling up in it with her hand under her cheek and with her dress wrapped around her feet.

She wondered with curiosity whether the other wives were like her, whether they had made a mistake and had been un-happy, and then had loved someone else. One by one she considered the women of Fjordby. Then she thought about Mrs. Boye. Niels had told her about Mrs. Boye, and she had always seemed a titillating mystery to Fennimore, that female whom she hated and felt humiliated by.

Erik had also told her once that he had been wildly in love with Mrs. Boye.

If only you knew everything about her!

She laughed at the thought of Mrs. Boye's new husband.

And the whole time that she was preoccupied with this, she longed for and listened for Niels, and she imagined him on his way, still on his way out there on the ice. She was not aware that for two hours a little black spot from a totally different direction had been working its way across the snow-white fields with completely different news for her than what she was ex-pecting from across the fjord. It was only a man in homespun and oiled leather, and now he was knocking on the kitchen window and frightening the maid.

"It's a letter," said Trine as she came in to her mistress.

Fennimore took it; it was a telegram. Calmly she gave the maid the receipt and let her go, she was not the least bit wor-ried; lately Erik had sent her telegrams many times to tell her that he would be coming home the next day with a couple of strangers.

Then she read it.

She turned pale at once, jumped up from her chair, dis-traught, and stared with expectant horror at the door.

She didn't want it inside, she didn't dare, and with a leap she threw herself against the door, leaning on it with her shoulder and turning the key until it cut into her hand. But it refused to lock, no matter how hard she forced it. Then she let go. Oh, that's right — it wasn't here at all, it was far away from her in some strange house.

She began to shake, her knees couldn't hold her up any longer, and she slid down along the door to the floor.

Erik was dead. The horses had bolted, had thrown the carriage against a streetcorner and flung Erik headfirst into the wall. His head had been crushed, and now he lay dead in Aalborg. That's what had happened, and most of it was described in the telegram. No one else had been with him in the carriage except the pale-necked tutor, the Arab, and he was the one who had sent the telegram.

She lay quietly moaning on the floor; with both her hands pressed flat against the carpet, with her eyes downcast, expressionless and rigid, she rocked her body helplessly from side to side.

Only a moment ago it had been so bright and fragrant around her, and she could not immediately let it all go for the pitch-black night of grief and remorse, no matter how much she wanted to. It was not her fault, but her consciousness was still haunted by uncertain, dazzling glimpses of the happiness of love and the desire of passion; and strong, foolish wishes swirled up, striving for the bliss of forgetfulness or, with a wildly convulsive grasp, trying to push back the rolling wheel of events.

But this soon passed.

In black swarms, from every direction, the dark thoughts came flying like ravens, lured by the corpse of her happiness, and pecked at it, beak after beak, while the warmth of life still lingered in it. And they flayed and tore at it and made it repulsive and unrecognizable; every feature was disfigured and distorted until the whole thing was a carrion-heap of odiousness and horror.

She stood up and walked around, leaning like an invalid on chairs and tables, and she glanced up in despair, as if seeking a spider's web of help, merely a look of solace, a little caress of sympathy, but her eyes met only the brightly illuminated family portraits, all those strangers who had been witness to her fall and her guilt, somnolent old men, prudish-mouthed matrons, and the eternal gnome child that they had everywhere, the girl with the big round eyes and the protruding, high-domed forehead. All these unfamiliar possessions had gradually acquired plenty of memories: that table over there, that chair, the footstool with the black poodle on it, and the drapes that resembled a dressing gown — she had saturated all of them with memories, memories of fornication, which they now spewed out and flung at her. Oh, it was horrible to be locked in with all these ghosts of sin and with herself; she shivered for herself, she threatened herself, that ignominious Fennimore who crawled at her feet; she pulled her dress away from her pleading hands. Mercy! No, there was no mercy, how could there be mercy from those dead eyes in that strange town, those eyes which, now that they were shattered, saw how she had cast his honor in the dirt, lied to his lips, been unfaithful to his heart.

She could feel the way they were fixed on her, those dead eyes, she didn't know from where, she writhed beneath them to escape them but they continued to follow her, gliding over her like two icy rays; and as she stared downward and every thread in the carpet, every stitch in the footstools became unnaturally distinct to her eyes in that bright, sharp light of the room, then she noticed how it was moving around her with the steps of dead men and felt it brush against her clothes so that she screamed in terror and jumped aside; but then it was there in front of her like hands, and yet not like hands, something that slowly grabbed at her, grabbed scornfully and exultantly at her heart, that marvel of deception, that yellow pearl of faithlessness! And she shrank back until she bumped into the table, but it was still there, and her breast was no protection against it; it clawed through skin and flesh like . . . She almost died of fright as she stood there, helplessly bending back over the table while all her nerves contracted in anticipation and her eyes stared as if they were about to be murdered in their sockets.

Then it was over.

She looked around with a frightened gaze, then fell to her knees and prayed for a long time. She repented and confessed, wildly and recklessly with ever increasing passion, with exactly the same fanatical hatred toward herself that makes a nun flagellate her own naked body. She sought eagerly for demeaning words and grew intoxicated on self-abasement and a submission that burned for insignificance.

After a while she got up. Her breast was heaving hard and irregularly, and there was a faint sheen on her pale cheeks, which seemed to have grown somehow fuller during her prayer.

She looked around the room with an expression as if she were quietly making a vow to herself about something, then she went into the dark adjoining room, closed the door behind her, stood still for a moment to get used to the darkness, and then fumbled her way to the door leading to the closed glass veranda, and stepped out.

It was lighter out there. The moon, which had now come out, shone through the bits of ice crystals on the frozen glass wall, yellowish through the panes themselves, red and blue through the rectangles of colored glass that formed a frame around the windows.

She thawed a hole in the ice with her hand and carefully wiped off the water with her handkerchief.

There was still no one visible out there on the fjord.

Then she started walking back and forth in her glass cage. There was no furniture except a bentwood wicker sofa, and it was full of withered ivy leaves from the vines up near the ceiling. Every time she went past it, the leaves would rustle faintly in the draft, and now and then her dress would catch a leaf on the floor and drag it along behind her with a scratching sound across the floorboards.

Back and forth she walked in her sad vigil, with her arms folded across her breast, bracing herself against the cold.

He came.

With a jerk she tore open the door and stepped out into the icy snow in her thin shoes.

She welcomed this, she would have gone barefoot to this meeting.

Niels had slowed his speed at the sight of the black figure against the snow, and approached the shore with hesitant, tentative strokes.

That skulking figure seemed to be burning into her eyes. Every movement, every feature she could make out struck her like a shameless reproach, as if boasting with degrading secrets. She quivered with hatred, her heart swelling with curses, and she could hardly control her mind.

"It's me," she shouted derisively out to him, "the whore Fennimore."

"What in God's name, my sweet?" he asked in amazement, now only a few steps away from her.

"Erik is dead."

"Dead! When?" He had to step into the snow with his skates in order not to fall. "Tell me!" and he anxiously took a step closer.

Now they were standing face to face, and she had to stop herself from striking those pale, disturbed features with her clenched fist.

"I'll tell you, all right," she said. "He's dead, as I said, his horses bolted in Aalborg, and his head was crushed while we were here betraying him."

"That's terrible," gasped Niels, putting his hands to his temples. "Who would have thought... Oh, if only we had been true to him, Fennimore. Erik, poor Erik! If only it had been me!" and he sobbed aloud, doubled up with pain.

"I hate you, Niels Lyhne!"

"Oh, who cares about *us*," Niels moaned impatiently, "if only we had *him* back. Poor Fennimore," he corrected himself, "don't pay any attention to me. Did you say that you hate me? You may very well, yes, you may." He straightened up suddenly. "Let's go inside," he said, "I don't know what I'm saying myself. Who did you say sent the telegram?"

"Inside!" shrieked Fennimore, who was furious that he paid so little attention to her hostility. "Inside! Never will you set your cowardly, dishonest foot in this house again. How dare you think of that, you wretch, you devious dog, who came sneaking in here and stole your friend's honor because it was so poorly guarded. What, didn't you steal it right from under his nose because he thought you were honest, you thief!"

"Hush, hush, are you crazy? What's come over you? Just listen to the words you're using!" He had clasped her hard by the arm and pulled her closer and looked with astonishment into her face. "Pull yourself together," he continued in a milder tone. "What good will it do, dear, to fling ugly words around?"

She tore her arm away from him so that he stumbled on his unsteady feet.

"Can't you hear that I hate you," she screeched, "and haven't you got enough of an honest man's brain that you can comprehend this? How blind I must have been to love you, you fake of a man, while I had him at my side who was ten thousand times better than you. I will hate and despise you to the end of my life. When you arrived I was honorable, I had never done any harm, but then you came along with your poetry and your filth, and your lies dragged me down into the dirt with you. What had I done to you that you couldn't leave me alone, I who was supposed to be more sacred to you than anyone else. Day after day I will have to live with this stigma on my soul, and never will I meet anyone so degraded that I won't know in my heart that I am even more degraded. You have poisoned all the memories of my youth. Now what do I have left to think about that is pure and good? Everything has been sullied by you, everything. He isn't the only one who's dead. Everything of goodness and light that was between us is all dead and rotten too. Oh, God help me, is it fair that I can have no revenge on you, after all that you have done to me?

Make me honorable again, Niels Lyhne. Make me spotless and good again. No, no — but it *ought* to be possible for you to be tortured into righting your wrongs. Can you, can you bring everything back with lies? Don't stand there crawling under your helplessness; suffer here before my eyes, writhe in pain and despair and be miserable. Let him be miserable, Lord, don't let him steal my revenge from me too. Go, you wretch, go, I cast you away from me, but I will drag you along with me, believe me, through all the torments I can bring down upon you with hatred."

She had stretched out her arms toward him, threatening; now she turned around and walked away, and the veranda door rattled gently after her.

Niels stood and stared with astonishment, almost with disbelief, in the direction she had gone; it seemed to him that it was still there in front of him, that pale, vindictive face, so incredibly mean-spirited and raw in its passion, entirely devoid of its usual delicate beauty, as if all its features had been plowed up by some rough, barbaric hand.

He tottered cautiously down to the ice and began to skate slowly out toward the mouth of the fjord with the moonlight in front of him and the wind at his back. Gradually he skated faster as his thoughts drew his attention away from his surroundings, and the chips of ice from his skate blades swished with him across the shiny surface, blown by the ever increasing icy wind.

So this was the end! So this was the way he had rescued that female soul and raised it up and given it happiness! How beautiful was his relationship to his dead friend, his childhood friend, for whom he wanted to sacrifice his future, his life, everything! He with his rescuing and sacrificing! Heaven and earth should look at him, then they would see a man who kept his life on the heights of honor, without a defect or a blemish, so that he would not cast a shadow on that Idea which he served, and which he was called to proclaim.

He raced onward.

It was also one of his grandiloquent ideas that his petty life might have the power to besmirch the sun of the Idea. Good Lord, he always had to make things so lofty, it was in his blood. If he couldn't be anything better, then at least he could be a Judas and call himself Iscariot in magnificent gloom. At least that sounded like something. Was he always going to parade around as if he were a responsible minister of the Idea and a member of its Privy Council, who had everything regarding humanity at first hand? Couldn't he ever learn, in all humility, to strive to fulfill his obligations in the garrison service of the Idea, as a footsoldier of a quite inferior class?

There were red flames out on the ice, and he came so close to them that a gigantic shadow shot out from his feet for a moment, swept forward, and vanished.

He thought about Erik and about the kind of friend he had been to him. Oh, Erik! The memories of his childhood wrung their hands over him, the dreams of his youth covered their heads and wept over him, his entire past stared at him with one long gaze, full of reproach. He had betrayed it all for the sake of a love as base and petty as himself. There *had* been nobility in that love, nevertheless; and he had betrayed that too. Where should he flee from all these tentative efforts that always ended in the ditch? His whole life had been like this, and it would be no different in the future, he knew, he was so sure of it, and he despaired at the prospect of all those futile encounters and wished with all his soul that he might escape and be free from this meaningless fate. If only the ice would shatter beneath him as he raced forward, and everything would be over with a gasp and a spasm down in the cold water.

He stopped, exhausted from the skating, and looked back. The moon had disappeared, and the fjord lay long and dark between the white hills of the shore. Then he turned around and worked his way against the wind. It was so strong now, and he was tired. He turned in to seek the shelter of the high embankment, but as he made his way forward, he came out on a thin spot in the ice, created by a wind off the hills, and the thin ice gave underneath him with a laborious, creaking groan.

How lighthearted he felt all the same when he got out onto solid ice again! Most of his weariness had vanished with his fear, and he pushed energetically onward.

While he was struggling out there, Fennimore sat in the brightly lit parlor, disappointed and tormented. She felt herself betrayed by her revenge; she didn't know what she had expected, but it had been something entirely different. She had had a vague idea of something noble and magnificent, something like swords and red flames, or maybe not — something that would raise her up and place her on a throne, and now it had all turned out so petty and ordinary, and she had felt more like a quarrelsome woman than someone who was pronouncing a curse . . .

She had learned something from Niels, after all.

Early the next morning, while Niels was still asleep, overwhelmed with weariness, she went away.

X I I

For the better part of two years Niels Lyhne wandered abroad.

He was so lonely. He had no family, no friend who was dear to his heart. But there was a greater loneliness about him than that; for a person may well feel anguished and forsaken if on the whole enormous earth there is not one small place he can bless and wish well, someplace he can turn his heart toward when his heart insists on swelling, a place he can long for when longing insists on spreading its wings; but if he has the clear, steady star of a life's goal shining overhead, then there is no night so lonely that he is entirely alone. But Niels Lyhne had no star. He didn't know what to do with himself and his abilities. He did have talent, but he just couldn't use it; he went around feeling like a painter without hands. How he envied the others, great and small, who, no matter where they reached in life, always found something to hold on to! Because he could not find anything to hold on to. It seemed to him that all he could do was sing the old romantic songs over again, and everything that he had accomplished had been nothing more than this. It was as if his talent were something remote in him, a quiet Pompeii, or like a harp he could take out of a corner. It was not omnipresent, it did not run down the street with him, it did not reside in his eyes, it did not tingle in his fingertips, not at all; his talent did not have a hold on him. At times it seemed to him that he had been born half a century too late, at other times that he had arrived much too early. The talent within him was rooted in something from the past which was the only thing that could give it life. It could not draw nourishment from his opinions, his convictions, his sympathies, it could not assimilate them and give them form; they floated away from each other, these two parts, like water and oil, they could be shaken together but could not be mixed, never become one.

After a while he began to realize this, and it made him boundlessly discouraged and gave him a sarcastic, suspicious view of himself and his past. There must be some defect in him, he would tell himself, some incurable flaw in the innermost marrow of his being, for a human being *could* become whole by living, he did believe that.

It was in this state of mind, during his last year abroad, that he settled down in the little town of Riva on the banks of Lago di Garda in the beginning of September.

Right after he had arrived the country was closed off by a wall of difficulties and travel restrictions which kept all foreigners away. In fact, cholera had broken out around Venice and to the south in Desenzano and northward around Trento. Under these circumstances Riva was not particularly lively; the hotels had emptied at the first rumors, and travelers to Italy took a detour around the region.

So those who remained drew even closer together.

The most extraordinary among them was the famous opera singer whose real name was Madame Odéro. Her stage name had a much more famous ring to it. She, her lady companion, Niels, and a deaf Viennese doctor were the only guests at the town's foremost hotel, the *Sole d'oro*.

Niels became very attached to her, and she surrendered to that sincerity there was in his nature, as there is so often in people who live in disharmony with themselves and therefore must resort to finding comfort in others.

Madame Odéro had been living there for seven months in order to recover, in total peace and quiet, from the aftereffects of a throat infection that had threatened her voice. The doctor had forbidden her to sing for an entire year, and so that she would not be tempted he had forbidden all music as well. Not until the year was up would he allow her to attempt to sing, and if it was then apparent that not a trace of weariness resulted, she would be completely cured.

Niels had a kind of civilizing effect on Madame Odéro, who had an emotional, fiery temperament with very few subtleties. It had been a terrible sentence for her to hear that for an entire year she must live in silence, far removed from admiration and adulation, and in the beginning she was in great despair, staring with terror at the future of those twelve months as if it were a deep black grave she was to be put into alive; but everyone seemed to feel that it was something that could not be avoided, so one morning she had suddenly fled to Riva. She could have stayed at a livelier and more popular place, but that is exactly what she did not want. She felt ashamed and behaved as if she bore an externally visible, physical guilt, and she thought she could see in people how they pitied her for her infirmity and talked about it with one another. So she had avoided all socializing at her new residence, and lived largely in her rooms, whose doors had to swallow many curses when this voluntary imprisonment became too intolerable. Now that everyone had left, she reappeared once more and thus came into contact with Niels Lyhne, for she was not at all afraid of people on an individual basis.

A person did not have to be with her for very long before it became obvious whether she liked him or not, because she would show it with sufficient clarity. What Niels Lyhne was allowed to see was very encouraging, and they had not sat alone together for very many days in that magnificent hotel garden, with its pomegranate trees and myrtles, its gazebos with flowering oleanders, and its glorious view, before they had grown quite intimate.

There was no question of them being in love with one another, or at any rate not very much; it was one of those vague, comfortable relationships that can arise between men and women who are past the first youth with its flaring up and striving for some unknown happiness. It was a kind of fleeting summer in which you stroll primly side by side and shower yourself with bouquets, pat yourself with the other person's hand, admire yourself with the other's eyes. All the beautiful secrets you possess, all the lovely, irrelevant things you keep hidden, all the knickknacks of the soul are brought forth and passed from hand to hand and held up appraisingly in an artistic search for the best lighting while you compare and explain.

Naturally it is only during the pleasant hours of life that there is peace and quiet for this sort of Sunday relationship, but there by the lovely lake they had ample time, those two. It was Niels who had initiated the relationship by draping Madame Odéro, through words and glances, in an attractive melancholy. At the very beginning she was many times on the verge of tearing away the whole costume and stepping forth as the barbarian she was, but when she found that it suited her so grandly, she seized hold of the melancholy as if it were a role, and did not merely stop herself from slamming doors but sought out within herself the moods and gestures that might suit this new costume, and it was astonishing the way she gradually discovered how little she had really known about herself. Her life had been much too emotional and mercurial for her to find time previously to take stock of herself, and actually she was just now approaching the age when women who have experienced much and seen a great deal of the world start to preserve their memories, to look back at themselves and put together a past.

From the beginning the relationship developed rapidly and surely, and they became quite indispensable to each other. They were only half alive when they were alone.

Then one morning, as Niels was setting out for a sail, he heard Madame Odéro singing in the garden. His first impulse was to turn back and scold her, but before he had really considered this, he had glided out of earshot; besides, the wind was so tempting for a sail to Limone, and he would be back by noon. So he kept on sailing.

Madame Odéro had come down to the garden unusually early. The fresh scent out there, the curving waves which, smooth and clear as glass, rose and fell beneath the garden wall, and the whole exuberance of colors on all sides — blue lake and sunburned mountains, and white sails that fled across the lake, and red flowers in the arch above her head — all this and then a dream she could not forget that was still cradled against her heart . . . she could not remain silent, she had to take part in all this life.

And then she had to sing.

Fuller and fuller rang the joy of her voice; she was intoxicated by its melody, she trembled with the pleasurable feeling of its power. And she kept on, she couldn't stop, it bore her too delightfully onward through wonderful dreams of future triumphs.

And there was no weariness, she could leave, leave immediately, shake off at once all these months of nothingness, and go forth again and live.

By noon everything was ready for her departure.

Just as the carriages pulled up to the door, she remembered Niels Lyhne. She took from her pocket a sorry little notebook that she always carried and filled it with words of farewell to Niels, for the pages were so small that there was only room for three or four words on each; she put it into an envelope and made her departure.

When Niels returned home in the afternoon — he had been detained by the health authorities in Limone — she had long since reached Mori and was on the train.

He was not surprised, merely dejected, not angry at all, and he even had a little resigned smile for this new hostility of fate. But in the evening when he sat in the empty, moonlit garden and told the hotel owner's little boy the story about the princess who found her feathers again and flew away from her beloved, back to the land of the fairies, he felt an endless longing for Lønborggaard, for something that would enclose him like a home, pull him to it and hold him tight, no matter what. He could not stand the indifference of life any longer, of being released at every turn and always thrown back on himself. No home on earth, no God in heaven, no goal out there in the future! He wanted a home at least; he would love that place, both the great and the small: every stone, every tree, whether inanimate or alive, he would share his heart with everything so that it would never let go of him again.

XIII

Niels Lyhne had been living at Lønborggaard for about a
year, managing its affairs as well as he could and as much
as his foreman would permit. He had put down his shield,
erased its motto, and surrendered. Humanity would have to
get along without him. He had learned to know the happiness
that is found in purely physical labor: to watch the heap grow
under his hands; to be really finished so that you *are* finished;
to know that when you walk away exhausted, the energy you
have invested would remain there behind you in your work
and that the work would continue to exist, would not be eaten
away by doubt during the night, would not be dispersed by
criticism on a morose morning. There was no stone of Sisyphus
in agriculture.

And then to have worked your body to exhaustion; the
pleasure there was in going to bed and regaining your energies
in sleep, to put them to use once again as regularly as day
follows night, without being hindered by the whims of your
mind, without needing to guard yourself cautiously like a
tuned guitar with worn-out pegs.

He was truly quite happy, and he could often be seen sitting
the way his father had sat, on a fence or a boundary stone, and
staring, in a strangely vegetative trance, out across the golden
wheat or the top-heavy oats.

As yet he had not begun to seek out any kind of social
interaction with the families of the region; the only place he
went with any kind of regularity was to Councilor Skinnerup's
in Varde. They had come to the town while his father was still
alive, and since the Councilor was one of the elder Lyhne's old
friends from the university, the two families had spent a lot of

time together. Skinnerup, a gentle, balding man with sharp features and kind eyes, was a widower now, and his house was more than full with four daughters, the eldest seventeen and the youngest twelve.

Niels enjoyed having a chat with the well-read Councilor on all sorts of aesthetic topics; just because he had started using his hands didn't mean he had suddenly turned into a peasant. And he was fond of the slightly comical caution with which he had to express himself as soon as there was any mention of a comparison between Danish and foreign literature, or any time at all when Denmark was to be measured by something that wasn't Danish; because it *was* necessary to be cautious. The gentle Councilor was one of those good, ferocious patriots who existed at that time, people whom you might persuade to admit irritably that Denmark was not the most significant of the great powers, but who would not confess to anything else that might place the nation or anything belonging to the nation anywhere but in the forefront. The other thing that made him fond of these conversations, but quite vaguely and without placing the least weight on it, was to see the joyous admiration in the eyes of seventeen-year-old Gerda as she gazed at him when he spoke. And she always tried to be present whenever he was there; she followed along so intently that he would often see her blush with delight when he said something that she thought was especially wonderful.

Quite innocently he had become the young lady's ideal; at first because, when he came riding to town, he wore a gray, foreign cape cut in a very romantic fashion. There was also the way he always said "Milano" instead of "Milan," and things like that; the fact that he was alone in the world; and the rather melancholy expression on his face. In so many ways he was different from everyone else in both Varde and Ringkøbing.

One hot summer day Niels came down the little street behind the Councilor's garden. The sun was beating down over the little houses, brown as bricks; over there on the river lay the small boats with mats hanging over the sides so that the pitch wouldn't melt out of the seams, and all the doors stood wide open around him in order to create a coolness inside that was not to be found outdoors. Inside the open street doors sat the children reading aloud from their homework, buzzing in competition with the bees out in the garden, and a swarm of sparrows swooped silently from tree to tree, all of them up at once and all of them back down together.

Niels went into a little house adjacent to the garden and was left alone in a clean, neat little room that smelled of starched clothing and golden wallflowers while the woman ran to get her husband from the neighbors' house.

When he had finished looking at the pictures, the two dogs on the sideboard, and the conch shells on the lid of the sewing basket, he stepped over to the open window. He heard Gerda's voice right next to him, and there stood all four of the Skinnerup girls very close to the house in the Councilor's bleaching grounds.

The chrysanthemums and the other flowers on the windowsill concealed him, and he settled down to listen and to watch.

It was obvious that there was a quarrel in progress and that the three younger sisters were making a unified attack on Gerda. They all had lemon-yellow sticks in their hands, and the youngest had placed three or four rings bound with red on her head like a kind of turban.

She was the one speaking now.

"She says he looks like Themistocles on the tile stove in the office," she said to her two cohorts and put on a dreamy expression, with her eyes turned skyward.

"Oh, pooh," said the middle sister, a fierce little lady who had been confirmed that spring, "do you think Themistocles was hunchbacked?" And she imitated Niels Lyhne's slightly forward-drooping posture. "Themistocles, far from it!"

"There's something so manly in his eyes, he's a real man!" quoted the twelve-year-old.

"Him!" That was the middle sister again. "He wears perfume, is that manly? The other day his gloves were lying there, reeking of *Mille fleur*."

"Perfection itself!" exclaimed the twelve-year-old with swooning delight and tottered poignantly backwards.

They pretended that they were directing these remarks to each other and not to Gerda, who was standing a little apart, blushing and boring her yellow stick into the ground. Suddenly she raised her head. "You're all naughty girls," she said, "to talk about someone when you're not even worthy of his glance."

"He's just a person like the rest of us," admonished the eldest of the three mildly, as if wanting to mediate.

"No, he is *not*," said Gerda.

"He does have his faults, too," continued her sister, pretending that she hadn't heard what Gerda said.

"No, he doesn't!"

"Dear Gerda! You know that he never goes to church."

"What does he need to do that for? He's *much* wiser than the pastor."

"Yes, but unfortunately he doesn't even believe in God, Gerda!"

"Well, you can be sure, dear sister, that if he doesn't, then he must have a *very good* reason for it."

"Shame on you, Gerda, how can you say that?"

"You'd almost think..." interrupted the recently confirmed sister.

"What would you almost think?" asked Gerda fiercely.

"Nothing, nothing, don't bite my head off!" replied her sister, and was suddenly enormously placating.

"Tell me at once what you meant!"

"No, no, no, no, no; I should think I'm allowed to keep my mouth shut when I want to."

She went away, accompanied by the twelve-year-old, and they put their arms around each other's shoulders in sisterly camaraderie.

Behind them walked the eldest of the three, bristling with indignation.

Gerda stood alone, staring defiantly ahead while she chopped at the air with her yellow stick.

There was a slight pause and then from the other end of the garden could be heard the twelve-year-old's hoarse voice singing:

> You ask, my boy,
> What I want with that withered violet...

Niels understood the teasing quite well; he had recently given Gerda a book with a dried grape leaf in it from the garden in Verona where Juliet's grave is. He could hardly keep himself from laughing. Then the woman returned with her husband, whom she had finally found, and Niels placed his order for the piece of carpentry he had come for.

From that day on Niels paid more attention to Gerda, and day by day he became more aware of how sweet and marvelous she was, and gradually his thoughts would turn more and more often toward that trusting little girl.

And she *was* lovely; she had so much of that gentle, touching beauty that almost brings tears to your eyes. In her figure, despite its early maturity, the voluptuousness of a woman seemed to be made harmless by some of the plumpness of a child. Her small, softly formed hands, which were about to lose the pink color of puberty, were so innocent too and had none of the nervous, trembling curiosity of that age. She had such a strong little neck, such firmly curving cheeks, such a low, dreamy little feminine forehead, where thoughts that are great are so rare and almost hurt, so that the full brows frown. And her eyes — what eyes she had! So dark blue and deep, but deep only like a lake in which the bottom is visible; and the full, soft corners of her eyes where her smile rested, concealed beneath eyelids that rose with languid astonishment. That is how she looked, little Gerda, white and pink and blonde, with all her short, shiny golden hair gathered in a demure, prim bun.

They often talked with each other, Niels and Gerda, and he grew more and more beguiled by her; in a calm, tender, and open way at first, until one day there was a change in the air around them, a little spark of what it is too clumsy to call sensuality, but which still drives the hands, the mouth, and the eyes to grasp for what the heart cannot pull close enough to its heart. And so one day, a short time later, Niels went to Gerda's father because Gerda was so young and because he was so sure of her love. And her father said yes, and Gerda did too.

In the springtime they were married.

It seemed to Niels Lyhne that existence had become so infinitely clear and simple, life was so easy to live, and happiness was so close and as easy to attain as the air he drew in with a breath.

He loved her, this young wife he had won with all the goodness of his thoughts and his heart, with all the great, deep tenderness that resides in a man who knows love's tendency to sink and believes in love's ability to rise. He was so protective of this young soul who leaned toward him with nameless trust and who pressed herself to him with the same caressing confidence, the same secure conviction — that he could not intend anything but good toward her — as the lamb in the parable had for its shepherd when it ate from his hand and drank from his goblet. He didn't have the heart to take her God away from her, to exile all those white flocks of angels who hover, singing, all day in heaven and then come down to earth in the evening, spreading themselves out from bed to bed in a faithful vigil, filling the darkness of night with a protective, invisible light. He was so reluctant for his more melancholy, imageless view of life to intervene between her and the gentle blue of heaven and make her feel afraid and forsaken. But that is not what she wanted; she wanted to share everything with him. Nowhere in heaven or on earth would their ways part, and no matter what he said to hold her back she would refute it all, if not with the words of the Moabite woman, then still with the same stubborn thought that lay in those words: "Your people shall be my people, and your God shall be my God." And so he began in earnest to teach her, and he explained to her how all gods were human inventions and could not endure forever, like everything made by humans; they had to deteriorate, one generation of gods after another, because humanity is perpetually developing and changing and growing around its ideals. And a god whom the noblest and greatest of a generation did not endow with their richest spiritual legacy, a god who did not receive his light from humanity but who was supposed to illuminate himself, a god who was not in the process of development but who was frozen in the historic plaster of dogma, he was no longer a god but an idol, and therefore Judaism had power over Baal and Astarte, and Christianity had power over Jupiter and Odin, for an idol is nothing in the world. From god to god humanity had moved forward, and thus Christ could say, on the one hand, turning against the old God, that he had not come to dissolve the law but to manifest the law and, on the other hand, point beyond himself to a still higher ideal of God, with those mysterious words about the sin that cannot be forgiven, the sin against the Holy Spirit.

He also taught her that the belief in a personal God who rules everything for His own good, and in another life punishes and rewards, was a flight from harsh reality, a futile attempt to remove the thorn from the bleak arbitrariness of life. He showed her how this dulled humanity's sympathy with the unfortunate and made them less willing to apply all their forces to help, since they could reassure themselves with the thought that whatever was loathsome here in this short life on earth forged the way for the sufferer to an eternity of glory and joy.

He pointed out to her what power and independence it would give humanity when a person, believing in himself, sought to live his life in harmony with what the individual, in his best moments, valued the most of what dwelled within him, instead of placing it outside himself in a controlling deity. He made his beliefs as beautiful and beneficent as he could, but he also did not hide from her how oppressively heavy and inconsolable the truth of atheism could be to bear during hours of sorrow, in comparison with that bright, joyous dream about a heavenly father who guides and rules. But she was brave. Many of his teachings certainly shook her to the very depths of her soul, and frequently it was those that he would least expect, but her faith in him knew no bounds, her love carried her with him away from all heavens, and she was convinced by love. And then, with time, as she grew accustomed to and familiar with the new ideas, she became intolerant to a high degree and fanatical, as has always happened with young disciples who loved their masters dearly. Niels would often reprove her, but that was something she could never understand: if their own ideas were truth, then why weren't the ideas of others repulsive and reprehensible?

For three years they lived a happy life together, and much of that happiness shone from the face of a little child, a little boy they had in the second year of their marriage.

Happiness generally makes people good, and Niels strove earnestly in every way to shape their lives so nobly, beautifully, and usefully that there would never be a pause in the development of their souls toward the human ideal in which they both believed. But for him there was never any more talk of bearing the banner of this ideal out among the people; it was enough for him to follow it. Once in a while he might take out his old attempts at writing, but he was continually amazed that he was actually the one who had written all those beautiful, ingenious things, and he would regularly get tears in his eyes over his own poems. And yet, he would not for all the world have traded places with that poor soul who had written them.

Suddenly, in the spring, Gerda fell ill, and she was going to die.

Early one morning — the last morning — Niels was watching at her bedside. The sun was about to come up and it cast a red glow on the white shades, while the morning light coming in at the edge of the shades was still blue and made the shadow blue on the white folds of the bed and under Gerda's pale, thin hands as they lay clasped in front of her on the sheet. Her cap had slipped off and she was lying with her head tilted back, completely changed, so strangely elegant with the sharp, pointed features of illness. She was moving her lips as if to moisten them, and Niels reached for the glass with the dark red liquid, but she shook her head in refusal. Then, all at once, she turned her face toward him and stared tensely at his anguished features. The longer she looked at the deep sorrow they displayed and all the hopelessness they revealed, the more her anxious foreboding gave way to a fearful certainty.

She struggled to sit up but could not.

Niels quickly bent over her, and she seized his hand.

"Is it death?" she said, muting her weak voice as if to avoid pronouncing it too distinctly.

He just looked at her as he exhaled heavily with a whimpering sigh.

Gerda clasped his hand hard and threw herself toward him in her terror. "I'm afraid!" she said.

He let himself slip down to his knees next to the bed, and put his arm under her pillow so he was practically holding her to his chest. The tears were blinding him so he could not see her, running one after the other down his cheeks. He guided her hand with a corner of the sheet to his eyes; then he managed to control his voice. "Tell me everything, little Gerda," he said, "don't let anything stop you. Is it the pastor?" He could not believe this was true, and there was a little doubt in his voice.

She did not answer, she closed her eyes and dropped her head back a little, as if to be alone with her thoughts.

This lasted for some time. The long, soft whistle of a blackbird sounded from beneath the windows, then another whistled, and then a third; a whole series of whistling notes continued to pierce through the silence inside.

Then she looked up again. "If you were going along," she

said, leaning more heavily against the pillow, which he was supporting. There was a caress in this movement, and he felt it... "If you were going along — but alone!" and she clasped his hand gently and then released it. "I'm afraid." Her eyes grew anxious. "You must go and get him, Niels, I don't dare go up there alone like this. We never thought that I would die first, it was always you who was going to go ahead. I know... but what if we were wrong after all, it *is* possible, Niels, isn't it? You don't think so; and yet it would be so strange if *everybody* was mistaken and there wasn't anything at all, all the great churches... and when they bury them, the bells... I have always thought that the bells..." She lay still as if she were listening for them and could hear them.

"It's impossible, Niels, for everything to be over at death. You can't feel it, you who are healthy, you think it must kill us completely because we grow so listless and everything disappears, but that is only true outwardly, inside there is just as much soul as before — there is, Niels, I have it all inside, everything that I've been given, the same eternal world, only quieter, more alone with itself, the way it is when you close your eyes. It's just like a light that they're carrying away from you, and you can't see it, but it's shining just as brightly over there where it is. Far away. I had always thought that I would be an old, old woman and that I would stay here with all of you, but now I can't stay any longer; they're taking me away from everything and letting me go all alone. I'm afraid, Niels — where I'm going, it is our Lord who rules, and He has no interest in our cleverness here on earth, He knows what He wants and nothing else, and it's so far away from me, all that He wants. I haven't done much evil, have I? But that's not it... Get the pastor for me, I want so much to speak to him."

Niels stood up at once and went to get the pastor; he was grateful that this had not come at the very last moment.

The pastor came and remained alone with Gerda.

He was a handsome, middle-aged man with fine, regular features and large brown eyes. Naturally, he knew of the relationship Niels Lyhne and Gerda had to the church, and he had occasionally heard reports of various anticlerical expressions of the young woman's fanaticism, but it did not occur to him to speak to her as if she were a heathen or an apostate. He understood so well that it was her great love alone that had led her astray, and he also understood so well that feeling which, now that her love could not follow her any longer, made her fearfully yearn for reconciliation with the God she had known before, and so, as he talked, he sought primarily to reawaken her slumbering memories, and he read passages from the Gospels and the Psalms which he thought she might know best.

And he was not mistaken.

How those words rang out, so familiar and festive, like the chiming of the bells on a Christmas morning, and that land appeared at once before her eyes, the land in which our imagination first felt at home, where Joseph dreamed and where David sang, where the ladder stands that goes from earth to heaven! With figs and with mulberries it lay there, and the Jordan flashed silver-clear through the morning fog; Jerusalem lay red and sad in the evening sun, but over Bethlehem there was the glorious night with great stars in the dark blue. How her childhood faith poured forth again! She became that same little girl who had gone to church holding her mother's hand, and sat and shivered and wondered why people sinned so much. Then she grew up again under the mighty words of the Sermon on the Mount and she lay there like the sick sinner when the pastor spoke about the holy mysteries, about the sacraments of baptism and communion. Then the right desire won out in her heart — the deep submission before the almighty, judging God; the bitter tears of remorse before the forsaken, blasphemed, and tortured God; and the humble, bold yearning for the new pact of bread and wine with the inscrutable God.

The pastor left; later in the morning he returned and gave her the last rites.

Her strength diminished rapidly with a strange flickering,

but even in the darkness, when Niels took her in his arms for the last time to bid her farewell before the shadow of death came too near, she was still fully conscious. But the love that had been the greatest happiness of his life was extinguished in her gaze. She was no longer his; even now her wings had begun to grow; she longed only for her God.

At midnight she died.

Those were hard times, the days that followed. Time swelled up into something monstrous and hostile; each day was an endless desert of emptiness, each night was an abyss of memories. Not until months later, when summer was almost over, did the tearing, foaming torrent of grief wear itself a riverbed down in his soul so that it could flow away like a murmuring, heavily undulating stream of longing and sorrow.

Then one day when he came home from the fields he found his little boy very ill. He had not been feeling well for a few days, and he had been restless the night before, but no one had realized that it was of any importance; now he lay in his little bed, alternately hot and cold with fever, moaning in pain.

The carriage was sent to Varde at once for a doctor, but none of them were home, and it had to wait there for many hours. By bedtime it had still not returned.

Niels sat at his son's bedside; at least every half hour he would send someone out to look and see whether the carriage had come. A messenger on horseback was also sent off to meet the carriage, but he found none and rode all the way to Varde.

This waiting for help that did not come made it even more painful to witness the sick child's suffering. And the illness made rapid progress. Toward eleven at night the first convulsions started, and after that they came at shorter and shorter intervals.

At a little past one the messenger on horseback came back with word that the carriage could not be expected for at least several hours, since none of the doctors had returned home by the time he left the town.

Then everything fell apart for Niels. He had held off despair as long as it was possible to hope; now he couldn't do it any longer. He went into the dark parlor next to the sickroom and gazed out through the dark windowpanes as his fingernails dug into the wood of the window frame; his eyes seemed to devour the darkness, looking for hope, his mind crouched for a leap toward a miracle. Then it was clear for a moment, and quiet, and in that clarity he moved away from the window and threw himself across a table standing there, and sobbed without tears.

When he went into the sickroom again, the child was having convulsions. He looked as if he were going to kill himself with them, those small hands that clenched, white with pale blue nails, those rigid eyes that rolled back in their sockets, that contorted mouth in which his teeth were grinding against each other with the sound of iron on stone; it was terrible, and yet it wasn't the worst of all. No, for when the convulsions had stopped and his body became soft and pliant again and surrendered to the happiness of the lesser pain, then the fear that appeared in the child's eyes when he noticed that the convulsions were coming back, that ever greater plea for help as the torture came closer and closer, no *that* was the worst of all, and then not being able to help, not with his heart's blood, not with everything that he owned and possessed — Niels raised his clenched fist threateningly toward heaven, he seized hold of his child with the insane thought of fleeing, and then he threw himself to his knees on the floor and prayed to that Lord who is in heaven, who keeps the kingdom of earth in fear with trials and admonitions, who sends poverty and sickness, suffering and death, who wants everyone's knees to bend with trembling, and from whom no escape is possible, not to the farthest ocean nor down into the abyss — He, God, who if He pleases will trample on the one you love most here in the world, and torture your loved ones underfoot, back into the dust from which He Himself has created them.

With thoughts like this, Niels prayed to God and threw

himself down helplessly before the throne of heaven, recognizing that His was the power, His alone.

But the child continued to suffer.

Toward morning, by the time the farm's old doctor drove in through the gate, Niels was alone.

XIV

It is autumn now, there are no more flowers on the graves up there in the cemetery, and the leaves lie brown and rotting in dampness beneath the trees in the garden at Lønborggaard.

In the empty rooms Niels Lyhne walks around in bitter melancholy. Something broke inside him that night when the child died; he lost confidence in himself, lost his faith in the power of humanity to bear the life it must live. The seams of existence were leaking, and its contents were seeping away meaninglessly on all sides.

It would do no good for him to say that the prayer he had made was a father's insane cry for help for his child, even though he knew that no one could hear his cry. In the midst of his despair, he had known what he was doing. He had been tempted and he had fallen; it *was* a fall from grace, a fall away from himself and from the Idea. It was probably true that tradition had been too strong in his blood; for so many thousands of years the human race had always cried to heaven in its need, and now he had yielded to this inherited urge. But he should have resisted it as if it were an evil instinct, because he knew right to the innermost fibers of his mind that gods were dreams and that it was a dream he had fled to as soon as he prayed — just as he knew in the old days, when he threw himself into the arms of fantasy, that it *was* fantasy. He had not been able to endure life as it was; he had been in the struggle for Greatness, and in the violence of the battle he had forsaken the banner to which he was sworn. Atheism, the New, truth's holy cause — what purpose did they all serve? What were they but names of tinsel for the one simple idea: to endure life as it was!

Endure life as it was and let life shape itself according to its own laws.

It seemed to him as though his life had ended on that tormented night; whatever came afterwards would never be anything but uninteresting scenes tacked on to the fifth act, after the plot was played to the end. He could take up his old view of life again if he wanted to, but he had fallen the Fall one time, and whether he would later repeat it or not was absolutely irrelevant.

This was the mood in which he most frequently wandered.

Then came that November day when the king died, and the threat of war grew greater and greater.

Quickly he arranged his affairs at Lønborggaard and enlisted as a volunteer.

The boredom of training was quite easy for him to bear; it meant so much not to be a superfluous person anymore. Then, when he went into the army, the endless struggle with the cold, the vermin, and discomforts of every kind—all the things that drove his thoughts to shelter so that they could deal only with what was right outside the door—made him almost cheerful, and his health, which had suffered greatly from the sorrows of the past year, became quite robust again.

Then one dreary day in March he was shot in the chest.

Hjerrild, who was a doctor at the field hospital, saw to it that he was placed in a smaller room where there were only four beds. One of the men in there had been shot in the spine and lay quite still; another man had a wound in the chest, he had been lying there for several days, hallucinating for hours on end with hastily uttered, clipped words. And finally, the third man, who was lying next to Niels, was a big, strong farm hand with plump, round cheeks. He had been hit in the brain by a piece of shrapnel, and incessantly, hour after hour, almost every thirty seconds, he would lift his right arm and right leg at the same time and then let them fall back at once, accompanying this movement with an audible, but dull and toneless "Hah, ho," always in the same tempo, always exactly the same. "Hah" when he lifted his limbs, "ho" when he let them fall again.

There lay Niels Lyhne. The bullet had penetrated his right lung and had not come out. During a war there is no time for beating around the bush, and he was told that his prospects for survival were not good.

This surprised him, since he didn't feel as though he was dying and didn't have much pain from his wound. But soon a lethargy appeared which told him that the doctor was right.

So this was to be the end. He thought about Gerda, he thought a lot about her that first day, but he was still disturbed by that strange, cool gaze she had had when he took her in his arms for the last time. How wonderful it would have been, painfully wonderful, if she had clung to him to the very end and had not let go of him with her eyes until death made them dull; content to have lived her life to the very last breath with the heart that had loved her so much, instead of turning away from him at the last moment to redeem herself for more life, ever more life.

On his second day in the field hospital, Niels grew more and more despondent from the nauseating stench in the room, and a yearning for fresh air and the desire to live had become strangely intertwined in his mind. And yet there had been much beauty in his life, he thought, when he recalled the fresh breeze on the shore at home, the cool rustling in the beech forests of Sjælland, the pure mountain air of Clarens, and the gentle evening zephyr of Lago di Garda. But when he thought about the people, his mind would feel sick again. He called them up before him, one by one, and all of them walked past him and left him alone, and not one of them remained. But how had *he* held on to them? Had he been faithful? It was simply that he had been slower to let go. No, that was not it at all. It was the great sadness that a soul is always alone. Any belief in the merging of one soul with another is a lie. Not the mother who took you onto her lap, not a friend, not the wife who rested next to your heart . . .

Toward evening his wound began to ache, and the pain grew worse and worse.

Hjerrild came and sat with him for a moment in the evening and returned at midnight and sat there for a long time. Niels was suffering greatly and moaning in pain.

"A word in all seriousness, Lyhne," said Hjerrild. "Do you want a pastor?"

"I have no more to do with pastors than you do," whispered Niels bitterly.

"This has nothing to do with me; I'm alive and healthy. Don't lie there and torture yourself with your ideas. People who are about to die don't have ideas, and the ones they do have don't matter at all. Ideas are good only for living; life is where they serve their purpose. Will it help a single human being if you die with one idea instead of another? Believe me, we all have bright, tender memories from our childhood. I have seen so many die; it's always a comfort to call forth those memories. Let's be honest — we can be whatever we may call it, but we can never completely remove that God from heaven; our minds have imagined Him up there too many times, it has been chimed into us and sung into us ever since we were very small."

Niels nodded.

Hjerrild leaned down toward him to hear whether he wanted to say something.

"You mean well," whispered Niels, "but . . ." and he shook his head firmly.

It was quiet in the room for a long time, only the perpetual "hah-ho, hah-ho" of the farm hand slowly hammered the time into bits.

Hjerrild stood up. "Goodbye, Lyhne," he said. "It's a beautiful death, to die for our poor country."

"Yes," said Niels, "but that's not the way we dreamed about doing our utmost, that time long, long ago."

Hjerrild left; when he reached his room, he stood at the window for a long time and looked up at the stars. "If I were

God," he muttered to himself, and in his thoughts he continued, "I would much rather bless the one who does not change his mind at the end."

The pain grew stronger and stronger for Niels, mercilessly stabbing and stabbing inside his chest, and it kept on so unbearably. It would have been so good to have a god to whom he could complain and pray.

Toward morning he began to hallucinate. The infection was spreading rapidly.

And it continued for two more days and nights.

The last time Hjerrild looked in on Niels Lyhne he was lying there raving about his armor, saying that he wanted to die on his feet.

And then finally he died the death — the difficult death.

AFTERWORD

Among the creators of the modern novel Jens Peter Jacobsen is unique. Jacobsen was a scientist, a student of botany, and a translator of the works of Charles Darwin. His more famous contemporary (and sincere admirer) August Strindberg was also at one time bent on a scientific career, but with his special penchant for the bizarre he really preferred alchemy to chemistry. Jacobsen's interest in science was genuine, however, although he was also a poet, and therein lie the seeds of a conflict that was to be vividly dramatized in *Niels Lyhne,* the remarkable second and last novel of his all too brief life.

Jens Peter Jacobsen was born in 1847 in the commercial port of Thisted on the shores of Limfjord near the west coast of Denmark. His father, a shipping magnate, was one of the leading citizens of the town. The young Jacobsen developed into a precocious dreamer, writing poetry at the age of nine and botanizing in the countryside. When he entered the University of Copenhagen in 1867 he was torn between his interest in science and his love of poetry. He quickly adopted a thoroughly naturalistic and atheistic world view, in the process rejecting the Christian faith as a myth, a comforting illusion, in conflict with the laws of nature (not surprisingly losing his girlfriend as a consequence). Although he also immersed himself in contemporary literature, in the works of Kierkegaard, Hans Christian Andersen, Edgar Allan Poe, and Ivan Turgenev, among others, the focus of his studies was on science, and his plan was to get an advanced degree in natural history. When Jacobsen finally abandoned science and turned exclusively to writing, it was actually by default, as it were, illness having broken his strength to continue.

One result of Jacobsen's studies in science was a prize-winning essay on algae. More important, however, was his discovery of the writings of Charles Darwin. Jacobsen — unlike his contemporaries Zola and Strindberg, for instance, who were to use the theory of evolution to concoct a rather dismal and despairing naturalistic philosophy stressing "the survival of the fittest" in a war to the death — used Darwinian ideas, along with others, to build a positive faith in nature's own laws, a religion of nature supplanting the Christian belief in a special creation. Darwin's works were of course already known in Denmark among experts, but Jacobsen helped bring them to the attention of a larger public. Between 1871 and 1874 he undertook the arduous and formidable task of translating *On the Origin of Species* (1859) and *The Descent of Man* (1871) into Danish. In addition he published a number of substantial articles summarizing Darwin's theories.

In the meantime his efforts to have his poetry published met with no success. So instead he turned to fiction, initially with the brilliant novella *Mogens,* which appeared in the leading journal of the time, and then with the much more ambitious novel *Marie Grubbe* in 1876. Although the latter is a historical novel set in the seventeenth century, it presents essentially the same naturalistic view of life as *Mogens.* Like Flaubert's *Madame Bovary* (1857), with its stress on the importance of self-knowledge, it was praised by the most influential critics of the day in Denmark, the brothers Georg and Edvard Brandes. Like *Niels Lyhne* it is a Scandinavian classic widely read and appreciated. Although this is not generally known, *Marie Grubbe* also served as an inspiration for Strindberg's most famous modern drama, *Miss Julie* (1888). In part, at least, equally sado-masochistic, Jacobsen's novel shocked some contemporary readers, mainly on account of its objective and matter-of-fact portrayal of a lady of the aristocracy who in the end surrenders all her romantic illusions about love (initially fostered by her reading of romances) and finds happiness in the arms of a crude farm hand who beats her, happiness obviously being envisioned as a life lived in conformity with the laws of a person's natural inclinations and desires.

Unfortunately, before his success with *Marie Grubbe*, destiny dealt the young writer a deadly blow. On a journey to Italy in 1873 Jacobsen was taken ill in Venice and then suffered a hemorrhage in Florence. Forced to return to Denmark, he was confronted with the bitter truth of the professional diagnosis: advanced tuberculosis without much hope of a cure. Incredibly Jacobsen managed to stay alive until 1885, but the continuous battle for survival necessarily colors everything he was to create—including *Niels Lyhne*, his second and last novel. The positive faith and promise embedded in his early fiction is gradually replaced by a darker vision reflecting the ever present threat of death.

Niels Lyhne, undoubtedly Jacobsen's supreme achievement, was begun shortly after *Marie Grubbe* was completed, but the writing was a slow and painful process because of his failing health. He traveled abroad a good deal, especially to Italy, but to little avail, and he missed his friends and Copenhagen, a city he dearly loved. Some years he only managed to write a few pages. That he finally was able to complete the novel (in 1880) is a testament to his remarkable courage and great devotion to his art. Equally remarkable is the fact that the impeccable style and tone of the novel is preserved throughout, the brief but highly charged sentences on the last page echoing in the mind with the same power as on the opening page. With *Niels Lyhne* finally completed, Jacobsen thus managed against all odds to take his place among those few Scandinavian writers (Herman Bang and Jonas Lie, to name the most distinguished) bent on perfecting the novel as a serious art form capable of providing total aesthetic satisfaction and challenging the supremacy of lyric poetry and drama.

Although the problem of belief is central in the novel, *Niels*

Lyhne is a rich and complex work touching on a variety of
human concerns: art, sex, and manners, to name a few. A brief
history of its reception over the past century provides ample
evidence of its wealth of meaning and significance.

Not surprisingly the novel had a great and immediate im-
pact, reflecting as it clearly did the vital concerns of a generation of sensitive spirits who shared the hero's feelings of living
in an age of transition, born either twenty years too soon or
twenty years too late, torn between the old values and the new,
between romanticism and realism, between faith and reason.
Succeeding generations were to read the novel in a different
light. Thus the writers of the turn of the century saw in Niels
Lyhne a decadent aesthete, a Hamlet figure caught in a dream
world, incapable of action like the characters in a Chekhov
drama. In the 1940s and '50s, a generation thoroughly disen-
chanted by the events of World War II and its aftermath, a
generation that had been reading Camus and Sartre, looked
upon Niels Lyhne as an existentialist hero confronting the
anguish of the human condition without the comforting illusions of the Christian faith. The young Algerian novelist and
philosopher Albert Camus (who incidentally also suffered
from tuberculosis and experienced a similar intimacy with the
thought of his own death) was not familiar with the works of
Jacobsen as far as I know, but had he been, he would undoubtedly have recognized in Niels Lyhne the ideal of the hero he
sought to sketch in his famous essay *The Myth of Sisyphus* in
1942, the man trying to live religiously by the concept of the
absurd. Similarly, Jean-Paul Sartre's insistence on his own
brand of existentialism as a new form of humanism was clearly
anticipated in *Niels Lyhne*, especially in Niels' manifesto
"There is no God and the human being is His prophet," along
with Dr. Hjerrild's warning that atheism will make much
greater demands on human beings than Christianity does.

And what about the readers of today? Given the literary
and critical climate of the late 1980s, the likelihood is that they
would focus on the *erotic* rather than the atheistic aspects of

Niels Lyhne, that is, on the women in Lyhne's life, characters like Mrs. Boye and Fennimore and their efforts to teach him about women's refusal to be reduced to the objects of men's fantasies and dreams, about their demands to be treated as equals, as human beings, obviously another vital aspect of the humanistic gospel embedded in the novel.

So much for the reception in Scandinavia. Abroad, *Niels Lyhne* is of course less well known, suffering the customary fate of so many other remarkable Nordic works of literature. Not surprisingly, the French do regard Jacobsen as another (but lesser!) Flaubert, not failing to detect the remarkable similarities between Niels Lyhne and Frédéric Moreau, the ineffectual and unheroic hero of *Sentimental Education* (1869), who also had his difficulties with women. But on the whole, Jacobsen's name is not known in French literary circles.

In the German-speaking countries, on the other hand, his works have fared much better. Jacobsen became an important mentor to the great Austrian poet Rainer Maria Rilke, whose powerful works convey a similar and very striking combination of aestheticism and humanism. To Rilke, Jacobsen obviously ranked with Kierkegaard and Ibsen in importance along with his other great mentor, the sculptor Auguste Rodin. The following excerpt from a letter to the Swedish feminist author Ellen Key, dated April 2, 1904, tells us much about Rilke's feelings about Jacobsen and his works:

> I first read Jacobsen in 1896—97 in Munich. I was very immature then and read sensing rather than observing, first *Niels Lyhne,* later *Marie Grubbe.* Since then these books, to which were added in 1898 the "six short stories" and the letters, have been influential in all my developments; and even today my experience with them is that, wherever I may be standing, always, every time I want to go on, I find the next, the next higher, the approaching stage of my growth sketched out and already created in them. In these books much of what the best people are

seeking even today is already found, derived from one life, at least. Jacobsen and Rodin, to me they are the two inexhaustible ones, the masters. Those who can do what I would sometime like to be able to do. Both have that penetrating, devoted observation of nature, both the power to transform what they have seen into reality enhanced a thousandfold. Both have made things, things with many sure boundaries and countless intersections and profiles: that is how I feel their art and their influence. . . .

And indeed, Rilke's own novel, *The Notebooks of Malte Laurids Brigge* (1910), with its strong northern European atmosphere, is obviously inspired by the reading of *Niels Lyhne.*

Another great German writer, the novelist Thomas Mann, in his youth was an admirer of Jacobsen's *Niels Lyhne*; this is most obviously reflected in his equally elegant, elegiac, and ironic early masterpiece, the short novel *Tonio Kröger* (1903).

In the United States, finally, Jacobsen's novels have clearly failed to arouse an interest similar to the generous reception afforded the works of Knut Hamsun, Sigrid Undset, or Isak Dinesen. Like Flaubert and Thomas Mann, the novelists with whom he has most in common, Jacobsen is a superb stylist, and it is difficult to do justice to his supple and sensuous prose in translation. The difficulties inherent in rendering *Niels Lyhne* into English are also clearly evident in the 1919 translation. It is my hope that this new translation, with its much greater fidelity to the original Danish text, will at last bring this profound and moving novel to the attention of a larger audience. Along with Martin Andersen Nexø's *Pelle the Conqueror* and Herman Bang's *Katinka, Niels Lyhne* is indeed a splendid addition to the rapidly growing number of Danish classics published by Fjord Press.

Eric O. Johannesson
University of California
Berkeley

BIBLIOGRAPHY

J ens Peter Jacobsen had only three books published during his short lifetime. Older English translations of all his works are out of print, and Fjord plans to do new translations of his short stories and his first novel.

Fru Marie Grubbe. Interieurer fra det syttende Aarhundrede (Madame Marie Grubbe: Interiors from the Seventeenth Century). Copenhagen: Gyldendal, 1877 (novel).

Niels Lyhne (Niels Lyhne). Copenhagen: Gyldendal, 1880 (novel). Seattle: Fjord Press, 1990.

Mogens og andre Noveller (Mogens and Other Stories). Copenhagen: Gyldendal, 1882 (short stories).

Digte og Udkast (Poems and Drafts). Copenhagen: Gyldendal, 1886.

Samlede Værker (Collected Works). 5 vols. Copenhagen: Gyldendal, 1924 – 1929 (novels, short stories, poems, scientific writings; includes unpublished works).

Samlede Værker (Collected Works). 6 vols. Copenhagen: Rosenkilde & Bagger, 1972 – 1974 (novels, short stories, poems, personal papers, letters; illustrated).

Niels Lyhne. Ed. Jørn Vosmar. Danish Classics Series; The Danish Language and Literature Association. Copenhagen: Borgen, 1986.

Acknowledgments:
Omkring Niels Lyhne. Ed. Niels Barfoed (Copenhagen: Reitzel, 1970).
J. P. Jacobsens spor i ord, billeder og toner. Ed. F. J. Billeskov Jansen (Copenhagen: Reitzel, 1985).
Jens Peter Jacobsen. By Niels Lyhne Jensen (Boston: Twayne, 1980).

TRANSLATOR'S ACKNOWLEDGMENTS

Fifteen years ago I read *Niels Lyhne* for the first time in a class taught by Professor Niels Ingwersen at the University of Wisconsin. Vivid memories of entire scenes from the novel have stayed in my mind ever since, along with a great admiration for Jacobsen's beautifully lyrical prose. Three years ago I decided that a completely new English translation might be able to resurrect this long-neglected classic and bring it the attention it deserves among English-speaking readers. I am indebted to Jørn Vosmar for his extensive notes to the definitive Danish edition of *Niels Lyhne,* on which this translation is based. I would also like to thank Inge and Klaus Rifbjerg for their invaluable assistance in untangling and explaining some of the more puzzling literary intricacies of Jacobsen's Danish. Grateful acknowledgment is also due to Stephen Mitchell for his translations of Rilke — the author whose enthusiasm for *Niels Lyhne* has sent many readers in a vain search for an English edition. Finally, I would like to thank my editor for his patience, grammatical skill, and flair for finding just the right word when my translator's mind occasionally failed me.

Forthcoming translations from Fjord Press

Pelle the Conqueror, Vol. 2: Apprenticeship by Martin Andersen Nexø
Translated from the Danish by Steven T. Murray & Tiina Nunnally
$9.95 paper, $19.95 cloth

Love & Solitude: Selected Poems, 1916–1923 by Edith Södergran
Translated from the Finland-Swedish by Stina Katchadourian
$9.95 paper, Third bilingual edition

Idealists by Hans Scherfig
Translated from the Danish by Frank Hugus
$9.95 paper, $19.95 cloth

Katinka by Herman Bang
Translated from the Danish by Tiina Nunnally
$8.95 paper, $17.95 cloth

Titles now available:

Peasants and Masters by Theodor Kallifatides
Translated from the Swedish by Thomas Teal
$8.95 paper, $17.95 cloth

Another Metamorphosis and Other Fictions by Villy Sørensen
Translated from the Danish by Tiina Nunnally & Steven T. Murray
$8.95 paper, $17.95 cloth

Pelle the Conqueror, Vol. 1: Childhood by Martin Andersen Nexø
Translated from the Danish by Steven T. Murray
$9.95 paper, $19.95 cloth

Stolen Spring by Hans Scherfig
Translated from the Danish by Frank Hugus
$7.95 paper, $15.95 cloth

The Missing Bureaucrat by Hans Scherfig
Translated from the Danish by Frank Hugus
$8.95 paper, $17.95 cloth

Laterna Magica by William Heinesen
Translated from the Danish by Tiina Nunnally
$7.95 paper, $15.95 cloth

Witness to the Future by Klaus Rifbjerg
Translated from the Danish by Steven T. Murray
$8.95 paper, $17.95 cloth

Please write for a catalog: Fjord Press, P.O. Box 16501, Seattle, WA 98116

This book was typeset by Fjord Press Typography
in 11/14 Stempel Garamond, a modern adaptation
by the Stempel foundry, Frankfurt,
of the classic French typeface
designed by Claude Garamond
in the 16th century.